L·I·T·L·E
WOMEN
LOUISA   MAY   ALCOTT

Abridgment by Muriel Fuller

Illustrated by Gabe Keith
Cover by Nancy Stahl

SCHOLASTIC INC.
New York Toronto London Auckland Sydney Tokyo

from

Grandpa + Grandma

Stafford

Christmas 1991

ISBN 0-590-08556-5

12 11 10 9 8 7 6 5 4 3 2 1   9   3 4 5 6 7/8

Printed in the U.S.A.   01

CONTENTS

Part I

CONTENTS

Part II

L·I·T·T·L·E
WOMEN

PART I

Chapter 1

PLAYING PILGRIMS

"CHRISTMAS won't be Christmas without any presents," grumbled Jo, lying on the rug.

"It's so dreadful to be poor!" sighed Meg, looking down at her old dress.

"I don't think it's fair for some girls to have plenty of pretty things, and other girls nothing at all," added little Amy, with an injured sniff.

"We've got Father and Mother and each other," said Beth contentedly, from her corner.

The four young faces on which the firelight shone brightened at the cheerful words, but darkened again as Jo said sadly: "We haven't got Father, and shall not have him for a long time." She didn't say "perhaps never," but each silently added it, thinking of Father far away, where the fighting was.

Nobody spoke for a minute, then Meg said in an altered tone: "You know the reason Mother proposed not having any presents this Christmas was because it is going to be a hard winter for everyone, and she thinks we ought not to spend money for pleasure, when our men are suffering so in the army. We can't do much, but we can make our little sacrifices, and ought to do it gladly. But I'm afraid I don't," and Meg shook her head, as she thought of the pretty things she wanted.

"But I don't think the little we should spend would do any good. We've each got a dollar, and the army wouldn't be

much helped by our giving that. I agree not to expect anything from Mother or you, but I do want to buy *Undine and
Sintram* for myself; I've wanted it *so* long," said Jo, who was
a bookworm.

"I planned to spend mine in new music," said Beth with a
sigh.

"I shall get a nice box of drawing pencils," said Amy decidedly.

"Mother didn't say anything about our money, and she
won't wish us to give up everything. Let's each buy what
we want, and have a little fun. I'm sure we work hard
enough to earn it," cried Jo.

"I know *I* do, teaching those tiresome children nearly all
day, when I'm longing to enjoy myself at home," began
Meg.

"You don't have half such a hard time as I do," said Jo.
"How would you like to be shut up for hours with a fussy old
lady who is never satisfied?"

"I think washing dishes and keeping things tidy is the
worst work in the world," said Beth. "My hands get so stiff, I
can't practice well."

"You don't have to go to school with girls who laugh at
your dresses, and label your father if he isn't rich," cried
Amy.

"If you mean *libel,* I'd say so, and not talk about *labels,*
as if Papa was a pickle bottle," advised Jo laughing.

"I know what I mean, and you needn't be *statirical* about
it. It's proper to use good words, and improve your *vocabi-
lary,*" returned Amy with dignity.

"Don't peck at one another, children. Don't you wish we
had the money Papa lost when we were little, Jo? Dear me,
how happy and good we'd be, if we had no worries!" said
Meg, who could remember better times.

The four sisters sat knitting away in the twilight, while the
December snow fell quietly without, and the fire crackled
cheerfully within. It was a comfortable old room, though the
carpet was faded and the furniture plain. A good picture or

two hung on the walls, books filled the recesses, chrysanthemums and Christmas roses bloomed in the windows, and there was an atmosphere of peace.

Margaret, the eldest of the four, was sixteen, and pretty; plump and fair, with large eyes, plenty of soft brown hair, a sweet mouth, and white hands of which she was rather vain. Fifteen-year-old Jo was tall, thin and brown, and reminded

one of a colt, for she never seemed to know what to do with her long limbs. She had a decided mouth, a comical nose, and sharp gray eyes, which appeared to see everything. Her long thick hair was her one beauty, but it was usually bundled into a net. Round shoulders had Jo, big hands and feet, a fly-away look to her clothes, and the uncomfortable appearance of a girl who was rapidly shooting up into a woman and didn't like it.

Elizabeth—or Beth, as everyone called her—was a rosy, smooth-haired, brighteyed girl of thirteen, with a shy manner, a timid voice, and a peaceful expression which was seldom disturbed. "Mouse" was the pet of the family. Her father called her "Little Tranquillity," and the name suited her for she seemed to live in a happy world of her own. Amy, though the youngest, was a most important person—in her own opinion at least. A snow maiden, with blue eyes and yellow hair curling on her shoulders, pale and slender, always carrying herself like a young lady mindful of her manners.

The clock struck six, and having swept up the hearth Beth put a pair of slippers there to warm. Somehow the sight had a good effect upon the girls, for Mother was coming and everyone brightened to welcome her. Meg lighted the lamp, Amy got out of the easychair without being asked, and Jo forgot how tired she was as she held the slippers nearer the blaze. "They are quite worn out. Marmee must have a new pair."

"I thought I'd get her some with my dollar," said Beth.

"No, I shall!" cried Amy.

"I'm the oldest," Meg began, but Jo cut in.

"I'm the man of the family now Papa is away, and *I* shall provide the slippers, for he told me to take special care of Mother while he was gone."

"I'll tell you what we'll do," said Beth. "Let's each get her something for Christmas, and not get anything for ourselves."

"That's like you, dear!" exclaimed Jo. "What will we get?"

Everyone thought for a minute, then Meg announced, "I shall get her a nice pair of gloves."

"Army shoes, best to be had," cried Jo.

"Some handkerchiefs, all hemmed," said Beth.

"I'll get a little bottle of cologne. She likes it, and it won't cost much, so I'll have some left to buy my pencils," added Amy.

"Let Marmee think we are getting things for ourselves, and then surprise her. We ought to rehearse tonight for the play. Come here, Amy, and do the fainting scene. You are as stiff as a poker."

"I can't help it. I never saw anyone faint," returned Amy, who was not gifted with dramatic power.

"Do it this way—clasp your hands so and stagger across the room," and away went Jo with a thrilling scream.

Amy followed, but she jerked herself along as if she went by machinery. Jo groaned and the rehearsal ended in a general burst of laughter.

"Glad to find you so merry, my girls," said a voice at the door, and they turned to welcome a tall, motherly lady. She was not elegantly dressed but a noble-looking woman, and the girls thought the gray cloak and unfashionable bonnet covered the most splendid mother in the world.

"Well, dearies, how have you got on today? There was so much to do, getting the boxes ready to go tomorrow, that I didn't come home to dinner. Has anyone called, Beth? How is your cold, Meg? Jo, you look tired to death. Come and kiss me, baby."

Mrs. March got her wet things off, her warm slippers on, and sitting down in the easychair, drew Amy to her lap, prepared to enjoy the happiest hour of her busy day. Meg arranged the tea table; Jo brought wood and set chairs; Beth trotted to and fro between parlor and kitchen; while Amy gave directions to everyone.

As they gathered about the table, Mrs. March said happily, "I've got a treat for you after supper."

A quick bright smile went around like a streak of sunshine. Beth clapped her hands, and Jo tossed up her napkin, crying, "A letter! Three cheers for Father!"

"Yes, a nice long letter. He is well and thinks he shall get through the cold season better than we feared. He sends all sorts of loving wishes for Christmas and an especial message to you girls," said Mrs. March.

"I think it was splendid in Father to go as a chaplain when he was too old to be drafted and not strong enough for a soldier," said Meg.

"When will he come home, Marmee?" asked Beth.

"Not for many months, dear, unless he is sick. He will stay and do his work faithfully as long as he can, and we won't

ask for him back a minute sooner than he can be spared.
Now hear the letter."

They all drew to the fire, Mother in the big chair with
Beth at her feet, Meg and Amy perched on either arm of the
chair, and Jo leaning on the back, where no one would see
any sign of emotion. It was a cheerful, hopeful letter, full of
lively descriptions of camp life, marches, and military news.
Only at the end did the writer's heart overflow with love and
longing for the girls at home.

> *Give them all my dear love and a kiss. Tell them
> I think of them by day, pray for them by night, and
> find my best comfort in their affection at all times.
> A year seems very long to wait before I see them,
> but remind them that while we wait we may all
> work, so that when I come back to them I may be
> fonder and prouder than ever of my little women.*

Everybody sniffed and Jo wasn't ashamed of the tear that
dropped off the end of her nose. Amy hid her face on her
mother's shoulder and sobbed, "I *am* a selfish girl, but I'll
truly try to be better, so he mayn't be disappointed in me."

"We all will!" cried Meg. "I think too much of my looks,
and hate to work, but won't any more if I can help it."

"I'll try and be what he loves to call me, 'a little woman,'
and not be rough and wild," said Jo.

Beth said nothing but wiped away her tears with the blue
army sock, and began to knit with all her might. Mrs. March
broke the silence that followed Jo's words. "Do you remember how you used to play *Pilgrim's Progress* when you were
little things? Nothing delighted you more than to have me
tie my piece bags on your backs for burdens, give you hats
and sticks and rolls of paper, and let you travel through the
house from the cellar, which was the City of Destruction,
up, up to the housetop, where you had all the lovely things
you could collect to make a Celestial City."

"What fun it was, especially going by the lions, fighting

Apollyon, and passing through the Valley where the hob-goblins were!" said Jo.

"I liked the place where the bundles fell off," said Meg.

"My favorite part was when we came out on the flat roof where our flowers were, and we all sung for joy in the sunshine," said Beth, smiling.

"I don't remember much about it, except I was afraid of the cellar and liked the cake and milk we had at the top. If I wasn't too old for such things, I'd rather like to play it over again," said Amy, who began to talk of renouncing childish things at the mature age of twelve.

"We never are too old for this, my dear, because it is a play we are playing all the time in one way or another. Our burdens are here, our road is before us, and the longing for goodness and happiness is the guide that leads us through many troubles and mistakes to the peace which is a true Celestial City. Now, my little pilgrims, suppose you begin again, not in play but in earnest, and see how far on you can get before Father comes home."

"Let us do it," said Meg thoughtfully. "It is only another name for trying to be good, and the story may help us."

"We were in the Slough of Despond tonight, and Mother came and pulled us out as Help did in the book. We ought to have our roll of directions, like Christian," said Jo.

"Look under your pillows Christmas morning and you will find your guidebook," replied Mrs. March.

Chapter 2

A MERRY CHRISTMAS

JO was first to wake Christmas morning. No stockings hung at the fireplace, and for a moment she felt disappointed. Then she remembered her mother's promise and, slipping her hand under her pillow, drew out a little crimson book. She knew it very well, for it was that beautiful old story of the best life ever lived, and Jo felt that it was a true guidebook for any pilgrim going the long journey.

She woke Meg with a "Merry Christmas," and bade her see what was under her pillow. A green book appeared, with the same picture inside. Presently Beth and Amy woke, to rummage and find their little books, one dove-colored, the other blue. Then the rooms were very still while the pages were softly turned, and the winter sunshine crept in to touch the bright heads and serious faces with a Christmas greeting.

"Where is Mother?" asked Meg, as she and Jo ran down to thank her for their gifts half an hour later.

"Goodness only knows. Some poor creeter come a-beggin', and your ma went straight off to see what was needed," replied Hannah, who had lived with the family since Meg was born, and was considered by them all more as a friend than a servant.

"She will be back soon, I think, so have everything ready," said Meg, looking over the presents which were collected in a basket under the sofa. "Why, where is Amy's bottle of cologne?" she added.

"She took it out and went off to put a ribbon on it," replied Jo, dancing about the room to take the stiffness off the new army slippers.

"How nice my handkerchiefs look, don't they? Hannah washed and ironed them for me, and I marked them all myself," said Beth, looking proudly at the somewhat uneven letters.

"There's Mother. Hide the basket, quick!" cried Jo, as a door slammed and steps sounded in the hall.

Amy came in hastily, and looked abashed when she saw her sisters all waiting for her.

"Where have you been and what are you hiding behind you?" asked Meg, surprised that lazy Amy had been out so early.

"Don't laugh at me, Jo! I didn't mean anyone should know

till the time came. I only meant to change the little bottle for a big one, and I gave *all* my money to get it." As she spoke, Amy showed the handsome flask which replaced the cheap one. Beth ran to the window and picked her finest rose to ornament the stately bottle.

Another bang of the door sent the basket under the sofa and the girls to the table, eager for breakfast.

"Merry Christmas, Marmee! Many of them! Thank you for our books. We read some and mean to every day," they cried in chorus.

"Merry Christmas, little daughters! I'm glad you began at once, and hope you will keep on. But I want to say one word before we sit down. Not far from here lies a poor woman with a newborn baby. Six children are huddled into one bed to keep from freezing, for they have no fire. There is nothing to eat over there. My girls, will you give them your breakfast as a Christmas present?"

They were all hungry, having waited an hour, and for a minute no one spoke. Then Jo exclaimed, "I'm so glad you came before we began!"

"I shall take the cream and muffins," Amy said, heroically giving up what she most liked.

Meg was already covering the buckwheats and piling the bread into one big plate.

"I thought you'd do it," said Mrs. March, smiling as if satisfied. "You shall all go and help me, and when we come back we will have bread and milk for breakfast, and make it up at dinnertime."

They were soon ready and the procession set out. A poor, bare, miserable room it was, with broken windows, no fire, ragged bedclothes, a sick mother, wailing baby, and a group of pale hungry children cuddled under one old quilt trying to keep warm. How the big eyes stared and the blue lips smiled as the girls went in!

"*Ach*, it is good angels come to us!" said the poor woman, crying for joy.

"Funny angels in hoods and mittens," said Jo, and set them laughing.

Hannah, who had carried wood, made a fire and stopped up the broken panes with old hats and her own cloak. Mrs. March gave the mother tea and gruel, and comforted her with promises of help while she dressed the baby. The girls spread the table, set the children around the fire, and fed them like so many hungry birds, laughing, talking, and trying to understand the funny broken English.

"*Das ist gut! Die Engel-kinder!*" they cried as they ate, and warmed their purple hands at the comfortable blaze. The girls had never been called angel children before, and thought it very agreeable. That was a happy breakfast though they didn't get any of it. When they went away, leaving comfort behind, there were not in all the city four merrier people than the hungry girls who gave away their breakfast and contented themselves with bread and milk on Christmas morning.

"That's loving our neighbor better than ourselves, and I like it," said Meg, as they set out their presents while their mother was upstairs collecting clothes for the poor Hummels.

There was a great deal of love done up in the few little bundles, and the tall vase of red roses, white chrysanthemums and vines gave an air to the table.

"She's coming! Strike up, Beth! Open the door, Amy! Three cheers for Marmee!" cried Jo.

Beth played her gayest march, Amy threw open the door, and Meg enacted escort with great dignity. Mrs. March was both surprised and touched, and smiled with her eyes full as she examined her presents, and read the little notes which accompanied them. The slippers went on at once, a new handkerchief was slipped into her pocket, well scented with Amy's cologne, the rose was fastened in her bosom, and the nice gloves were pronounced a perfect fit.

The rest of the day was devoted to preparations for the evening. Being still too young to go often to the theater, and not rich enough to afford any great outlay, the girls put their wits to work and made whatever they needed. No gentlemen were admitted, so Jo played male parts to her heart's content. The smallness of the company made it necessary for the two principal actors to take several parts apiece.

On Christmas night, a dozen girls piled on to the bed which was the dress circle, and the five acts of *The Witch's Curse: An Operatic Tragedy* began. Tumultuous applause followed the final curtain, and then Hannah appeared, with "Mrs. March's compliments, and would the ladies walk down to supper?"

This was a surprise, even to the actors, and when they saw the table they looked at one another in amazement. There was ice cream, pink and white, and cake and fruit and distracting French bonbons, and in the middle of the table four great bouquets of hothouse flowers!

"Is it fairies?" asked Amy.

"It's Santa Claus," said Beth.

"Mother did it," and Meg smiled her sweetest.

"Aunt March had a good fit and sent the supper," cried Jo.

"All wrong. Old Mr. Laurence sent it," replied Mrs. March.

"The Laurence boy's grandfather! What in the world put such a thing into his head? We don't know him!" exclaimed Meg.

"Hannah told one of his servants about your breakfast party. He is an odd old gentleman, but that pleased him. He knew my father, years ago, and he sent me a polite note this afternoon, saying he hoped I would allow him to express his friendly feeling toward my children by sending them a few trifles in honor of the day."

"That boy put it into his head, I know he did! He's a capital fellow, and I wish we could get acquainted. He's bashful, and Meg is so prim she won't let me speak to him when we pass," said Jo.

"You mean the people who live in the big house next door?" asked one of the girls. "Mother knows old Mr. Laurence, but says he's very proud and doesn't like to mix with his neighbors. He keeps his grandson shut up, when he isn't riding or walking with his tutor, and makes him study very hard. We invited him to our party but he didn't come. Mother says he's very nice."

"Our cat ran away once and he brought her back. We talked over the fence and were getting on capitally—all about cricket and so on—when he saw Meg coming and walked off. I mean to know him someday, for he needs fun, I'm sure he does," said Jo decidedly.

"I never had such a fine bouquet before! How pretty it is!" said Meg.

"They *are* lovely, but Beth's roses are sweeter to me," said Mrs. March, smelling the half-dead posy in her belt.

Beth whispered softly, "I wish I could send my bunch to Father. I'm afraid he isn't having a merry Christmas."

Chapter 3

THE LAURENCE BOY

"JO! JO! Where are you?" cried Meg, at the foot of the garret stairs.

"Here!" answered a husky voice from above. Running up, Meg found her sister eating apples and crying over *The Heir of Redclyffe*, wrapped up in a comforter on an old, three-legged sofa by the sunny window.

"An invitation from Mrs. Gardiner for tomorrow night!" cried Meg, waving it. "*Mrs. Gardiner would be happy to see Miss March and Miss Josephine at a little dance on New Year's Eve.* Marmee is willing we should go. Now what *shall* we wear?"

"What's the use of asking that, when you know we shall

wear our poplins, because we haven't got anything else?" answered Jo.

"If I only had a silk!" sighed Meg. "Mother says I may when I'm eighteen, perhaps, but two years is an everlasting time to wait."

"I'm sure our pops look like silk, and they are nice enough for us. Yours is as good as new, but I forgot the burn and the tear in mine. Whatever shall I do? The burn shows badly."

"You must sit still all you can, and keep your back out of sight. The front is all right. I shall have a new ribbon for my hair, and Marmee will lend me her little pearl pin, and my new slippers are lovely, and my gloves will do, though they aren't as nice as I'd like."

"Mine are spoiled with lemonade, and I can't get any new ones, so I shall have to go without," said Jo, who never troubled about dress.

"You *must* have gloves or I won't go," said Meg.

"I can hold them so no one will know how stained they are. No! I'll tell you. We can each wear *one* good one and carry a bad one."

"Your hands are bigger than mine, and you will stretch my glove dreadfully," began Meg, whose gloves were a tender point with her.

"Then I'll go without. I don't care what people say!" cried Jo.

"You may have it, you may! Only don't stain it, and do behave nicely. Don't put your hands behind you, or stare, will you?"

"Don't worry about me. I'll be as prim as I can. Now go away and let me finish this story."

On New Year's Eve the parlor was deserted, for the two younger girls played maids, and the two elder were absorbed in the all-important business of getting ready for the party. There was a great deal of running up and down, and laughing and talking.

Meg was finished at last, and by the united exertions of

the family Jo's hair was got up and her dress on. They looked very well in their simple suits—Meg in silvery drab, with a blue velvet snood, lace frills, and the pearl pin; Jo in maroon, with a stiff, gentlemanly linen collar, and a white chrysanthemum for her only ornament. Each put on one nice light glove, and carried one soiled one. Meg's high-heeled slippers were tight and hurt her, though she would not own it, and Jo's nineteen hairpins all seemed stuck straight into her head.

"Have a good time, dearies!" said Mrs. March, as the sisters went down the walk. "Don't eat much supper, and come away at eleven, when I send Hannah for you." As the gate clashed behind them, a voice cried from a window, "Girls, girls! *Have* you both got nice pocket-handkerchiefs?"

"Yes, yes," cried Jo, adding with a laugh, "I do believe Marmee would ask that if we were running away from an earthquake."

"It is quite proper, for a real lady is always known by neat shoes, gloves, and handkerchief," replied Meg.

"Is my sash right?" asked Meg, as she turned from the glass in Mrs. Gardiner's dressing room.

"I know I shall forget. If you see me doing anything wrong, just remind me by a wink, will you?" returned Jo, giving her collar a twitch and her head a hasty brush.

"No, winking isn't ladylike. I'll lift my eyebrows if anything is wrong, and nod if you are all right. Now hold your shoulders straight, and take short steps, and don't shake hands if you are introduced to anyone. It isn't the thing."

"How *do* you learn all the proper ways? I never can. Isn't that music gay?"

Down they went, feeling a trifle timid, for they seldom went to parties, and, informal as this little gathering was, it was an event to them. Mrs. Gardiner, a stately old lady, greeted them kindly, and handed them over to the eldest of her six daughters. Meg knew Sallie, and was at her ease very soon, but Jo, who didn't care much for girls or girlish gossip, stood about, with her back carefully against the wall, feeling out of place.

Half a dozen jovial lads were talking about skates in another part of the room and she longed to join them, for skating was one of the joys of her life. She telegraphed her wish to Meg, but the eyebrows went up so alarmingly that she dared not stir. No one came to talk to her, and one by one the group near her dwindled away until she was left alone. She could not roam about and amuse herself, for the burned place would show, so she stared at people rather forlornly until the dancing began.

Meg was asked at once, and the tight slippers tripped about so briskly that none would have guessed the pain their wearer suffered smilingly. Jo saw a big redheaded youth approaching her corner, and, fearing he meant to engage her, she slipped into a curtained recess, intending to peep and enjoy herself in peace. Unfortunately, another bashful person had chosen the same refuge, for as the curtain fell behind her she found herself face to face with the "Laurence boy."

"I didn't know anyone was here," stammered Jo, preparing to back out as speedily as she had bounced in.

But the boy laughed and said pleasantly, though he looked a little startled, "Don't mind me. Stay if you like."

"Sha'n't I disturb you?"

"Not a bit. I only came here because I don't know many people, and felt rather strange at first, you know."

"So did I. Don't go away, please, unless you'd rather."

The boy sat down again and looked at his pumps. Jo said, "I think I've had the pleasure of seeing you before. You live near us, don't you?"

"Next door!" He looked up and laughed, for Jo's prim manner was rather funny when he remembered how they had chatted about cricket when he brought the cat home.

That put Jo at her ease, and she laughed as she said, "We did have such a good time over your nice Christmas present."

"Grandpa sent it."

"But you put it into his head, didn't you?"

"How is your cat, Miss March?" asked the boy, trying to look sober while his black eyes shone with fun.

"Nicely, thank you, Mr. Laurence, but I am not Miss March. I'm only Jo," returned the young lady.

"I'm not Mr. Laurence. I'm only Laurie."

"Laurie Laurence. What an odd name!"

"My first name is Theodore, but I don't like it, for the fellows called me Dora so I made them say Laurie."

"I hate my name, too—so sentimental! I wish everyone would say Jo, instead of Josephine. How did you make the boys stop calling you Dora?"

"I thrashed 'em."

"I can't thrash Aunt March so I shall have to bear it," Jo sighed.

"Don't you like to dance, Miss Jo?" asked Laurie.

"I like it well enough if there is plenty of room and everyone is lively. In a place like this I'm sure to upset something, tread on people's toes, or do something dreadful, so I keep out of mischief and let Meg sail about. Don't you dance?"

"Sometimes. You see I've been abroad a good many years, and haven't been here long enough yet to know how you do things."

"Abroad!" cried Jo. "Oh, tell me about it!"

Laurie didn't seem to know where to begin, but Jo's eager questioning soon set him going, and he told her how he had been at school in Vevey, where the boys had a fleet of boats on the lake, and went on walking trips about Switzerland.

They chatted until they felt like old acquaintances. Laurie's bashfulness soon wore off, for Jo's demeanor amused and set him at ease, and Jo was her merry self again. She liked the "Laurence boy" better than ever, and took several good looks at him, so that she might describe him to the girls; for they had no brothers, few male cousins, and boys were almost unknown creatures.

"Curly black hair, brown skin, big black eyes, handsome nose, fine teeth, small hands and feet, taller than I am, very polite, for a boy, and altogether jolly. Wonder how old he is?"

It was on the tip of Jo's tongue to ask, but she checked herself, and with unusual tact tried to find out in a roundabout way. "I suppose you are going to college soon?"

Laurie smiled but didn't seem shocked, and answered with a shrug, "Not for a year or two. I won't go before seventeen, anyway."

"Aren't you but fifteen?" asked Jo, looking at the tall lad.

"Sixteen, next month."

"How I wish I was going to college! You don't look as if you liked it."

"I hate it! Nothing but grinding or skylarking. And I don't like the way the fellows do either, in this country."

"What do you like?"

"To live in Italy, and to enjoy myself in my own way."

Jo wanted to ask what his own way was, but his black brows looked threatening, so she changed the subject. "That's a splendid polka. Why don't you go and try it?"

"If you will come too," he answered, with a gallant little bow.

"I can't, for I told Meg I wouldn't because—" There Jo stopped, and looked undecided whether to tell or to laugh.

"Because what?" asked Laurie curiously.

"You won't tell?"

"Never!"

"Well, I have a bad trick of standing before the fire, and so I burn my frocks and I scorched this one; and, though it's nicely mended, it shows, and Meg told me to keep still so no one would see it. You may laugh if you want to. It is funny, I know."

But Laurie didn't laugh. He only looked down a minute and the expression of his face puzzled Jo, when he said gently, "Never mind that. I'll tell you how we can manage. There's a long hall out there and we can dance and no one will see us. Please come?"

Jo thanked him and gladly went, wishing she had two

neat gloves when she saw the pearl-colored ones her partner wore. The hall was empty and they had a grand polka, for Laurie danced well, and taught her the German step, which delighted Jo, being full of swing and spring. When the music stopped, they sat down on the stairs to get their breath. Laurie was in the midst of an account of a students' festival at Heidelberg, when Meg appeared. She beckoned, and Jo followed her into a side room, where she found her on a sofa, holding her foot and looking pale.

"I've sprained my ankle. That stupid high heel turned and gave me a sad wrench. It aches so, I can hardly stand, and I don't know how I'm ever going to get home," she said, rocking in pain.

"I knew you'd hurt your feet with those silly shoes. I'm sorry. But I don't see what you can do, except get a carriage," answered Jo, rubbing Meg's ankle.

"I can't have a carriage, without its costing ever so much. I dare say I can't get one at all, for most people come in their own, and it's a long way to the stable, and no one to send."

"I'll go."

"No, indeed! It's past nine. I can't stop here, for Sallie has some girls staying with her, and the house is full. I'll rest till Hannah comes."

"I'll ask Laurie. He will go," said Jo, looking relieved as the idea occurred to her.

"Mercy, no! Don't ask anyone. Get my rubbers and put these slippers with our things. I can't dance any more. As soon as supper is over, watch for Hannah and tell me the minute she comes."

"They are going out to supper now. I'll stay with you. I'd rather."

"No, dear, run along and bring me some coffee. I'm so tired."

So Meg reclined, with rubbers well hidden, and Jo went blundering away to the dining room. Making a dart at the table, she secured the coffee, which she immediately spilled, thereby making the front of her dress as bad as the back.

"Oh, dear, what a blunderbus I am!" exclaimed Jo, finishing Meg's glove by scrubbing her gown with it.

"Can I help you?" said a friendly voice, and there was Laurie, with a full cup in one hand and a plate of ice in the other.

"I was trying to get something for Meg, who is very tired, and someone shook me, and here I am, in a nice state," answered Jo, glancing dismally from the stained skirt to the coffee-colored glove.

"Too bad! I was looking for someone to give this to. May I take it to your sister?"

"Oh, thank you! I'll show you where she is. I don't offer to take it myself, for I should only get into another scrape if I did."

Jo led the way, and as if used to waiting on ladies Laurie drew up a little table, brought a second instalment of coffee and ice for Jo, and they had a merry time. When Hannah appeared, Meg forgot her foot and rose so quickly that she was forced to catch hold of Jo with an exclamation of pain.

"Hush! Don't say anything," she whispered, adding aloud, "It's nothing. I turned my foot a little, that's all," and limped upstairs to put her things on.

Slipping out, Jo ran down and, finding a servant, asked if he could get her a carriage. It happened to be a hired waiter, who knew nothing about the neighborhood. Jo was looking around for help, when Laurie, who had heard what she said, came up and offered his grandfather's carriage, which had just come.

"It's so early! You can't mean to go yet?" began Jo, looking relieved, but hesitating to accept the offer.

"I always go early. I do, truly! Please let me take you home. It's all on my way, you know, and it rains, they say."

That settled it. Telling him of Meg's mishap, Jo gratefully accepted, and rushed up to bring down the rest of the party. They rolled away in the luxurious carriage, feeling festive and elegant. Laurie went on the box, so Meg could keep her foot up, and the girls talked over their party in freedom.

"I had a capital time, did you?" asked Jo, rumpling her hair.

"Yes, till I hurt myself. Sallie's friend, Annie Moffat, took a fancy to me and asked me to come and spend a week with her when Sallie does. She is going in the spring, when the opera comes. It will be perfectly splendid, if Mother only lets me go," answered Meg.

Jo told her adventures and by the time she had finished they were at home. With many thanks, they said good night and crept in, hoping to disturb no one. But the instant their door creaked, two little nightcaps bobbed up and two sleepy but eager voices cried, "Tell about the party! Tell about the party!"

Jo had saved some bonbons for the little girls, and they soon subsided, after hearing the most thrilling events.

"I declare, it really seems like being a fine young lady, to come home from the party in a carriage and sit in my dressing gown, with a maid to wait on me," said Meg, as Jo bound up her foot with arnica and brushed her hair.

"I don't believe fine young ladies enjoy themselves a bit more than we do, in spite of old gowns, one glove apiece, and tight slippers that sprain our ankles when we are silly enough to wear them," Jo replied.

Chapter 4

BURDENS

"OH DEAR, how hard it does seem to take up our packs and go on," sighed Meg, the morning after the party.

"I wish it was Christmas or New Years all the time, Wouldn't it be fun?" answered Jo, yawning dismally.

"We shouldn't enjoy ourselves half so much as we do now.

But it does seem so nice to go to parties and drive home, and not work. I'm so fond of luxury," said Meg, trying to decide which of two shabby gowns was the least shabby.

Everyone seemed rather out of sorts at breakfast, and inclined to croak. Beth had a headache, and lay on the sofa, trying to comfort herself with the cat and three kittens. Amy was fretting because her lessons were not learned, and she couldn't find her rubbers. Jo *would* whistle and make a great racket getting ready. Mrs. March was very busy trying to finish a letter, which must go at once, and Hannah had the grumps.

"There never *was* such a cross family!" cried Jo, when she had upset an inkstand, broken both bootlacings, and sat on her hat.

"Beth, if you don't keep these horrid cats down cellar I'll have them drowned," exclaimed Meg angrily, as she tried to get rid of the kitten, which had scrambled up her back, and stuck like a burr.

Jo laughed, Meg scolded, Beth implored, and Amy wailed because she couldn't remember how much nine times twelve was.

"Girls, girls, do be quiet one minute! I *must* get this off by the early mail," cried Mrs. March.

There was a momentary lull, broken by Hannah, who stalked in, laid two hot turnovers on the table, and stalked out again. These turnovers were an institution, and the girls called them "muffs," for they had no others. The hot pies were comforting to their hands on cold mornings.

"Cuddle your cats, and get over your headache, Bethy. Good-by, Marmee. We are a set of rascals this morning but we'll come home regular angels. Now then, Meg!" and Jo tramped away, feeling that the pilgrims were not setting out as they ought to do.

They always looked back before turning the corner, for their mother was always at the window, to nod and smile, and wave her hand to them. Somehow it seemed as if they couldn't have got through the day without that, for whatever their mood might be the last glimpse of that motherly face was like sunshine.

"If Marmee shook her fist instead of kissing her hand to us, it would serve us right, for more ungrateful wretches than we are were never seen," cried Jo.

"Don't use such dreadful expressions," said Meg from the depths of her veil.

"I like good strong words that mean something," replied Jo, catching her hat as it took a leap off her head.

"Call yourself any names you like, but *I* am neither a rascal nor a wretch and I don't choose to be called so."

"You're a blighted being and decidedly cross today because you can't sit in the lap of luxury all the time. Poor dear, just wait till I make my fortune, and you shall revel in carriages and ice cream and high-heeled slippers."

"How ridiculous you are, Jo," but Meg laughed.

Jo gave her sister an encouraging pat on the shoulder as they parted for the day, each going a different way.

When Mr. March lost his property in trying to help an unfortunate friend, the two oldest girls begged to be allowed to do something toward their own support. Believing that they could not begin too early to cultivate energy, industry, and independence, their parents consented, and both fell to work with hearty good will. Margaret found a place as nursery governess, and felt rich with her small salary. She found poverty harder to bear than the others, because she could remember a time when home was beautiful, life full of ease and pleasure, and want of any kind unknown. She tried not to be discontented, but it was natural that the young girl should long for pretty things, gay friends, and a happy life. At the Kings' she daily saw all she wanted, for the children's older sisters were just out, and Meg caught frequent glimpses of dainty ball dresses and bouquets, and heard lively gossip of theaters and parties. Poor Meg seldom complained, but a sense of injustice made her feel bitter sometimes.

Jo happened to suit Aunt March, who was lame and needed an active person to wait on her. The childless old lady had offered to adopt one of the girls and was much offended because her offer was declined. Other friends told the Marches that they had lost all chance of being remembered in the rich old lady's will, but the unworldly Marches only said, "We can't give up our girls for a dozen fortunes. Rich or poor, we will keep together and be happy."

The old lady wouldn't speak to them for a time, but happening to meet Jo at a friend's, something in her comical face and blunt manners struck the old lady's fancy, and she proposed to take her for a companion. This did not suit Jo at all, but she accepted the place since nothing better appeared, and to everyone's surprise got on remarkably well with her irascible relative. The real attraction was a library of fine books. The moment Aunt March took her nap, or was busy with company, Jo hurried to this quiet place and devoured poetry, romance, history, travels, and pictures.

Jo's ambition was to do something splendid. What it was she had no idea as yet, and meanwhile found her greatest affliction in the fact that she couldn't read, run, and ride as much as she liked.

Beth was too bashful to go to school. It had been tried, but she suffered so much that it was given up, and she did her lessons at home with her father. Even when he went away, and her mother was called to devote her skill and energy to Soldiers' Aid Societies, Beth went faithfully on by herself and did the best she could. She helped Hannah keep home neat. She had her troubles as well as the others. She loved music dearly, tried hard to learn, and practiced away patiently at the jingling old piano. She sang like a lark about her work, never was too tired to play for Marmee and the girls, and day after day said hopefully to herself, "I know I'll get my music sometime, if I'm good."

If anybody had asked Amy what the greatest trial of her life was, she would have answered at once, "My nose." When she was a baby, Jo had accidentally dropped her into the coal hod, and Amy insisted that the fall had ruined her nose forever. It was not big or red. It was only rather flat, and all the pinching in the world could not give it an aristocratic point. Amy felt deeply the want of a Grecian nose, and drew whole sheets of handsome ones to console herself.

"Little Raphael," as her sisters called her, had a decided talent for drawing, and was never so happy as when copying flowers, designing fairies, or illustrating stories. One thing rather quenched her vanities—she had to wear her cousin's clothes. Amy suffered deeply at having to wear a red instead of a blue bonnet, unbecoming gowns, and fussy aprons that did not fit.

Meg was Amy's confidant and monitor, and by some strange attraction of opposites Jo was gentle Beth's. To Jo alone did the shy child tell her thoughts, and over her big, harum-scarum sister Beth unconsciously exercised more influence than anyone in the family.

"Has anybody got anything to tell?" asked Meg, as they sat sewing together that evening. "It's been such a dismal day I'm really dying for some amusement."

"I had a queer time with Aunt today, and as I got the best of it I'll tell you about it," began Jo. "I was reading that everlasting Belsham's *Essays*. Aunt soon drops off, and then I take out some nice book and read like fury till she wakes up. The minute her cap began to bob, I whipped *The Vicar of Wakefield* out of my pocket and read away, with one eye on him and one on Aunt. I'd just got to where they all tumbled into the water, when I forgot and laughed out loud. Aunt woke up, and being more good-natured after her nap told me to read a bit. I did my best, and she liked it though she only said, 'I don't understand what it's about. Go back and begin it.'"

"Did she own she liked it?" asked Meg.

"Oh, bless you, no! But she let old Belsham rest, and when I ran back after my gloves this afternoon, there she was, so hard at the *Vicar* that she didn't hear me laugh. I don't envy her much, in spite of her money. Rich people have as many worries as poor ones, I think," added Jo.

"That reminds me," said Meg. "It isn't funny, like Jo's

story, but I thought about it a good deal as I came home. At the Kings' today, one of the children said that her oldest brother had done something dreadful, and Papa had sent him away. I heard Mrs. King crying, and Mr. King talking very loud. Grace and Ellen turned away their faces when they passed me, so I shouldn't see how red their eyes were. I didn't ask any questions, of course, but I felt so sorry for them, and was rather glad I hadn't any wild brothers to do wicked things and disgrace the family."

"I think being disgraced in school is a great deal try*inger* than anything bad boys can do," said Amy, shaking her head. "Susie Perkins came to school today with a lovely red carnelian ring. I wanted it dreadfully. Well, she drew a picture of Mr. Davis, with a monstrous nose and a hump, and the words, 'Young ladies, my eye is upon you!' coming out of his mouth in a balloon thing. We were laughing over it, when all of a sudden his eye *was* on us, and he ordered Susie to bring up her slate. She was *parry*lized with fright, but she went, and oh, what *do* you think he did? He took her by the ear, led her to the recitation platform, and made her stand there half an hour, holding that slate so everyone could see. Susie cried quarts, I know she did. I didn't envy her then, for I felt that millions of carnelian rings wouldn't have made me happy after that."

"I saw something that I liked this morning, and I meant to tell it at dinner but I forgot," said Beth, putting Jo's topsy-turvy basket in order as she talked. "When I went to get some oysters for Hannah, Mr. Laurence was in the fish shop, but he didn't see me, for I kept behind a barrel, and he was busy with Mr. Cutter, the fish man. A poor woman came in with a pail and a mop, and asked Mr. Cutter if he would let her do some scrubbing for a bit of fish, because she hadn't any dinner for her children, and had been disappointed of a day's work. Mr. Cutter was in a hurry, and said 'No,' rather crossly. So she was going away looking hungry and sorry, when Mr. Laurence hooked up a big fish with the crooked end of his cane and held it out to her. She was so glad and

surprised, she took it right in her arms and thanked him over
and over. He told her to 'go along and cook it,' and she hurried off, so happy! Wasn't it good of him? Oh, she did look
so funny, hugging the big slippery fish, and hoping Mr.
Laurence's bed in heaven would be 'aisy.' "

When they had laughed at Beth's story, they asked their
mother for one. After a moment's thought she said soberly:
"As I sat cutting out blue flannel jackets today, at the rooms,
I felt very anxious about Father, and thought how lonely
and helpless we should be if anything happened to him. An
old man came in, with an order for some clothes. He sat
down near me, and I began to talk to him, for he looked poor
and tired and anxious.

" 'Have you sons in the army?' I asked.

" 'Yes ma'am. I had four, but two were killed, one is a
prisoner, and I'm going to the other, who is very sick in a
Washington hospital,' he answered quietly.

" 'You have done a great deal for your country, sir,' I said,
feeling respect now instead of pity.

" 'Not a mite more than I ought, ma'am. I'd go myself, if
I was any use. As I ain't, I give my boys.'

"He spoke so cheerfully, looked so sincere, and seemed so
glad to give his all, that I was ashamed of myself. I'd given
one man and thought it too much, while he gave four without grudging them. I felt so rich, so happy, thinking of my
blessings, that I made him a nice bundle, gave him some
money, and thanked him for the lesson he had taught me."

Chapter 5

BEING NEIGHBORLY

"WHAT in the world are you going to do now, Jo?" asked
Meg one snowy afternoon, as her sister came tramping

through the hall in rubber boots and hood, a broom in one hand and a shovel in the other.

"Going out for exercise," answered Jo with a twinkle.

Meg went back to toast her feet and read *Ivanhoe*, and Jo began to dig paths with great energy. The snow was light, and she soon swept a path all around the garden which sep· arated the Marches' house from that of Mr. Laurence. Both stood in a suburb of the city which was still countrylike, with groves and lawns, large gardens, and quiet streets. On one side of the low hedge was an old brown house, looking rather bare and shabby, robbed of the vines that in summer covered its walls, and the flowers which then surrounded it. On the other side, was a stately stone mansion, plainly betokening every sort of comfort and luxury, from the big coach house and well-kept grounds to the conservatory and the glimpses of lovely things one caught between the rich curtains.

To Jo's lively fancy, this fine house seemed a kind of enchanted palace, full of splendors and delights. She had long wanted to behold these hidden glories and to know the "Laurence boy." Since the party she had been more eager than ever, and had planned many ways of making friends with him. But he had not been seen lately, and Jo began to think he had gone away, when one day she spied a brown face at an upper window, looking wistfully down into their garden where Beth and Amy were snowballing one another.

"That boy is suffering for society and fun," she said to herself. "His grandpa does not know what's good for him, and keeps him shut up all alone. He needs somebody young and lively. I've a great mind to go over and tell the old gentleman so!"

The idea amused Jo, who liked to do daring things. The plan was not forgotten, and when the snowy afternoon came Jo resolved to try what could be done. She saw Mr. Laurence drive off, and then sallied out to dig her way down to the hedge, where she paused and took a survey. All quiet— nothing human visible but a curly black head leaning on a thin hand at the upper window.

"I'll toss up a snowball and make him look out," Jo thought.

Up went a handful of soft snow and the head turned at once. The face lost its listless look, the big eyes brightened and the mouth began to smile. Jo nodded and laughed, as she called, "How do you do? Are you sick?"

Laurie opened the window and croaked, "Better, thank you. I've had a bad cold and been shut up a week."

"I'm sorry. What do you amuse yourself with? Don't you read?"

"Not much. They won't let me."

"Can't somebody read to you?"

"Grandpa does sometimes, but my books don't interest him and I hate to ask Brooke all the time."

"Have someone come and see you then."

"There isn't anyone I'd like to see. Boys make such a row."

"Isn't there some nice girl who'd read and amuse you?"

"Don't know any."

"You know us," began Jo, then laughed and stopped.

"So I do! Will you come, please?" cried Laurie.

"I'm not quiet and nice, but I'll come, if Mother will let me. I'll go ask her. Shut that window, like a good boy."

With that Jo shouldered her broom and marched into the house, wondering what they would all say to her. Laurie was in a flutter of excitement at the idea of having company, and flew about to get ready. Presently there came a loud ring, then a decided voice asking for "Mr. Laurie," and a servant came to announce a young lady.

"All right, show her up. It's Miss Jo," said Laurie, going to the door of his little parlor to meet Jo, who appeared with a covered dish in one hand and Beth's three kittens in the other.

"Here I am, bag and baggage," she said briskly. "Mother sent her love and was glad if I could do anything for you. Meg wanted me to bring some of her blancmange, and Beth thought her cats would be comforting. I knew you'd laugh at them, but I couldn't refuse."

It so happened that Beth's funny loan was just the thing, for in laughing over the kits, Laurie forgot his bashfulness. "That looks too pretty to eat," he said, smiling with pleasure as Jo uncovered the blancmange.

"Tell the girl to put it away for your tea. It's so simple it will slip down without hurting your sore throat. What a cozy room this is!"

"It might be if it was kept nice."

"I'll right it up in two minutes. It only needs to have the hearth brushed, so, and the things made straight on the mantelpiece, so, and the books put here and the bottles there, and your sofa turned from the light, and the pillows plumped up a bit." As she laughed and talked, Jo whisked things into place, and gave a different air to the room. Laurie watched her in respectful silence, and when she beckoned him to his sofa he sat down with a sigh of satisfaction, saying gratefully: "How kind you are! Please take the big chair and let me amuse my company."

"No, I came to amuse you. Shall I read aloud?"

"Thank you, I've read all those. If you don't mind, I'd rather talk," answered Laurie.

"Not a bit. I'll talk all day. Beth says I never know when to stop."

"Is Beth the rosy one who stays at home a good deal, and sometimes goes out with a little basket?" asked Laurie with interest.

"Yes. She's my girl, and a regular good one she is, too."

"The pretty one is Meg, and the curly-haired one is Amy."

"How did you find that out?"

Laurie colored but answered frankly, "Why, you see, I often hear you calling to one another, and I can't help looking over at your house. I beg your pardon for being so rude, but sometimes you forget to put down the curtain at the window where the flowers are, and when the lamps are lighted it's like looking at a picture to see the fire and you all around the table with your mother. Her face is right opposite, and it looks so sweet behind the flowers. I haven't got any mother, you know," and Laurie poked the fire to hide a little twitching of the lips that he could not control.

The solitary hungry look in his eyes went straight to Jo's warm heart. Laurie was sick and lonely, and feeling how rich she was in home love and happiness, she gladly tried to share it with him. Her sharp voice was unusually gentle as she said: "We'll never draw that curtain any more, and I give you leave to look as much as you like. I just wish, though, instead of peeping you'd come over and see us. Mother is so splendid, she'd do you heaps of good, and we'd have jolly times. Wouldn't your grandpa let you?"

"I think he would, if your mother asked him. He's very kind and he lets me do what I like, pretty much, only he's afraid I might be a bother to strangers," began Laurie.

"We are not strangers, we are neighbors, and you needn't think you'd be a bother. We *want* to know you."

"You see, Grandpa lives among his books. Mr. Brooke, my tutor, doesn't stay here, and I have no one to go about with me, so I just stop at home."

"That's bad. You ought to make an effort, and go visiting everywhere you are asked. Then you'll have plenty of friends and places to go. Never mind being bashful. It won't last long."

"Do you like your school?" asked the boy, changing the subject.

"Don't go to school. I'm a businessman—girl, I mean. I go to wait on my great-aunt, and a dear, cross old soul she is, too," answered Jo.

She gave him a lively description of the old lady, her fat poodle, the parrot that talked Spanish, and the library where she reveled. Laurie enjoyed it immensely. Then they got to talking about books, and to Jo's delight she found that he loved them as well as she did.

"Come down and see ours," said Laurie, getting up. "Grandpa is out, so you needn't be afraid."

"I'm not afraid of anything," returned Jo, with a toss of her head.

Laurie led the way from room to room, letting Jo stop to examine whatever struck her fancy. At last they came to the library, where she clapped her hands and pranced, as she always did when delighted. It was lined with books, and there were pictures and statues and distracting little cabinets full of coins and curiosities, and sleepy-hollow chairs, and queer tables, and bronzes. Best of all, there was a great open fireplace with quaint tiles all around it.

"What richness!" sighed Jo, sinking into the depth of a velvet chair. "Theodore Laurence, you ought to be the happiest boy in the world."

"A fellow can't live on books," said Laurie.

Before he could say more, a bell rang. Jo flew up, exclaiming with alarm, "Mercy me! It's your grandpa!"

"Well, what if it is? You are not afraid of anything, you know."

"I think I am a little bit afraid of him, but I don't know why I should be. Marmee said I might come," said Jo, composing herself.

"I'm a great deal better for it, and ever so much obliged," said Laurie gratefully.

"The doctor to see you, sir," and the maid beckoned as she spoke.

Laurie went away, and Jo was standing before a fine portrait of the old gentleman when the door opened again. Without turning, she said: "I'm sure now that I shouldn't be afraid of him, for he's got kind eyes, though his mouth is grim, and he looks as if he had a tremendous will. He isn't as handsome as *my* grandfather but I like him."

"Thank you, ma'am," said a gruff voice behind her, and there, to her great dismay, stood old Mr. Laurence.

Poor Jo blushed and her heart began to beat uncomfortably fast. A wild desire to run away possessed her, but she resolved to stay and get out of the scrape as she could. A second look showed her that the living eyes under the bushy gray eyebrows were kinder even than the painted ones, and there was a sly twinkle in them, which lessened her fear a good deal.

The gruff voice was gruffer than ever, as the old gentleman said abruptly after that dreadful pause, "So you're not afraid of me, hey?"

"Not much, sir."

"And you don't think me as handsome as your grandfather?"

"Not quite, sir."

"And I've got a tremendous will, have I?"

"I only said I thought so."

"But you like me in spite of it?"

"Yes, I do, sir."

That answer pleased the old gentleman. He gave a short laugh, shook hands with her, and putting his finger under her chin turned up her face, examined it gravely, and said with a nod: "You've got your grandfather's spirit, if you haven't his face. He *was* a fine man, my dear, but what is better he was a brave and an honest one, and I was proud to be his friend."

"Thank you, sir," and Jo was quite comfortable after that.

"What have you been doing to this boy of mine, hey?" was the next question, sharply put.

"Only trying to be neighborly, sir," and Jo told of her visit.

"You think he needs cheering up a bit, do you?"

"Yes, sir. He seems a little lonely. We should be glad to help if we could, for we don't forget the Christmas present you sent us," said Jo eagerly.

"Tut, tut, tut! That was the boy's affair. How is the poor woman?"

"Doing nicely, sir," and Jo told about the Hummels in whom her mother had interested friends.

"Just her father's way of doing good. I shall come and see your mother, some fine day. Tell her so. There's the tea bell. We have it early on the boy's account. Come down and go on being neighborly."

"If you'd like to have me, sir."

"Shouldn't ask you if I didn't," and Mr. Laurence offered her his arm with old-fashioned courtesy.

"What *would* Meg say to this?" thought Jo.

"Hey! Why, what the dickens has come to the fellow?" said the old gentleman as Laurie came running downstairs and stopped with a start of surprise at the sight of Jo arm in arm with his grandfather.

"I didn't know you'd come, sir."

The old gentleman did not say much as he drank his four cups of tea, but he watched the young people and the change in his grandson did not escape him. There was color, light and life in the boy's face now, vivacity in his manner, and genuine merriment in his laugh.

"She's right, the lad *is* lonely. I'll see what these girls can do for him," thought Mr. Laurence. He liked Jo, for her odd blunt ways suited him, and she seemed to understand the boy as well as if she had been one herself.

When they rose, Jo proposed to go, but Laurie said he had something more to show her, and took her to the conservatory which had been lighted for her benefit. It seemed quite fairylike to Jo, as she went up and down the walks, enjoying the blooming walls on either side, the soft light, the damp sweet air, and the wonderful vines and trees that hung above her, while her new friend cut the finest flowers until his hands were full. Then he tied them up, saying, with the happy look Jo liked to see, "Please give these to your mother, and tell her I like the medicine she sent me very much."

They found Mr. Laurence standing before the fire in the great drawing room, but Jo's attention was entirely absorbed by a grand piano which stood open. "Do you play?" she asked, turning to Laurie.

"Sometimes," he answered modestly.

"Please do now. I want to hear it so I can tell Beth."

So Laurie played and Jo listened, with her nose buried luxuriously in heliotrope and tea roses. Her regard for the "Laurence boy" increased, for he played remarkably well. She wished Beth could hear him, but she did not say so; only praised him until he was quite abashed and his grand-father came to the rescue.

"That will do, young lady. His music isn't bad, but I hope he will do as well in more important things. Going? Well, I'm much obliged to you, and I hope you'll come again. My respects to your mother. Good night, Doctor Jo."

He shook hands kindly but looked as if something did not please him. When they got into the hall Jo asked Laurie if she had said anything amiss.

He shook his head. "He doesn't like to hear me play."

"Why not?"

"I'll tell you someday. You will come again, I hope?"

"If you promise to come and see us after you are well."

"I will."

"Good night, Laurie!"

"Good night, Jo, good night!"

When the afternoon's adventures had been told, the family felt inclined to go visiting in a body, for each found some-thing attractive in the big house on the other side of the hedge. Mrs. March wanted to talk of her father with the old man who had not forgotten him. Meg longed to walk in the conservatory. Beth sighed for the grand piano, and Amy was eager to see the pictures and statues.

"Mother, why didn't Mr. Laurence like to have Laurie play?" asked Jo, who was of an inquiring disposition.

"I am not sure, but I think it was because his son, Laurie's father, married an Italian lady, a musician, which displeased the old man, who is very proud. The lady was good and lovely and accomplished, but he did not like her and never saw his son after he married. They both died when Laurie was little, and then his grandfather took him home. I fancy the boy, who was born in Italy, is not very strong and the old man is afraid of losing him, which makes him so careful. Laurie comes naturally by his love of music, and I dare say his grandfather fears that he may want to be a musician, and his skill reminds him of the woman he did not like."

"Dear me, how romantic!" exclaimed Meg.

"How silly!" said Jo. "Let him be a musician, if he wants to, and not plague him. We'll all be good to him, because he hasn't any mother, and he *may* come over and see us, mayn't he, Marmee?"

"Yes, Jo, your friend is very welcome."

"I was thinking about our *Pilgrim's Progress*," answered Beth. "How we got out of the Slough and through the Wicket Gate by resolving to be good, and up the steep hill by trying. It may be the house over there, full of splendid things, is going to be our Palace Beautiful."

"We have got to get by the lions first," said Jo.

Chapter 6

BETH FINDS THE PALACE BEAUTIFUL

THE BIG HOUSE did prove a Palace Beautiful, though it took some time for all to get in, and Beth found it very hard to pass the lions. Old Mr. Laurence was the biggest one, but after he had called, said something funny or kind to each one of the girls, and talked over old times with their mother, nobody felt much afraid of him except Beth. The other lion was the fact that they were poor and Laurie rich, for this made them shy of accepting favors which they could not return. But after a while they found that he considered them the benefactors, and could not do enough to show how grateful he was. So they soon forgot their pride, and interchanged kindnesses without stopping to think which was the greater.

What good times they had! Such plays and tableaux, such sleigh rides and skating frolics, such pleasant evenings in the old parlor, and now and then such gay little parties at the great house. Meg could walk in the conservatory whenever she liked, Jo browsed over the new library, and Amy copied pictures and enjoyed beauty to her heart's content.

But Beth, though yearning for the grand piano, could not pluck up courage to go to the "Mansion of Bliss," as Meg called it. She went once with Jo, but the old gentleman stared at her so hard from under his heavy eyebrows and said "Hey!" so loud, that he frightened her so much she ran away, declaring she would never go there any more not even for the piano. No persuasions or enticements could overcome her fear, until the fact came to Mr. Laurence's ear in some mysterious way and he set about mending matters.

During one of his brief calls he artfully led the conversation to music, and talk about great singers he had heard, and told such charming anecdotes that Beth found it impossible

to stay in her distant corner, but crept nearer and nearer.
At the back of his chair she stopped and stood listening, her
great eyes wide open and her cheeks red with the excitement of this unusual performance. Taking no more notice of
her than if she had been a fly, Mr. Laurence talked on about
Laurie's lessons and teachers, and then, as if the idea had
just occurred to him, said:

"The boy neglects his music now and I'm glad of it, for
he was getting too fond of it. But the piano suffers for want
of use. Wouldn't some of your girls like to run over and practice now and then, just to keep it in tune, you know,
ma'am?"

Beth took a step forward and pressed her hands tightly
together to keep from clapping them. The thought of prac-
ticing on that splendid instrument quite took her breath
away. Before Mrs. March could reply, Mr. Laurence went
on with an odd little smile and nod: "They needn't see or
speak to anyone, but run in at any time. I'm shut up in my
study at the other end of the house, Laurie is out a great
deal, and the servants are never near the drawing room
after nine o'clock. But if they don't care to come, never
mind."

Here he rose as if going, and Beth made up her mind to
speak. A little hand slipped into his and Beth looked up at
him with a face full of gratitude, as she said in her earnest
yet timid way, "Oh, sir, they do care, very much!"

"Are you the musical girl?" he asked without any startling
"Hey!"

"I'm Beth. I love it dearly, and I'll come if you are quite
sure nobody will hear me—and be disturbed," she added,
fearing to be rude.

"Not a soul, my dear. The house is empty half the day,
so come and drum away as much as you like, and I shall
be obliged to you."

Beth blushed under his friendly look, but she was not
frightened now, and gave the big hand a grateful squeeze
because she had no words to thank him for the gift. The

old gentleman softly stroked the hair off her forehead and, stooping down, kissed her, saying in a tone few people ever heard, "I had a little girl once with eyes like these. God bless you, my dear! Good day, madam." And away he went, in a great hurry.

How blithely Beth sang that evening, and how they all laughed at her because she woke Amy in the night by playing the piano on her face in her sleep. Next day, having seen both the old and young gentlemen out of the house, Beth, after two or three retreats, got in at the side door and made her way as noiselessly as any mouse to the drawing room. Some easy music lay on the piano and with trembling fingers and frequent stops to listen and look about, Beth at last touched the great instrument. She straightway forgot her fear, herself, and everything but the unspeakable delight which the music gave her, for it was like the voice of a beloved friend. She stayed until Hannah came to take her home to dinner, but she had no appetite and could only sit and smile upon everyone.

After that, the little brown hood slipped through the hedge nearly every day, and the great drawing room was haunted by a tuneful spirit that came and went unseen. She never knew that Mr. Laurence often opened his study door to hear the old-fashioned airs he liked. She never saw Laurie mount guard in the hall to warn the servants away. She never suspected that the exercise books and new songs which she found in the rack were put there for her special benefit.

"Mother, I'm going to work Mr. Laurence a pair of slippers. He is so kind to me, I must thank him. Can I do it?" asked Beth, a few weeks after the eventful call.

"Yes, dear. It will please him very much and be a nice way of thanking him. The girls will help you, and I will pay for the making up."

After many serious discussions with Meg and Jo, the pattern was chosen, the materials bought, and the slippers begun. A cluster of grave yet cheerful pansies on a deeper purple ground was pronounced pretty, and Beth worked away early and late, with occasional lifts over the hard parts. She was a nimble little needlewoman and the slippers were finished before anyone got tired of them. Then she wrote a short simple note and with Laurie's help got them smuggled on to the study table one morning before the old gentleman was up.

When this excitement was over, Beth waited to see what would happen. All that day passed and a part of the next before any acknowledgement arrived, and she was beginning to fear she had offended her crotchety friend. On the afternoon of the second day she went out to do an errand. As she came up the street she saw four heads popping in and out of the parlor window. The moment they saw her several hands were waved, and several joyful voices screamed, "Here's a letter from the old gentleman! Come quick and read it!"

"Oh, Beth, he's sent you—" began Amy, but she got no further, for Jo slammed the window.

Beth hurried on in a flutter of suspense. At the door her sisters seized her and bore her to the parlor in a triumphial procession, all pointing and saying at once, "Look there! Look there!"

Beth did look and turned pale with delight, for there stood a little cabinet piano with a letter lying on the glossy lid for "Miss Elizabeth March."

"For me?" gasped Beth, holding on to Jo.

"Yes, all for you! Isn't it splendid of him? Here's the key in the letter. We didn't open it but we are dying to know what he says," cried Jo.

"You read it. I can't, I feel so queer. Oh, it is too lovely!" and Beth hid her face in Jo's apron.

Jo opened the paper and read:

> *Miss March:*
> *Dear Madam,—*
> *I have had many pairs of slippers in my life, but*
> *I never had any that suited me so well as yours.*

Heart's-ease is my favorite flower, and these will always remind me of the gentle giver. I like to pay my debts, so I know you will allow "the old gentleman" to send you something which once belonged to the little granddaughter he lost. With hearty thanks and best wishes, I remain

Your grateful friend and humble servant,
James Laurence

"There, Beth, that's an honor to be proud of! Laurie told me how fond Mr. Laurence used to be of the child who died, and how he kept all her little things carefully. Just think, he's given you her piano. That comes of having big blue eyes and loving music," and Jo tried to soothe Beth, who trembled and looked excited.

"See the cunning brackets to hold candles, and the green silk puckered up with a gold rose in the middle, and the pretty rack and stool, all complete," added Meg, opening the instrument.

"*Your humble servant, James Laurence.* Only think of his writing that to you. I'll tell the girls," said Amy, much impressed.

"Try it, honey. Let's hear the sound of the baby pianny," said Hannah, who always took a share in the family joys and sorrows.

So Beth tried it, and everyone pronounced it the most remarkable piano ever heard. It had evidently been newly tuned and put in applepie order. Beth lovingly touched the beautiful black-and-white keys and pressed the bright pedals.

"You'll have to go and thank him," said Jo, joking.

"Yes, I mean to. I guess I'll go now before I get frightened thinking about it." And to the amazement of the assembled family Beth walked deliberately down the garden, through the hedge, and in at the Laurences' door.

They would have been still more amazed if they had seen what Beth did. She knocked at the study door before she gave herself time to think. When a gruff voice called out, "Come in!" she did go in, right up to Mr. Laurence, who looked quite taken aback and held out his hand. With only a small quaver in her voice she said, "I came to thank you sir, for—" But she didn't finish, for he looked so friendly that she forgot her speech, and only remembering that he had lost the little girl he loved, she put both arms around his neck and kissed him.

If the roof of the house had suddenly flown off, the old gentleman wouldn't have been more astonished, but he was so touched and pleased by the confiding little kiss that all his crustiness vanished. He set her on his knee and laid his wrinkled cheek against her rosy one, feeling as if he had his own little granddaughter back again. Beth ceased to fear him from that moment.

When she went home, he walked with her to her own gate, shook hands cordially, and touched his hat as he marched back again, looking very stately and erect.

Chapter 7

AMY'S VALLEY OF HUMILIATION

"THAT BOY is a perfect Cyclops, isn't he?" said Amy one day, as Laurie clattered by on horseback, with a flourish of his whip as he passed.

"How dare you say so, when he's got both his eyes, and very handsome ones they are, too," cried Jo.

"I didn't say anything about his eyes. I admire his riding."

"The little goose means a centaur, and she called him a Cyclops," exclaimed Jo with a burst of laughter.

"You needn't be so rude; it's only a 'lapse of lingy,' as Mr. Davis says," retorted Amy, finishing Jo with her Latin.

"I just wish I had a little of the money Laurie spends on that horse," she added.

"Why?" asked Meg kindly.

"I need it so much. I'm dreadfully in debt, and it won't be my turn to have the rag money for a month."

"In debt, Amy? What do you mean?" and Meg looked sober.

"Why, I owe at least a dozen pickled limes, and I can't pay till I have money, for Marmee forbade my having anything charged."

"Tell me all about it. Are limes the fashion now?"

"The girls are always buying them and unless you want to be thought mean, you must do it, too. If one girl likes another, she gives her a lime. They treat by turns, and I've had ever so many, but haven't returned them, and I ought, for they are debts of honor."

"How much will pay them off and restore your credit?" asked Meg, taking out her purse.

"A quarter would more than do it, and leave a few cents over for a treat for you. Don't you like limes?"

"Not much. You may have my share. Here's the money."

"Oh, thank you! It must be so nice to have pocket money! I'll have a grand feast, for I haven't tasted a lime this week."

Next day Amy was rather late at school, but could not resist the temptation of displaying with pardonable pride a moist brown paper parcel before she consigned it to the inmost recess of her desk. During the next few minutes the rumor that Amy March had twenty-four delicious limes—she ate one on the way—and was going to treat, circulated through her set, and the attentions of her friends became quite overwhelming. Even Jenny Snow, who had twitted Amy upon her limeless state, offered to furnish answers to certain sums. But Amy had not forgotten Miss Snow's cutting remarks, and returned, "You needn't be so polite all of a sudden for you won't get any."

A distinguished personage happened to visit the school that morning and Amy's beautifully drawn maps received praise, which honor rankled in the soul of Miss Snow and caused Miss March to assume the airs of a studious young peacock. No sooner had the guest bowed himself out, than Jenny, under pretense of asking an important question, informed Mr. Davis, the teacher, that Amy March had pickled limes in her desk.

Now Mr. Davis had declared limes a contraband article, and vowed to ferrule publicly the first person who was found breaking the law. His yellow face flushed, and he rapped on his desk with an energy which made Jenny skip to her seat. "Young ladies, attention, if you please!"

At the stern order the buzz ceased, and fifty pairs of eyes were obediently fixed upon his awful countenance.

"Miss March, come to the desk."

Amy rose with outward composure but a secret fear oppressed her, for the limes weighed upon her conscience.

"Bring with you the limes you have in your desk," was the unexpected command before she got out of her seat.

"Don't take all," whispered her neighbor.

Amy hastily shook out half a dozen and laid the rest before Mr. Davis. "Is that all?"

"Not quite," stammered Amy.

"Bring the rest immediately."

With a despairing glance she obeyed.

"You are sure there are no more?"

"I never lie, sir."

"So I see. Now take these disgusting things two by two and throw them out of the window."

Scarlet with shame, Amy went to and fro six dreadful times. As she returned from her last trip, Mr. Davis gave a portentous "Hem!" and said in his most impressive manner, "Young ladies, you remember what I said to you a week ago. I am sorry this has happened, but I never allow my rules to be infringed and I never break my word. Miss March, hold out your hand."

Amy started and put both hands behind her, turning on him an imploring look.

"Your hand, Miss March!" was the only answer her mute appeal received. Too proud to cry or beseech, Amy set her teeth, threw back her head defiantly, and bore without flinching several tingling blows on her little palm. For the first time in her life she had been struck and the disgrace was as deep as if he had knocked her down.

"You will now stand on the platform till recess," said Mr. Davis.

That was dreadful. It would have been bad enough to go to her seat, but to face the whole school with that shame fresh upon her seemed impossible. A bitter sense of wrong and the thought of Jenny Snow helped her to bear it. Taking the ignominious place, Amy fixed her eyes on the stove funnel above what now seemed a sea of faces and stood there, motionless and white. During the fifteen minutes that followed, the proud and sensitive little girl suffered a shame and pain which she never forgot. The fifteen minutes seemed an hour but they came to an end at last with the welcome word "Recess!"

"You can go, Miss March," said Mr. Davis.

He did not soon forget the reproachful glance Amy gave him as she went, without a word to anyone, straight into the anteroom, snatched her things, and left the place forever, as she passionately declared to herself. She was in a sad state when she got home, and when the older girls arrived sometime later, an indignation meeting was held at once. Mrs. March did not say much but looked disturbed and comforted her little daughter.

No notice was taken of Amy's flight except by her mates, but they discovered that Mr. Davis was quite benignant in the afternoon, also unusually nervous. Just before school closed, Jo appeared, wearing a grim expression as she stalked up to the desk and delivered a letter from her mother and collected Amy's property.

"Yes, you can have a vacation from school, but I want you to study a little every day with Beth," said Mrs. March that evening. "I don't approve of corporal punishment, especially for girls."

"That's good! I wish all the girls would leave and spoil his old school. It's perfectly maddening to think of those lovely limes," sighed Amy with the air of a martyr.

"I am not sorry you lost them, for you broke the rules and deserved some punishment," was the severe reply.

"Do you mean you are glad I was disgraced?"

"I should not have chosen that way of mending a fault," replied her mother, "but I'm not sure that it won't do you more good than a milder method. You are getting to be conceited. The great charm of all power is modesty."

"So it is!" cried Laurie, who was playing chess in a corner with Jo. "I knew a girl once who had a really remarkable talent for music, and she didn't know it, never guessed what sweet little things she composed, and wouldn't have believed it if anyone had told her."

"I wish I'd known that nice girl," said Beth, who was listening eagerly. "Maybe she would have helped me."

"You do know her and she helps you better than anyone else could," answered Laurie, looking at her with such mischievous meaning that Beth turned red.

Jo let Laurie win the game, to pay for that praise of her Beth. When he had gone home, Amy said suddenly, "Is Laurie an accomplished boy?"

"Yes, he has had an excellent education and has much talent," replied her mother. "He will make a fine man."

"And he isn't conceited, is he?" asked Amy.

"Not in the least. That is why he is so charming."

"I see. It's nice to have accomplishments but not to show off or get perked up," said Amy thoughtfully.

"These things are always seen and felt," said Mrs. March, "but it is not necessary to display them."

"Any more than it's proper to wear all your bonnets and gowns at once that folks may know you've got them," added Jo, and the lecture ended in a laugh.

Chapter 8

JO MEETS APOLLYON

"GIRLS, where are you going?" asked Amy, coming into their room one Saturday afternoon and finding them getting ready to go out.

"Never mind. Little girls shouldn't ask questions," returned Jo.

Amy bridled, and determined to find out the secret. Turning to Meg she said coaxingly, "Do tell me! You might let me go, too, for Beth is fussing over her piano and I haven't anything to do."

"I can't dear, because you aren't invited," began Meg, but Jo broke in impatiently, "Now Meg, be quiet, or you will spoil it all. You can't go, Amy, so don't be a baby."

"You're going somewhere with Laurie, aren't you?"

"Yes we are. Now do be still and stop bothering."

"I know, I know! You're going to the theater to see *The Seven Castles!*" she cried, adding, "and I *shall* go, for Mother said I might see it. I've got my rag money, and it was mean not to tell me in time."

"You can go with Beth and Hannah next week," Meg said soothingly, "and have a nice time."

"I don't like that half as well as going with you and Laurie. Please let me, I've been sick with this cold so long," pleaded Amy.

"I don't believe Mother would mind, if we bundle her up well," began Meg.

"If *she* goes, *I* shan't, and if I don't, Laurie won't like it. It will be very rude after he invited only us to go, to drag in Amy. I should think she'd hate to poke herself where she isn't wanted," Jo said crossly.

Her tone angered Amy, who began to put her boots on,

46

saying, "I *shall* go. Meg says I may, and if I pay for myself, Laurie hasn't anything to do with it."

"You can't sit with us, for our seats are reserved, and you mustn't sit alone, so Laurie will give you his place and that will spoil our pleasure. Or he'll get another seat for you, and that isn't proper when you weren't asked. You sha'n't stir a step, so you may just stay where you are," scolded Jo.

Amy began to cry and Meg to reason with her, when Laurie called from below and the two girls hurried down. Amy called over the banisters in a threatening tone, "You'll be sorry for this, Jo March!"

"Fiddlesticks!" returned Jo, slamming the door.

The Seven Castles of the Diamond Lake was as brilliant and wonderful as heart could wish, but in spite of the comical red imps, sparkling elves, and gorgeous princes and princesses, Jo's pleasure had a drop of bitterness in it. Between acts, she amused herself with wondering what her sister would do to make her sorry.

When they got home, they found Amy reading in the parlor. She assumed an injured air and never lifted her eyes from her book. Beth received a glowing description of the play. On going up to put away her best hat, Jo's first look was toward the bureau, for in their last quarrel Amy had soothed her feelings by turning Jo's top drawer upside down on the floor. Everything was in place, however, and Jo decided Amy had forgiven and forgotten her wrongs.

The next day Meg, Beth and Amy were sitting together, late in the afternoon, when Jo burst into the room. "Has anyone taken my book?" she demanded breathlessly.

Meg and Beth said "No," at once and looked surprised. Amy poked the fire and said nothing. Jo saw her color rise and was down on her in a minute. "Amy, you've got it!"

"No I haven't."

"You know where it is then!"

"No I don't."

"That's a fib!" cried Jo, taking her by the shoulders, looking fierce.

"It isn't. I haven't got it, don't know where it is, and don't care."

"You know something about it, and you'd better tell at once, or I'll make you," and Jo gave her a slight shake.

"You'll never see your silly old book again!" cried Amy.

"Why not?"

"I burned it up."

"My little book I was so fond of, and worked over, and meant to finish before Father got home? Have you really burned it?" said Jo, turning very pale, while her hands clutched Amy nervously.

"Yes, I did! I told you I'd make you pay for yesterday—"

Amy got no farther, for Jo's temper mastered her and she shook Amy until her teeth chattered, crying in grief and anger, "You wicked, wicked girl! I never can write it again, and I'll never forgive you."

Meg flew to rescue Amy, and Beth to pacify Jo, but Jo was beside herself. With a parting box on her sister's ear, she rushed out of the room up to the old sofa in the garret, and finished her fight alone.

When Mrs. March came home and heard the story, she soon brought Amy to a sense of the wrong she had done her sister. Jo's book was the pride of her heart, and was regarded by her family as having great promise. It was half a dozen little fairy tales which she had worked over patiently and hoped to make something good enough to print. She had just copied them with great care and destroyed the old manuscript, so Amy's bonfire had consumed the work of several years.

When the tea bell rang, Jo appeared looking so grim that it took all Amy's courage to say meekly, "Please forgive me, Jo. I'm very sorry."

"I shall never forgive you," was Jo's stern answer, and from that moment she ignored Amy entirely.

It was not a happy evening. As Jo received her goodnight kiss, Mrs. March whispered gently, "My dear, don't let the sun go down upon your anger. Forgive each other and begin again tomorrow."

Jo wanted to cry, but she winked hard, shook her head, and said gruffly, because Amy was listening, "It was an abominable thing, and she doesn't deserve to be forgiven." With that she marched off to bed.

The next day Jo still looked like a thundercloud, and nothing went well. "Everybody is so hateful," she said to herself that afternoon. "I'll ask Laurie to go skating. He will put me to rights, I know."

Amy heard the clash of skates and exclaimed, "There! She promised I should go next time, but it's no use to ask such a crosspatch."

"Don't say that. You were very naughty, and it is hard to forgive the loss of her precious book," said Meg. "Go after them. Don't say anything until Jo has got goodnatured with Laurie. Then kiss her, or do some kind thing, and I'm sure she'll be friends again."

"I'll try," and Amy ran after Laurie and Jo. It was not far to the river, but both were ready before Amy reached them. Jo saw her coming and turned her back. Laurie did not see, for he was carefully skating along the shore, sounding the ice, for a warm spell had preceded the cold snap. "I'll go on to the first bend and see if it's all right before we begin to race," Amy heard him say as he shot away.

Jo heard Amy putting her skates on, stamping her feet and blowing on her fingers, but she never turned and went slowly zigzagging down the river, taking a bitter satisfaction in her sister's troubles. As Laurie turned the bend, he shouted back, "Keep near the shore. It isn't safe in the middle."

Jo heard, but Amy was just struggling to her feet and did not catch a word. Laurie had vanished around the bend, Jo was just at the turn, and Amy, far behind, was striking out toward the smoother ice in the middle of the river. For a minute Jo stood still, with a strange feeling at her heart. Then she resolved to go on but something turned her around just in time to see Amy throw up her hands and go down with the sudden crash of rotten ice, the splash of water, and a cry that made Jo's heart stand still with fear. She tried to call Laurie but her voice was gone. She tried to rush forward but her feet seemed to have no strength in them. For a second she could only stand motionless, staring with terror-stricken face at the little blue hood above the black water.

Something rushed swiftly by her, and Laurie's voice cried, "Bring a rail. Quick, quick!"

How she did it she never knew, but for the next few minutes she worked as if possessed, blindly obeying Laurie who, lying flat, held Amy up by his arm and hockey stick until Jo dragged a rail from the fence. Together they got the child out, more frightened than hurt.

"Now then, we must walk her home as fast as we can. Pile things on her while I get off these confounded skates," cried Laurie, wrapping his coat around Amy and tugging away at the straps.

Shivering, dripping and crying, they got Amy home. After

an exciting time of it, she fell asleep rolled in blankets before a hot fire. During the bustle Jo had scarcely spoken, but flown about, looking pale and wild with her things half off, her dress torn, and her hands cut and bruised by ice and rails. When Amy was asleep, Mrs. March called Jo to her and began to bind up the hurt hands.

"Are you sure she is safe?" whispered Jo, full of remorse.

"Quite safe, dear. She is not hurt and won't even take cold, I think," replied her mother cheerfully.

"Laurie did it all. I only let her go. Mother, if she should die it would be my fault," and Jo dropped down beside the bed in a passion of penitent tears, telling all that had happened. "It's my dreadful temper. Oh, Mother, what shall I do?" cried poor Jo.

"Don't cry so bitterly, my child. You think your temper is the worst in the world, but mine used to be just like it."

"Yours, Mother? Why you are never angry," said Jo in surprise.

"I've been trying to cure it for forty years and have only succeeded in controlling it."

"What helped you?"

"Your father, Jo. He never loses patience, never doubts or complains, but always hopes and works and waits so cheerfully that one is ashamed to do otherwise before him."

"Oh Mother, if I'm ever half as good as you I shall be satisfied," cried Jo, much touched.

"I hope you will be a great deal better, dear," her mother replied.

Amy stirred and sighed in her sleep and Jo looked up with an expression on her face which it had never worn before. "I let the sun go down on my anger. I wouldn't forgive her and today, if it hadn't been for Laurie, it might have been too late! How could I be so wicked?" Jo said half aloud, as she leaned over her sister, softly stroking the wet hair scattered on the pillow.

As if she heard, Amy opened her eyes and held out her arms with a smile that went straight to Jo's heart. Neither said a word but they hugged one another close and everything was forgiven in a kiss.

Chapter 9

MEG GOES TO VANITY FAIR

"I DO THINK it was the most fortunate thing in the world that those children should have the measles just now," said Meg one April day, as she stood packing.

"And so nice of Annie Moffat not to forget her promise. A whole fortnight of fun will be splendid," replied Jo.

"I wish I was going to have a fine time and wear all these nice things," said Amy with her mouth full of pins.

"I wish you were all going. You've been so kind, lending me things and helping me get ready," said Meg, glancing around the room.

"What did mother give you out of the treasure box?" asked Amy, who had not been present at the opening of the cedar chest in which Mrs. March kept a few relics of past splendor as gifts for her girls.

"A pair of silk stockings, that pretty carved fan, and a lovely blue sash. I wanted the violet silk, but there isn't time to make it over, so I must be content with my old tarlatan."

"It will look nicely over my new muslin skirt and the sash will set it off beautifully," said Jo.

"There is a lovely old-fashioned pearl set in the treasure box, but Mother said real flowers were the prettiest ornament for a young girl, and Laurie promised to send me all I want," replied Meg. "Now let me see. There's my new gray walking suit, then my poplin for Sunday and the small party. It looks heavy for spring, doesn't it? The violet silk would be so nice!"

"Never mind. You've got the tarlatan for the big party and you always look like an angel in white," said Amy.

"It isn't low-necked, and it doesn't sweep enough, but it will have to do. My blue house dress looks so well, turned and freshly trimmed, that I feel as if I had a new one. My bonnet doesn't look like Sallie's. I didn't like to say anything but I was sadly disappointed in my umbrella. I told Mother black with a white handle, but she forgot and bought a green one with a yellowish handle. It's strong and neat, so I ought not to complain, but I know I shall feel ashamed of it beside Annie's silk one with a gold top," sighed Meg.

"Change it," advised Jo.

"I won't be so silly or hurt Marmee's feelings. My silk stockings and two pairs of new gloves are my comfort. You are a dear to lend me yours, Jo."

The next day was fine and Meg departed in style for a fortnight of novelty and pleasure.

The Moffats were very fashionable, and Meg was rather daunted at first by the splendor of the house and the elegance of its occupants. But they were kindly people and soon put their guest at ease. It was agreeable to do nothing but enjoy herself and suited her exactly. Soon she began to imitate the manners and conversation of those about her, to put on little airs and graces, use French phrases, crimp her hair, and take in her dresses.

The more Meg saw of Annie Moffat's pretty things, the more she envied her and sighed to be rich. The three young girls shopped, walked, rode, and called all day, and went to the theater and opera, or frolicked at home, in the evening. Annie's older sisters were very fine young ladies and one was engaged. Mr. Moffat knew Meg's father, and Mrs. Moffat petted her. Daisy, as they called her, was in a fair way to have her head turned.

When the evening for the small party came, Meg found that the poplin wouldn't do at all, for the other girls were putting on thin dresses, so out came the tarlatan, looking older and shabbier than ever beside Sallie's crisp new one. Meg saw the girls glance at it and then at one another, and her cheeks burned, for she was proud. No one said a word about it, but Sallie offered to dress her hair, and Annie to tie her sash, and Belle, the engaged sister, praised her white arms. In their kindness Meg saw only pity for her poverty, and her heart was heavy. The hard bitter feeling was getting pretty bad when the maid brought in a box of flowers. Before she could speak, Annie had the cover off and all were exclaiming at the lovely roses and ferns.

"It's for Belle," cried Annie. "George always sends her some."

"They are for Miss March, the man said. And here's a note," put in the maid, holding it out to Meg.

"What fun! Who are they from?" cried the girls.

"The note is from Mother, the flowers from Laurie," said Meg simply.

"Oh, indeed!" said Annie, with a funny look as Meg slipped the note into her pocket as a sort of talisman against envy. Feeling almost happy again, she laid by a few ferns and roses for herself and quickly made up the rest in dainty bouquets for her friends.

She enjoyed herself very much that evening for she danced to her heart's content. She had a nice time until she overheard a bit of conversation which disturbed her extremely. She was sitting just inside the conservatory, waiting for her partner to bring her an ice, when she heard a voice on the other side of the flowery wall ask, "How old is he?"

"Sixteen or seventeen, I should say," replied another voice.

"It would be a grand thing for one of those girls, wouldn't it? Sallie says the old man quite dotes on them."

"Mrs. M. has made her plans, I dare say, and will play her cards well, early as it is. The girl evidently doesn't think of it yet," said Mrs. Moffat.

"She told that fib about her mamma as if she did know, and colored when the flowers came. Poor thing! She'd be so nice if she was only got up in style. Do you think she'd be offended if we offered to lend her a dress for Thursday?" asked another voice.

"She's proud but I don't believe she'd mind, for that dowdy tarlatan is all she has. She may tear it tonight and that will be a good excuse for offering a decent one."

"We'll see. I shall ask young Laurence, as a compliment to her, and we'll have fun about it afterward."

Here Meg's partner appeared, to find her looking flushed and agitated. Her pride was useful then, for it helped her hide her anger and disgust at what she had heard. She tried to forget it but could not.

Poor Meg had a restless night and got up heavy-eyed and unhappy. She was half ashamed of herself for not speaking out frankly and setting everything right. As the girls sat at their worsted work, Miss Belle looked up from her writing and said, "Daisy, dear, I've sent an invitation to your friend Mr. Laurence for Thursday. We should like to know him, and it's only a proper compliment to you."

Meg colored but a mischievous fancy to tease the girls made her reply demurely, "You are very kind but I'm afraid he won't come."

"Why not, *chèrie?*" asked Miss Belle.

"He's too old."

"What do you mean? What is his age?" cried Miss Clara.

"Nearly seventy, I believe," answered Meg.

"You sly creature! We meant the young man," exclaimed Miss Belle.

"There isn't any. Laurie is only a little boy," Meg said.

"About your age," Nan said.

"Nearer my sister Jo's. I am seventeen in August," returned Meg.

"What shall you wear Thursday?" asked Sallie, changing the subject.

"My old white one again if I can mend it. It got sadly torn last night," said Meg, trying to speak easily.

"Why don't you send home for another?" asked Sallie.

"I haven't got any other." That cost Meg an effort.

Belle broke in kindly, "There's no need of sending home, Daisy, even if you have a dozen, for I have a sweet blue silk laid away which I've outgrown and you shall wear it to please me, won't you, dear?"

"You are very kind but I don't mind if you don't," said Meg.

"Now do let me please myself by dressing you up in style. We'll burst on them like Cinderella and her godmother," said Belle persuasively.

Meg couldn't refuse the offer so kindly made, so on Thursday evening Belle shut themselves up with her maid and they turned Meg into a fine lady. They crimped and curled her hair, polished her neck and arms with powder, touched her lips with coralline salve, to make them redder. They laced her into a sky-blue dress which was so tight she could hardly breathe, and so low in the neck that modest Meg blushed. A set of silver filigree was added—bracelets, necklace, brooch and even earrings. A cluster of rosebuds at the bosom and a ruche reconciled Meg to the display of her pretty white shoulders, and a pair of high-heeled blue silk boots satisfied the last wish of her heart. A lace handkerchief, a plumy fan, and a bouquet in a silver holder were the finishing touches, and Miss Belle surveyed her with satisfaction.

"Come and show yourself," she said, leading the way to the others. Meg went rustling after, with her long skirts trailing, her earrings tinkling, her curls waving, and her heart beating. Her friends were enthusiastic and chattered like a party of magpies, while Meg stood enjoying her borrowed plumes like the jackdaw in the fable.

"I'm afraid to go down, I feel so queer and half-dressed," said Meg to Sallie.

"You don't look a bit like yourself but you are very nice. I'm nowhere beside you for Belle has heaps of taste and you're quite French, I assure you. Let your flowers hang, and be sure you don't trip," and Sallie tried not to care that Meg was prettier than herself.

Keeping that warning carefully in mind, Margaret got safely downstairs and sailed into the drawing rooms, where the Moffats and a few early guests were assembled. Several young ladies who had taken no notice of her before were affectionate all of a sudden. Several young gentlemen, who had only stared at her at the other party, asked to be introduced, and said all manner of foolish but agreeable things. Margaret got on pretty well, but the tight dress gave her a side ache, the train kept getting under her feet, and she was in constant fear lest her earrings fly off and get lost or broken. She was flirting her fan and laughing, when she suddenly stopped and looked confused, for just opposite she saw Laurie. He was staring at her with undisguised surprise and disapproval, also, she thought. He bowed and smiled, yet something in his honest eyes made her blush and wish she had her old dress on. She rustled across the room.

"I'm glad you came. I was afraid you wouldn't."

"Jo wanted me to come and tell her how you looked, so I did," he said.

"What shall you tell her?" asked Meg, feeling ill at ease.

"I shall say I didn't know you, for you look so grown-up and unlike yourself. I'm quite afraid of you," and he fumbled at his glove button.

"How absurd! The girls dressed me up for fun and I rather like it. Don't you like me so?" she asked.

"No I don't," was the blunt reply.

"Why not?" in an anxious tone.

His expression abashed her more than his answer, which had not a particle of his usual politeness. "I don't like fuss and feathers."

That was too much from a lad younger than herself, and Meg walked away saying petulantly, "You are the rudest boy I ever saw." She went and stood at a quiet window to cool her cheeks. She leaned her forehead on the pane, never minding that her favorite waltz had begun. Someone touched her and turning, she saw Laurie, looking penitent.

"Please forgive my rudeness and come and dance with me," he said with his best bow and his hand out. "Come, I'll be good. I don't like your gown but I do think you are—just splendid."

Meg smiled and away they went, fleetly and gracefully. "Laurie, I want you to do me a favor, will you?" said Meg, as he stood fanning her when her breath gave out. "Please don't tell them at home about my dress tonight. I shall tell them myself all about it."

"I give you my word I won't, only what shall I say when they ask?"

"Just say I looked well and was having a good time."

"I'll say the first with all my heart, but how about the other? You don't look as if you were having a good time. Are you?"

"No, not just now. I wanted a little fun but I'm tired."

"Here comes Ned Moffat. What does he want?" asked Laurie.

"He put his name down for three dances and I suppose he's coming for them. What a bore!" said Meg with a languid air which amused Laurie.

He did not speak to her again until suppertime, when he saw her drinking champagne with Ned and his friend Fisher. "You'll have a splitting headache tomorrow if you drink much of that. I wouldn't, Meg. Your mother doesn't like it, you know."

"I'm not Meg tonight. Tomorrow I shall put away my fuss and feathers and be desperately good again."

"Wish tomorrow was here then," muttered Laurie walking off.

Meg was sick all the next day, and on Saturday went home. "It does seem pleasant to be quiet," she said Sunday night. "Home *is* a nice place though it isn't splendid."

"I'm glad to hear you say so, dear, for I was afraid home would seem dull after your fine quarters," replied her mother.

Meg had told her adventures gaily, and said over and over what a charming time she had had. When the younger girls were gone to bed, she sat thoughtfully staring at the fire, then suddenly left her chair and, taking Beth's stool, leaned her elbows on her mother's knee, saying bravely, "Marmee, I want to 'fess. I want you to know all the dreadful things I did at the Moffats'."

"We are prepared," said Mrs. March smiling.

"I told you they dressed me up but I didn't tell you they made me look like a fashion plate. Laurie thought I wasn't proper, though he didn't say so. They flattered me and I drank champagne and tried to flirt and was abominable."

"There is something more I think," and Mrs. March smoothed the soft cheek which suddenly grew rosy as Meg answered slowly:

"Yes. It's very silly but I want to tell it, because I hate to have people say and think such things about us and Laurie." Then she told the various bits of gossip she had heard, and Jo saw her mother fold her lips tightly, as if ill-pleased such ideas should be put in Meg's head.

"If that isn't the greatest rubbish I ever heard," cried Jo indignantly. "Why didn't you pop out and tell them so, on the spot?"

"I couldn't. It was so embarrassing. And I couldn't help hearing. Then I was so angry and ashamed, I didn't remember I ought to go away."

"Just wait till *I* see Annie Moffat and I'll show you how to settle such ridiculous stuff."

"No, never repeat that foolish gossip, and forget it as soon as you can," said Mrs. March gravely. "I was unwise to let you go among people of whom I know so little—kind, I daresay, but worldly, ill-bred, and full of these vulgar ideas about young people. I am sorry, Meg."

Margaret sat thinking a moment, while Jo looked interested. "Mother, do you have plans, as Mrs. Moffat said?" Meg asked.

"Yes my dear, I have a great many. All mothers do, but mine differ somewhat from Mrs. Moffat's. I want my daughters to be beautiful and good, to be admired, loved and respected, to have a happy youth, to be well and wisely mar-

ried, and to lead useful, pleasant lives with as little care
and sorrow to try them as God sees fit to send. But better
be happy old maids than unhappy wives. Your father and
I both trust and hope that our daughters, whether married
or single, will be the pride and comfort of our lives."

"We will, Marmee, we will!" cried both with all their
hearts.

Chapter 10

THE P.C. AND P.O

AS SPRING came on, a new set of amusements became the
fashion, and the lengthening days gave long afternoons for
work and play. The garden had to be put in order, and each
sister had a little plot to do what she liked with. Meg's had
roses and heliotrope, myrtle, and a little orange tree. Jo's
bed was never alike two seasons, for she was always trying
experiments. This year it was to be a plantation of sunflow-
ers, the seeds of which were to feed her family of chicks.
Beth had old-fashioned, fragrant flowers in her garden—
sweet peas and mignonette, larkspur, pinks, pansies, and
southernwood, with chickweed for the bird and catnip for
the pussies. Amy had a bower in hers, small but pretty,
with honeysuckles and morning-glories, tall white lilies and
delicate ferns.

Gardening, walks, rows on the river, and flower hunts em-
ployed the fine days. For rainy ones, they had house diver-
sions, some old, some new, all more or less original. One of
these was the "P.C." Secret societies were the fashion, and
as all the girls admired Dickens they called themselves the
Pickwick Club. With a few interruptions they had kept this
up for a year, and met every Saturday evening in the big
garret. Meg, as the eldest, was Samuel Pickwick; Jo, being of

a literary turn, Augustus Snodgrass; Beth, because she was round and rosy, Tracy Tupman; and Amy, who was always trying to do what she couldn't was Nathaniel Winkle. Pickwick, the president, read the weekly newspaper, *The Pickwick Portfolio*.

One evening as the president finished reading, Mr. Snodgrass rose to make a proposition. "I wish to propose the admission of a new member, one who highly deserves the honor, would be deeply grateful for it, and would add immensely to the spirit of the club. I propose Mr. Theodore Laurence as an honorary member of the P.C. Come now, do have him."

Jo's sudden change of tense made the girls laugh. "We'll put it to a vote," said the president. "All in favor of this motion say 'Ay.'"

"Ay! Ay! Ay!" replied three voices at once.

"Allow me to present the new member," and Jo threw open the door of the closet and displayed Laurie.

"You rogue! You traitor! Jo, how could you?" cried the three girls as Snodgrass led her friend triumphantly forth and, producing a chair and a badge, installed him.

The new member was equal to the occasion, and rising, with grateful salutation to the chair, said in the most engaging manner, "Mr. President and ladies, I beg your pardon, gentlemen, allow me to introduce myself as Sam Weller, the very humble servant of the club"

"Good, good!" cried Jo. "Hear, hear!"

"Go on, go on," added Winkle and Tupman.

"I merely wish to say that, as a slight token of my gratitude for the honor done me, and as a means of promoting friendly relations between adjoining nations, I have set up a post office in the hedge in the lower corner of the garden, a fine spacious building, with padlocks on the doors, and every convenience for the mails—also the females, if I may be allowed the expression. It's the old martin house, but I've stopped up the door and made the roof open, so it will hold all sorts of things, and save our valuable time. Letters, manuscripts, books and bundles can be passed in there, and as each nation has a key, it will be uncommonly nice, I fancy. Allow me to present the club key; and, with many thanks for your favor, take my seat."

Great applause as Mr. Weller deposited a little key on the table and subsided. The P.O. was a capital little institution and flourished wonderfully, for nearly as many queer things passed through it as through the real post office. Tragedies and cravats, poetry and pickles, garden seeds and long letters, music and gingerbread, rubbers, invitations, scoldings and puppies.

The old gentleman liked the fun and amused himself by sending odd bundles, mysterious messages, and funny telegrams. His gardener, who was smitten with Hannah's charms, actually sent a love letter in Jo's care. How they laughed, never dreaming how many love letters that little post office would hold in the years to come!

Chapter 11

EXPERIMENTS

"THE FIRST of June! The Kings are off to the seashore tomorrow and I'm free. Three months' vacation—how I shall enjoy it!" exclaimed Meg, coming home one warm day to find Jo laid upon the sofa in an unusual state of exhaustion, while Beth took off her dusty boots and Amy made lemonade.

"Aunt March went today, for which oh, be joyful!" said Jo.

"I shall lie abed late and do nothing," replied Meg from the depths of the rocking-chair.

"I've laid in a heap of books," said Jo, "and I'm going to read on my perch in the old apple tree."

"Don't let us do any lessons, Beth, for a while but play all the time and rest, as the girls mean to," said Amy.

"Well, I will, if Mother doesn't mind. I want to learn some new songs."

"May we, Mother?" asked Meg, turning to Mrs. March, who sat sewing in what they called "Marmee's corner."

"You may try your experiment for a week and see how you like it. I think by Saturday night you will find that all play and no work is as bad as all work and no play."

"Oh, dear no! It will be delicious, I'm sure," said Meg complacently.

Next morning, Meg did not appear until ten o'clock. Her solitary breakfast did not taste nice, and the room seemed lonely and untidy, for Jo had not filled the vases, Beth had not dusted, and Amy's books lay scattered about. Nothing was neat and pleasant but Marmee's corner, which looked as usual. There Meg sat, to rest and read, which meant yawn, and imagine what pretty summer dresses she would get with her salary. Jo spent the morning on the river with Laurie, and the afternoon reading and crying over *The Wide, Wide World* up in the apple tree. Beth began by rummaging everything out of the big closet, but getting tired before half done she left it topsy-turvy and went to her music, rejoicing that she had no dishes to wash. Amy arranged her bower, put on her best white frock, and sat down to draw under the honeysuckles, hoping someone would see and inquire who the young artist was. No one appeared but an inquisitive daddy-longlegs, so she went for a walk, got caught in a shower and came home dripping.

At tea time they compared notes, and all agreed that it had been a delightful though unusually long day. Meg discovered the blue muslin she had bought that afternoon wouldn't wash. Jo had burned the skin off her nose boating, and got a headache by reading too long. Beth was worried by the confusion of her closet, and the difficulty of learning three or four songs at once. And Amy deeply regretted the damage done her frock, for Katy Brown's party was to be the next day and she had nothing to wear. But they assured their mother the experiment was working finely. She smiled, said nothing, and with Hannah's help did their neglected work.

It was astonishing what a peculiar and uncomfortable state of things was produced by the "resting and reveling" process. The days kept getting longer, tempers were variable and an unsettled feeling possessed everyone. Meg found time hung heavily, and Jo read until her eyes gave out and got so fidgety even good-natured Laurie quarreled with her. Beth got on pretty well but Amy fared worst of all, for her resources were small.

No one would own that they were tired of the experiment, but by Friday night each acknowledged to herself that she was glad the week was nearly done. Hoping to impress the lesson more deeply, Mrs. March gave Hannah a holiday, and when they got up Saturday morning there was no breakfast in the dining room and no mother.

"Mercy on us, what has happened!" cried Jo.

Meg ran upstairs and soon came back, looking relieved but bewildered and a little ashamed. "Mother isn't sick, only tired, and she says she is going to stay quietly in her room all day and let us do the best we can. She says it has been a hard week for her."

"I like the idea," Jo said quickly.

It was an immense relief to them all to have a little work, and they took hold with a will, but soon realized the truth of Hannah's saying, "Housekeeping ain't no joke." Beth and Amy set the table while Meg and Jo got breakfast.

"I shall take some up to Mother though she said we were not to think of her," said Meg.

A tray was fitted out and taken up. The boiled tea was bitter, the omelet scorched, and the biscuits speckled with saleratus, but Mrs. March received her repast with thanks and laughed heartily after Jo had gone. Many were the complaints below and great the cook's chagrin.

"Never mind, I'll get dinner," said Jo, who knew less than Meg about culinary affairs.

Margaret retired to the parlor, which she hastily put in order by whisking the litter under the sofa and shutting the blinds to save the trouble of dusting. Jo, with perfect faith in her own powers, immediately put a note in the post office, inviting Laurie to dinner.

"You'd better see what you've got before you think of having company," said Meg, when informed of it.

"Oh, there's corned beef and plenty of potatoes, and I shall get some asparagus and a lobster. We'll have lettuce and make a salad. I don't know how, but the book tells. I'll have blancmange and strawberries for dessert, and coffee, too, if you want to be elegant."

"Don't try too many messes, Jo, for you can't make anything but gingerbread and molasses candy. I wash my hands of the dinner party."

"You'll give me your advice, won't you?" asked Jo.

"Yes, but I don't know much, except about bread. You had better ask Mother before you order anything," returned Meg prudently.

"Get what you like," said Mrs. March, when Jo spoke to her. "I'm going out to dinner and can't worry about things at home. I never enjoyed housekeeping and I'm going to take a vacation today, and read, write, go visiting and amuse myself."

The unusual spectacle of her busy mother rocking comfortably and reading, early in the morning, made Jo feel as if an eclipse, an earthquake, or a volcanic eruption would hardly have seemed stranger. "Everything is out of sorts somehow," she said to herself, going downstairs. "There's Beth crying. If Amy is bothering, I'll shake her."

Jo hurried into the parlor to find Beth sobbing over Pip, the canary, who lay dead in the cage with his little claws pathetically extended.

"It's all my fault. I forgot him. There isn't a seed or a

drop left. Oh Pip, oh Pip! How could I be so cruel to you?" cried Beth.

"Now don't cry, Bethy. The funeral shall be this afternoon and we'll all go." Leaving the others to console Beth, Jo departed to the kitchen, which was in a most discouraging state of confusion. Putting on a big apron she fell to work. Having rekindled the fire, she thought she would go to market while the water heated. The walk revived her spirits. She trudged home with a very young lobster, some very old asparagus, and two boxes of acid strawberries. By the time she got cleared up, the stove was red hot. Hannah had left a pan of bread to rise, Meg had worked it up early, set it on the hearth for a second rising, and forgotten it.

Meg was entertaining Sallie Gardiner in the parlor, when the door flew open and a floury, flushed, dishevelled figure appeared, demanding tartly, "I say, isn't bread 'riz' enough when it runs over the pans?"

Sallie began to laugh, but Meg nodded and lifted her eyebrows as high as they would go, which caused the apparition to vanish and put the sour bread into the oven. Mrs. March went out, and a strange sense of helplessness fell on the girls as the gray bonnet vanished around the corner. Despair seized them, when a few minutes later Miss Crocker appeared and said she had come to dinner. She was a thin spinster with a sharp nose and inquisitive eyes, who saw everything and gossiped.

The dinner Jo served became a standing joke. Fearing to ask any more advice, she did her best alone and discovered that something more than energy and good will is necessary to make a cook. She boiled the asparagus for an hour, and was grieved to find the heads cooked off and the stalks harder than ever. The bread burned black, for the salad dressing aggravated her so that she let everything else go until she had convinced herself she could not make it fit to eat. The lobster was a scarlet mystery to her, but she hammered and poked until it was unshelled, and then concealed its meager proportions in a grove of lettuce leaves. The potatoes had to be hurried, not to keep the asparagus waiting, and were not done. The blancmange was lumpy, and the strawberries not as ripe as they looked.

"Well, they can eat beef and bread and butter, if they are hungry," thought Jo, as she rang the bell half an hour later than usual.

Hot, tired and dispirited, she surveyed the feast. Laurie was accustomed to all sorts of elegance. Poor Jo would gladly have gone under the table, as one thing after another was tasted and left. Amy giggled, Meg looked distressed, Miss Crocker pursed up her lips, and Laurie laughed and talked with all his might to give a cheerful tone to the festive scene. Jo's one strong point was the fruit, for she had sugared it well, and had a pitcher of rich cream to eat with it. Her hot cheeks cooled a trifle, and she drew a long breath as the pretty glass plates went around and everyone looked graciously at the little rosy islands floating in a sea of cream. Miss Crocker tasted first, made a wry face and drank some water hastily. Jo, who had refused thinking there might not be enough, glanced at Laurie, but he was eating away manfully, though there was a slight pucker about his mouth and he kept his eyes fixed on his plate. Amy, who was fond of delicate fare, took a heaping spoonful, choked, hid her face in her napkin and left the table.

"Oh, what is it?" exclaimed Jo, trembling.

"Salt instead of sugar, and the cream is sour," replied Meg.

Jo groaned, fell back in her chair, and remembered that she had given a last hasty powdering to the berries out of one of the two boxes on the kitchen table, and had neglected to put the milk in the refrigerator. She turned scarlet and was on the verge of crying, when she met Laurie's eyes, which would look merry in spite of his heroic efforts. The comical side of the affair suddenly struck her, and she laughed until the tears ran down her cheeks. So did everyone else, even "Croaker," as the girls called the old lady, and the unfortunate dinner ended gaily with bread and butter, olives and fun.

"I haven't strength of mind enough to clear up now, so we will sober ourselves with a funeral," said Jo, as they rose.

At the conclusion of the ceremonies, Beth retired to her room overcome with emotion and lobster. But there was no place to repose, for the beds were not made, and she found her grief much assuaged by beating up pillows and putting things in order. Meg helped Jo clear away the remains of the feast, which took half the afternoon and left them so tired they agreed to be content with tea and toast for supper. Laurie took Amy to drive, which was a deed of charity, for the sour cream seemed to have had a bad effect upon her temper. As twilight fell, one by one they gathered in the porch where the June roses were budding, and each groaned or sighed as she sat down.

"What a dreadful day this has been!" began Jo.

"It has seemed short but so uncomfortable," said Meg.

"Not a bit like home," added Amy.

"It can't seem so without Marmee and little Pip," sighed Beth.

"Here's Mother, dear, and you shall have another bird tomorrow." As she spoke, Mrs. March came and took her place among them, looking as if her holiday had not been much pleasanter than theirs. "Are you satisfied with your experiment, girls, or do you want another week?"

"I don't!" cried Jo decidedly.

"Nor I," echoed the others.

"You think, then, that it is better to have a few duties and live a little for others, do you?"

"Lounging doesn't pay," observed Jo, shaking her head. "I'm tired of it and mean to go to work at something right off."

"Suppose you learn plain cooking. That's a useful accomplishment which no woman should be without," said Mrs. March, laughing inaudibly at the recollections of Jo's dinner party, for she had met Miss Crocker.

"Mother, did you go away and let everything be, just to see how we'd get on?" cried Meg.

"Yes. I wanted you to see how the comfort of all depends on each doing her share faithfully. While Hannah and I did your work, you got on pretty well, though I don't think you were every happy or amiable. Don't you feel that it is pleasanter to help one another so that home may be comfortable and lovely to us all?"

"We do, Mother, we do!" cried the girls.

"Very good! Then I am quite satisfied with the experiment," were Mrs. March's final words.

Chapter 12

CAMP LAURENCE

BETH was postmistress, for being most at home she could attend to it regularly, and dearly liked the daily task of unlocking the little door and distributing the mail. One July day she came in with her hands full and went about the house leaving letters and parcels.

"Here's your posy, Mother! Laurie never forgets that," she said putting the nosegay in the vase that stood in Marmee's corner.

"Miss Meg March, one letter and a glove," continued Beth, delivering the articles to her sister, who sat near her mother, sewing.

"Why, I left a pair over there and here is only one," said Meg, looking at the gay cotton glove. "I hate to have odd gloves! Never mind, the other may be found. My letter is only a translation of the German song I wanted. I think Mr. Brooke did it, for this isn't Laurie's writing."

"Two letters for Doctor Jo, a book, and a funny old hat which covered the whole post office stuck outside," said

Beth laughing, as she went into the study where Jo sat writing.

"What a sly fellow Laurie is! I said I wished bigger hats were the fashion because I burn my face every hot day. He said, 'Why mind the fashion? Wear a big hat and be comfortable!' I said I would if I had one, and he has sent me this to try me. I'll wear it for fun and show him I *don't* care for the fashion." Jo hung the antique broadbrim on a bust of Plato and read her letters. One from her mother made her cheeks glow and her eyes fill.

> *My dear:*
> *I write a little word to tell you with how much satisfaction I watch your efforts to control your temper. You say nothing about your trials, failures or successes, and think perhaps that no one sees them but the Friend Whose help you daily ask, if I may trust the well-worn cover of your guidebook. I, too, have seen them all and heartily believe in the sincerity of your resolution, since it begins to bear fruit. Go on, dear, patiently and bravely, and always believe that no one sympathizes more tenderly with you than your loving*
> *Mother*

"That does me good!" cried Jo. "Oh Marmee, I do try, I will keep on trying and not get tired, since I have you to help me." She opened her other letter. In a big dashing hand, Laurie wrote:

> *Dear Jo*
> *What ho!*
> *Some English girls and boys are coming to see me tomorrow and if it's fine I'm going to pitch my tent in Longmeadow, and row up the whole crew to lunch and croquet. They are nice people. Brooke will go, to keep us boys steady, and Kate Vaughn*

*to play propriety for the girls. I want you all to
come. Don't bother about rations—I'll see to that
and everything else—only do come, there's a good
fellow!*

*In a tearing hurry,
Yours ever, Laurie*

"Here's richness!" cried Jo, flying in to tell the news to
Meg. "Of course we can go, Mother? It will be such a help
to Laurie, for I can row, and Meg see to the lunch, and the
children be useful."

"I hope the Vaughns are not fine, grown-up people. Do
you know anything about them, Jo?" asked Meg.

"Only that there are four of them. Kate is older than you,
Fred and Frank, twins, about my age, and a little girl, Grace,
who is nine or ten. Laurie knew them abroad and liked the
boys. Let's fly around and do double duty today, so we can
play tomorrow with free minds."

When the sun peeped into the girls' room early next morning, to promise them a fine day, he saw a comical sight. Amy
had put a clothespin on her nose to uplift the offending feature. Jo woke first and roused all her sisters by a hearty
laugh at Amy's ornament. Soon there was a lively bustle in
both houses. Beth kept reporting what went on next door.

"There goes the man with the tent," she called. "I see Mrs.
Barker doing up the lunch in a hamper and a great basket.
Now Mr. Laurence is looking up at the sky and the weathercock. I wish he would go, too. There's Laurie, looking like a
sailor. Here's a carriage full of people, a tall lady, a little
girl and two dreadful boys. One is lame, poor thing; he's got
a crutch. Laurie didn't tell us that. Be quick, girls! It's getting late. Why there is Ned Moffat, I do declare. Look, Meg,
isn't that the man who bowed to you one day when we were
shopping?"

"So it is. How queer that he should come. I thought he
was at the mountains. There is Sallie. I'm glad she got back
in time. Oh Jo, you are not going to wear that awful hat?

It's too absurd," remonstrated Meg, as Jo tied down with a red ribbon the broad-brimmed, old-fashioned Leghorn Laurie had sent for a joke.

"I just will, for it's capital—so shady, light and big." With that, Jo marched away and the rest followed, all looking their best in summer suits with happy faces under the jaunty hat brims.

Laurie ran to meet and present them to his friends. Meg was grateful to see that Miss Kate, though twenty, was dressed with simplicity, and she was much flattered by Mr. Ned's assurances that he came especially to see her. Beth decided the lame boy was not dreadful, but gentle, and she would be kind to him. Amy found Grace a well-mannered, merry little person, and after staring dumbly at one another for a few minutes, they suddenly became very good friends.

Tents, lunch, and croquet set having been sent on beforehand, the party soon embarked, and the two boats pushed off together, leaving Mr. Laurence waving his hat on the shore, Laurie and Jo rowed one boat, Mr. Brooke and Ned the other. In the second boat, Meg was face to face with the two men, who admired the prospect. Mr. Brooke was a grave, silent young man, with handsome brown eyes and a pleasant voice. Meg liked his quiet manners and considered him a walking encyclopedia of useful knowledge. He never talked to her much, but he looked at her a good deal and she felt sure that he did not regard her with averison. Ned being in college, of course put on all the airs which freshmen think it their duty to assume. Sallie Gardiner was absorbed in keeping her white piqué dress clean, and chattering with Fred, who kept Beth in constant terror by his pranks.

It was not far to Longmeadow, but the tent was pitched and the wickets down by the time they arrived. A pleasant green field, with three widespreading oaks in the middle, and a smooth strip of turf for croquet.

"Welcome to Camp Laurence!" said the young host, as they landed with exclamations of delight. "Brooke is commander-in-chief, I am commissary general, the other fellows are staff officers, and you, ladies, are company. The tent is for your especial benefit and that oak is your drawing room. This is the mess room and the third is the camp kitchen. Now let's have a game before it gets hot, and then we'll see about dinner."

Frank, Beth, Amy and Grace sat down to watch the game played by the other eight. Mr. Brooke chose Meg, Kate and Fred. Laurie took Sallie, Jo and Ned. The English people played well, but the Americans played better, and contested every inch of ground. Jo and Fred had several skirmishes, and once narrowly escaped high words. Jo was through the last wicket and had missed the stroke, which failure ruffled her a good deal. Fred was close behind her and his turn came before hers. He gave a stroke, his ball hit the wicket, and stopped an inch on the wrong side. No one was very near, and running up to examine, he gave a sly nudge with his toe which put it an inch on the right side.

"I'm through! Now Miss Jo, I'll settle you and get in first," cried the young gentleman, swinging his mallet for another blow.

"You pushed it. I saw you. It's my turn now," said Jo sharply.

"Upon my word, I didn't move it. It rolled a bit perhaps, but that is allowed. So stand off, please, and let me have a go at the stake."

"We don't cheat in America but you can, if you choose," said Jo angrily.

"Yankees are a deal the most tricky, everybody knows. There you go!" returned Fred, croqueting her ball far away.

Jo opened her lips to say some thing rude but checked herself in time, colored up to her forehead, and stood a minute, hammering down a wicket with all her might, while Fred hit the stake and declared himself out with much exultation. She went off to get her ball and was a long time finding it among the bushes, but she came back looking cool and quiet, and waited her turn patiently. It took several strokes to regain the place she had lost, and when she got there, the other side had nearly won, for Kate's ball was the last but one and lay near the stake.

"By George, it's all up with us! Good-by, Kate. Miss Jo owes me one, so you are finished," cried Fred excitedly.

"Yankees have a trick of being generous to their enemies," said Jo, with a look that made the lad redden, "especially when they beat them," she added, as leaving Kate's ball untouched, she won the game by a clever stroke.

Laurie threw up his hat, then remembered that it wouldn't do to exult over the defeat of his guests. He whispered to his friend, "Good for you, Jo! He did cheat, I saw him. We can't tell him so, but he won't do it again, take my word for it."

Meg drew her aside, under pretense of pinning up a loose braid, and said approvingly, "It was dreadfully provoking, but you kept your temper and I'm so glad, Jo."

"Don't praise me, Meg, for I could box his ears this minute. I should certainly have boiled over if I hadn't stayed among the nettles until I got my rage under enough to hold my tongue. It's simmering now so I hope he'll keep out of my way," returned Jo, biting her lips as she glowered at Fred from under her big hat.

"Time for lunch," said Mr. Brooke, looking at his watch. "Commissary general, will you make the fire and get water, while Miss March, Miss Sallie and I spread the table? Who can make good coffee?"

"Jo can," said Meg, glad to recommend her sister. So Jo, feeling that her late lessons in cookery were to do her honor, went to preside over the coffeepot, while the children collected dry sticks and the boys made a fire and got water from a spring nearby. Miss Kate sketched, and Frank talked to Beth, who was making little mats of braided rushes to serve as plates.

The commander-in-chief and his aides soon spread the tablecloth with an inviting array, prettily decorated with green leaves. Jo announced the coffee was ready, and everyone settled themselves to a hearty meal. A very merry lunch it was, for everything seemed fresh and funny, and frequent peals of laughter startled a venerable horse who fed nearby.

"There's salt here, if you prefer it," said Laurie, as he handed Jo a saucer of berries.

"Thank you, I prefer spiders," she replied, fishing up two unwary little ones which had gone to a creamy death. "How dare you remind me of that horrid dinner party when yours is so nice in every way?" added Jo as they both laughed.

"I had an uncommonly good time that day and haven't got over it yet. This is no credit to me, you know. I don't do anything. It's you and Meg and Brooke who made it go, and I'm no end obliged to you. What shall we do after lunch?" asked Laurie.

"Have games till it's cooler. I brought Authors, and I daresay Miss Kate knows something new and nice. Go and ask her. She's company and you ought to stay with her more."

"Aren't you company too? I thought she'd suit Brooke, but he keeps talking to Meg."

Miss Kate did know several new games, and they all adjourned to the drawing room to play Rigmarole. "One person begins a story," Kate explained, "any nonsense you like, and tells as long as he pleases, only taking care to stop short at some exciting point, when the next one takes it up and does the same. It's very funny when well done. Please start it, Mr. Brooke," Kate commanded.

Lying on the grass at the feet of the two young ladies, Mr. Brooke obediently began the story, with the handsome brown eyes steadily fixed on the sunshiny river.

"What a piece of nonsense we have made!" exclaimed Sallie, after they had laughed over their story. "With practice we might do something quite clever. Do you know Truth?"

"What is it?" said Fred.

"Why, you pile up your hands, choose a number, and draw out in turn. The person who draws at the number has to answer truly any questions put by the rest. It's great fun."

"Let's try it," said Jo, who liked new experiments.

Miss Kate and Mr. Brooke, Meg, and Ned declined, but

Fred, Sallie, Jo and Laurie piled and drew. The lot fell to Laurie.

'Who are your heroes?" asked Jo.

"Grandfather and Napoleon."

"Which lady here do you think prettiest?" said Sallie.

"Margaret."

"Which do you like best?" from Fred.

"Jo, of course."

"What silly questions you ask!" and Jo gave a disdainful shrug as the rest laughed at Laurie's matter-of-fact tone.

"Try again. Truth isn't a bad game," said Fred.

"It's a very good one for you," retorted Jo.

His turn came next. "Let's give it to him," whispered Laurie to Jo, who nodded and asked at once, "Didn't you cheat at croquet?"

"Well, yes, a little bit."

"Good," said Laurie, as Jo nodded to Fred as a sign that peace was declared.

"I think Truth is a silly game," she said. "Let's have a sensible game of Authors to refresh our minds."

Ned, Frank and the little girls joined in this, and while it was on the three elders sat apart, talking. Miss Kate took out her sketch again, and Margaret watched her, while Mr. Brooke lay on the grass with a book which he did not read. "Did the German song suit, Miss March?" he inquired.

"Oh, yes. It was very sweet and I'm much obliged to whoever translated it for me," and Meg's face brightened as she spoke. "I don't read German well."

"Here is Schiller's *Mary Stuart* and a tutor who loves to teach," and Mr. Brooke laid his book on her lap with a smile.

"It's so hard I'm afraid to try," said Meg gratefully, but she obediently followed the long grass blade which her new tutor used to point with, read slowly and timidly, unconsciously making poetry of the hard words by the soft intonation of her musical voice. Down the page went the green guide, and presently, forgetting her listener in the beauty of the sad scene, Meg read as if alone, giving a little touch of tragedy to the words of the unhappy queen. If she had seen the brown eyes then, she would have stopped short, but she never looked up and the lesson was not spoiled for her.

"Very well indeed!" said Mr. Brooke as she paused, ignoring her many mistakes.

"I only wish I liked teaching as you do," Meg said.

"I think you would if you had Laurie for a pupil. I shall be very sorry to lose him next year," said Mr. Brooke.

"Going to college, I suppose?" Meg's lips asked the question but her eyes added, "And what becomes of you?"

"Yes, it's high time he went, for he is ready. As soon as he is off, I shall turn soldier. I am needed."

"I am glad of that!" exclaimed Meg, "I should think every young man would want to go, though it is hard for the mothers and sisters who stay at home," she added sorrowfully.

"I have neither, and very few friends, to care whether I live or die," said Mr. Brooke rather bitterly.

"Laurie and his grandfather would care a great deal, and we should all be very sorry to have any harm happen to you," said Meg heartily.

"Thank you, that sounds pleasant," and Mr. Brooke looked cheerful again.

An impromptu circus, fox and geese, and an amicable game of croquet finished the afternoon. At sunset the tent was struck, hampers packed, wickets pulled up, boats loaded, and the whole party floated down the river, singing at the tops of their voices.

CHAPTER 13

SECRETS

JO was very busy in the garret, for the October days began to grow chilly and the afternoons were short. For two or three hours the sun lay warmly in the high window, showing Jo seated on the old sofa, writing busily, with her papers spread out upon a trunk before her. Jo scribbled away until the last page was filled, when she signed her name with a flourish and threw down her pen, exclaiming, "There, I've done my best! If this won't suit I shall have to wait till I can do better."

Lying back on the sofa, she read the manuscript through carefully, making dashes here and there, and putting in many exclamation points, which looked like little balloons. Then she tied it up with a smart red ribbon and sat a minute looking at it with a wistful expression which plainly showed how earnest her work had been. Jo's desk up here was an old tin kitchen which hung against the wall. In it she kept her papers and a few books, safely shut away from Scrabble, her pet rat. From this tin receptacle Jo produced another manuscript, and putting both in her pocket crept quietly downstairs.

She put on her hat and jacket as noiselessly as possible, and going to the back entry window, got out upon the roof of a low porch, swung herself down to the grassy bank, and took a roundabout way to the road. Once there, she hailed a passing omnibus and rolled away to town.

On alighting, she went off at a great pace until she reached a certain number in a certain busy street. She went into the doorway, looked up the dirty stairs and after standing stock still a minute suddenly dived into the street and walked away as rapidly as she came. This manoeuver she repeated several times, to the great amusement of a black-eyed young gentleman lounging in the window of a building opposite. On returning for the third time, Jo gave herself a shake, pulled her hat over her eyes, and walked up the stairs.

A dentist's sign, among others, adorned the entrance, and after staring a moment at it, the young gentleman put on his coat, took his hat and went down to post himself in the opposite doorway. "It's like her to come alone," he thought with a shiver, "but if she has a bad time she'll need some-one to help her home."

In ten minutes Jo came running downstairs with a very red face. When she saw the young gentleman she looked anything but pleased, and passed him with a nod. But he followed, asking with an air of sympathy, "Did you have a bad time?"

"Not very."

"You got through quickly."

"Yes, thank goodness!"

"Why did you go alone?"

"Didn't want anyone to know."

"You're the oddest fellow I ever saw. How many did you have out?"

Jo looked as if she did not understand, then began to laugh. "There are two which I want to have come out but I must wait a week."

"What are you laughing at?" said Laurie, looking mysti-fied. "You are up to some mischief."

"So are you. What were you doing, sir, up in that billiard saloon?"

"Begging your pardon, ma'am, it wasn't a billiard saloon but a gymnasium and I was taking a lesson in fencing."

"You can teach me and when we play *Hamlet* we'll make a fine thing of the fencing scene."

Laurie laughed. "I'll teach you whether we play *Hamlet* or not. It's grand fun."

"I was glad that you were not in the saloon. I hope you never go to such places."

"Do you worry about me, Jo?"

"A little."

Laurie walked in silence a few minutes. "I'd like to walk with you," he said, "and tell you something interesting."

"I'd like to hear the news immensely."

"Then come on. It's a secret, and if I tell you, you must tell me yours."

"I haven't got any," began Jo, but stopped suddenly.

"You know you have. You can't hide anything, so up and 'fess or I won't tell," cried Laurie.

"Is your secret a nice one?"

"Oh, isn't it! All about people you know and such fun! You begin."

"You'll not say anything about it at home, will you?"

"Not a word."

"Well, I've left two stories with a newspaper man and he's to give his answer next week," whispered Jo in his ear.

"Hurrah for Miss March, the celebrated American authoress!" cried Laurie, throwing up his hat and catching it again.

"It won't come to anything, but I couldn't rest till I had tried."

"It won't fail. Won't it be fun to see them in print, and shan't we feel proud of our authoress?"

Jo's eyes sparkled. "Where's *your* secret? Play fair, Teddy, or I'll never believe you again."

"I may get into a scrape for telling, but I didn't promise not to. I know where Meg's glove is."

"Is that all?" said Jo, looking disappointed.

"It's quite enough, as you'll agree when I tell you where it is." Laurie bent and whispered three words in Jo's ear. She stared at him for a minute, looking displeased, then walked on, saying sharply, "How do you know?"

"Saw it."

"Where?"

"Pocket."

"All this time?"

"Yes, isn't that romantic?"

"No, it's horrid."

"I thought you'd be pleased."

"At the idea of anybody taking Meg away? No thank you. I don't think secrets agree with me. I feel rumpled in my mind since you told me."

"Race down this hill with me and you'll be all right," suggested Laurie.

No one was in sight and Jo darted away. Laurie reached the goal first, and Jo came panting up, hair flying. "I wish I was a horse. Then I could run for miles in this air and not lose my breath. Go pick up my things, like a cherub," said Jo, dropping down under a maple tree.

For a week or two Jo behaved so queerly that her sisters were bewildered. She rushed to the door when the postman rang, was rude to Mr. Brooke when they met, and would sit looking at Meg with woebegone face, occasionally jumping up to shake and then to kiss her, in a mysterious manner.

Laurie and she were always making signs to one another, and talked about *Spread Eagle* until the girls declared they had both lost their wits.

One Saturday, as Meg sat sewing, she was scandalized by the sight of Laurie chasing Jo all over the garden and finally capturing her in Amy's bower. Shrieks of laughter were heard, followed by the murmur of voices and a great flapping of newspaper. In a few minutes Jo bounced in, laid herself on the sofa and affected to read.

"Have you anything interesting there?" asked Meg with condescension.

"Nothing but a story," returned Jo, keeping the name of the paper out of sight.

"What's the name?" asked Beth.

"The Rival Painters."

"That sounds well. Read it," said Meg.

With a loud "Hem!" and a long breath, Jo began to read very fast. The girls listened with interest for the tale was romantic and somewhat pathetic, as most of the characters died in the end.

"I like that about the splendid picture," was Amy's remark.

"I prefer the lovering part. Viola and Angelo are two of our favorite names. Isn't that queer?" said Meg, wiping her eyes.

"Who wrote it?" asked Beth, who had caught a glimpse of Jo's face.

The reader suddenly sat up, cast away the paper, displaying a flushed countenance, and with a funny mixture of solemnity and excitement replied in a loud voice, "Your sister."

"You?" cried Meg, dropping her work.

"It's very good," said Amy critically.

"I knew it! Oh, my Jo, I *am* so proud!" and Beth ran to hug her.

How delighted they all were. Meg wouldn't believe it until she saw the words *Miss Josephine March* actually printed in the paper. Amy criticised the artistic parts of the story. Beth got excited, and Hannah came in to exclaim, "Sakes alive, well I never!" How proud Mrs. March was when she knew. Jo laughed, with tears in her eyes, as she declared she might as well be a peacock and done with it, as *The Spread Eagle* passed from hand to hand. She wondered if Miss Burney felt any grander over her *Evalina* than she did over her *Rival Painters*.

Having told how she disposed of her tales, Jo added, "And when I went to get my answer the man said he liked them both but didn't pay beginners, only let them print in his paper and noticed the stories. It was good practice, he said. And when the beginners improve, anyone would pay. So I let him have the two stories and today this was sent to me. Laurie caught me with it and insisted on seeing it, so I let him. He said it was good and I shall write more, and he's going to get the next paid for, and I *am* so happy, for in time I may be able to support myself and help the girls."

Jo's breath gave out and she wrapped her head in the paper, overwhelmed at what seemed to be the first step toward the happy end.

Chapter 14

A TELEGRAM

"NOVEMBER is the most disagreeable month in the whole year," said Margaret, standing at the window one dull afternoon looking out at the frost-bitten garden.

"That's the reason I was born in it," observed Jo pensively.

Beth, who sat at the other window, said smiling, "Two pleasant things are going to happen right away. Marmee is coming down the street and Laurie is tramping through the garden as if he had something nice to tell."

In they both came, Mrs. March with her usual question, "Any letter from Father, girls?" and Laurie to say, "Won't some of you come for a drive? Jo, you and Beth will go, won't you?"

"Of course we will."

"Can I do anything for you, Madam Mother?" asked Laurie, leaning over Mrs. March's chair, with the affectionate look and tone he always gave her.

"No thank you, except call at the post office. It's our day for a letter."

A sharp ring interrupted her, and a minute after, Hannah came in. "It's one of them horrid telegraph things, mum," she said, handling it as if she was afraid it would explode.

At the word *telegraph*, Mrs. March snatched it, read the two lines it contained, and dropped back into her chair as white as the little paper. Laurie dashed downstairs for water, while Meg and Hannah supported her, and Jo read aloud in a frightened voice:

MRS. MARCH:
YOUR HUSBAND IS VERY ILL. COME AT
ONCE. *S. HALE*
BLANK HOSPITAL, WASHINGTON

Mrs. March was herself again directly, read the message over and stretched out her arms to her daughters, saying in a tone they never forgot, "I shall go at once but it may be too late. Oh children, children, help me to bear it!"

For several minutes there was nothing but the sound of sobbing in the room, mingled with broken words of comfort and whispers that died away in tears. Poor Hannah was the first to recover.

"The Lord keep the dear man! I won't waste no time a-cryin', but git your things ready right away, mum," she said heartily, as she wiped her face on her apron.

"She's right. There's no time for tears now. Be calm, girls, and let me think. Where's Laurie?" she asked.

"Here, ma'am. Oh, let me do something!" cried the boy, hurrying from the next room where he had withdrawn.

"Send a telegram saying I will come at once. The next train goes early in the morning. I'll take that."

"What else? The horses are ready. I can go anywhere," he said.

"Leave a note at Aunt March's. Jo, give me that pen and paper."

Tearing off the blank side of one of her newly copied pages, Jo drew the table before her mother, well knowing that money for the long sad journey must be borrowed. Five minutes later, Laurie tore by the window, riding as if for his life.

"Jo, run to the rooms and tell Mrs. King that I can't come," Mrs. March said. "On the way get these things. They'll be needed and I must go prepared for nursing. Hospital stores are not always good. Beth, go and ask Mr. Laurence for a couple of bottles of old wine. I'm not too proud to beg for Father. He shall have the best of everything. Amy, tell Hannah to get down the black trunk, and Meg, come and help me find my things, for I'm half bewildered."

Everyone scattered, and the quiet happy household was broken up as suddenly as if the paper had been an evil spell. Mr. Laurence came hurrying back with Beth, bringing every comfort he could think of for the invalid, and promises of protection for the girls during the mother's absence which comforted her. He offered himself as escort, but Mrs. March would not hear of the old gentleman's undertaking the long journey. He marched abruptly away saying he'd be back directly. No one had time to think of him again until Meg, running through the entry with a pair of rubbers in one hand and a cup of tea in the other, came suddenly upon Mr. Brooke.

"I'm very sorry to hear of this, Miss March," he said. "I came to offer myself as escort to your mother. Mr. Laurence has commissions for me in Washington, and it will give me real satisfaction to be of service to her there."

Down dropped the rubbers and the tea was very near following as Meg put out her hand with a face so full of gratitude that Mr. Brooke would have felt repaid for a much greater sacrifice. "How kind you all are! Mother will accept, I'm sure, and it will be such a relief to know that she has someone to take care of her. Thank you very, very much!" Meg spoke earnestly and forgot herself entirely until something in the brown eyes looking down at her made her remember the cooling tea and lead the way into the parlor, saying she would call her mother.

Everything was arranged by the time Laurie returned with a note from Aunt March, enclosing the desired sum, and a few lines repeating what she had often said before —that she had always told them it was absurd for March to go into the army, always predicted that no good would come of it, and she hoped they would take her advice next time. Mrs. March put the note in the fire, the money in her purse, and went on with her preparations with her lips folded tightly in a way Jo would have understood if she had been there.

The short afternoon wore away. All the other errands were done, and Meg and her mother were busy at some necessary needlework, while Beth and Amy got tea and Hannah finished her ironing. But still Jo did not come. They began to get anxious, and Laurie went off to find her. He missed her and she came walking in with a queer expression which puzzled the family as much as did the roll of bills she gave her mother, saying with a little choke in her voice, "That's my contribution towards making Father comfortable and bringing him home!"

"My dear, where did you get it? Twenty-five dollars, Jo, I hope you haven't done anything rash?"

"No, it's mine honestly. I didn't beg, borrow or steal it. I don't think you'll blame me, for I only sold what was my own." As she spoke, Jo took off her bonnet and an outcry arose, for her hair was cut short.

As everyone exclaimed, and Beth hugged the cropped

head tenderly, Jo assumed an indifferent air which did not deceive anyone. She rumpled the brown bush and tried to look as if she liked it. "It will be good for my vanity," she said. "I was getting too proud of my wig. My head feels deliciously light and cool, and the barber said I could soon have a curly crop which will be boyish and easy to keep in order. I'm satisfied, so please take the money and let's have supper."

"What made you do it?" asked Amy, who would as soon have thought of cutting off her head as her pretty hair.

"Well, I was wild to do something for Father," replied Jo, as they gathered about the table. "I hate to borrow as much as Mother does and I knew Aunt March would croak. Meg gave all her quarterly salary toward the rent, and I only got some clothes with mine."

"My child, you had no winter things and got the simplest with your own hard earnings," said Mrs. March with a look that warmed Jo's heart.

"I hadn't the least idea of selling my hair at first but as I went along I kept thinking what I could do. In a barber's window I saw tails of hair with prices marked. One black tail, not so thick as mine, was forty dollars. Without stopping to think, I walked in, asked if they bought hair and what they would give for mine."

"I don't see how you dared to do it," said Beth in a tone of awe.

"The man stared at first, and said mine wasn't the fashionable color and he never paid much for it in the first place. It was getting late, so I begged him to take it and told him why I was in such a hurry. I got rather excited and his wife heard and said so kindly, 'Take it, Thomas, and oblige the young lady. I'd do as much for our Jimmy any day if I had a spire of hair worth selling.'"

"Who was Jimmy?" asked Amy.

"Her son, she said, who was in the army. She talked away all the time the man clipped, and diverted my mind nicely."

"Didn't you feel dreadfully when the first cut came?" asked Meg.

"I felt queer when I saw the dear old hair laid out on the table, and felt only the short rough ends on my head. It almost seemed as if I'd had an arm or a leg off. The woman picked out a long lock for me to keep. I'll give it to you, Marmee."

Mrs. March folded the wavy chestnut lock and laid it away with a short gray one in her desk. She only said, "Thank you, dearie," but something in her face made the girls change the subject. No one wanted to go to bed when, at ten o'clock, Mrs. March put by the last finished job and said, "Come, girls." Beth went to the piano and played the father's favorite hymn. All began bravely but broke down one by one, until Beth was left alone singing.

They went to bed silently. Beth and Amy soon fell asleep but Meg lay awake. Jo lay motionless and her sister fancied that she was asleep until a stifled sob made her exclaim, as she touched a wet cheek, "Jo, dear. What is it? Are you crying about Father?"

"No, not now."

"What then?"

"My—my hair!" burst out poor Jo. "I'm not sorry. I'd do it again tomorrow, if I could. It's only the vain selfish part of me that goes and cries in this silly way. Don't tell anyone. It's all over now."

Meg promised to make her hair curl, and the girls fell asleep. The clocks were striking midnight and the rooms were still, as a figure glided quietly from bed to bed, smoothing a coverlet here, settling a pillow there, and pausing to look tenderly at each unconscious face and to pray. As she lifted the curtain to look out into the dreary night, the moon broke suddenly from behind the clouds and shone upon her like a bright benignant face which seemed to whisper in the silence, "Be comforted! There is always light behind the clouds."

In the cold dawn the sisters lit their lamp and read their

chapter with an earnestness never felt before, for now the shadow of a real trouble had come, the little books were full of help and comfort. As they dressed, they agreed to say good-by cheerfully and hopefully, and send their mother on her anxious journey unsaddened by tears or complaints from them.

Everything seemed very strange when they went down, so dim and still outside, so full of light and bustle within. Breakfast at that early hour seemed odd, and even Hannah's familiar face looked unnatural as she flew about her kitchen with her nightcap on. The big trunk stood ready in the hall, Mother's cloak and bonnet lay on the sofa, and Mother herself sat trying to eat but looking so pale and worn with sleeplessness and anxiety that the girls found it very hard to keep their resolution. Nobody talked much.

The rattle of an approaching carriage made them all start and listen. That was the hard minute but the girls stood it well. They kissed their mother quietly and tried to wave their hands cheerfully when she drove away. Laurie and his grandfather came over to see her off, and Mr. Brooke looked so strong and sensible and kind that the girls christened him "Mr. Greatheart" on the spot.

"Good-by, my darlings! God bless and keep us all!" whispered Mrs. March as she kissed them and hurried into the carriage.

As she rolled away, the sun came out and looking back she saw it shining on the group at the gate like a good omen. They saw it also and smiled and waved their hands.

"I feel as if there had been an earthquake," said Jo, as their neighbors went home to breakfast.

"It seems as if half the house was gone," added Meg forlornly.

Hannah came to the rescue, armed with a coffeepot. "Now, my dear young ladies, come and have a cup of coffee all 'round, and then fall to work and be a credit to the family." In ten minutes they were all right again.

"*Hope and keep busy*. That's the motto for us, so let's

see who will remember it best," said Jo, as she sipped with returning spirit.

When she and Meg went out to their daily tasks, they looked sorrowfully back at the window where they were accustomed to see their mother's face. It was gone, but Beth had remembered the little household ceremony and there she was, nodding away at them.

News from their father comforted the girls very much, for though dangerously ill, the presence of his wife had already done him good. Mr. Brooke sent a bulletin every day, and as the head of the family Meg insisted on reading the dispatches, which grew more and more cheering as the week passed. Everyone was eager to write, and plump envelopes were carefully poked into the letterbox by one or the other of the sisters, who felt rather important with their Washington correspondence.

Chapter 15

DARK DAYS

FOR A WEEK the amount of virtue in the old house would have supplied the neighborhood. Relieved of their first anxiety about their father, the girls insensibly relaxed their efforts a little and began to fall back into the old ways. The house seemed like a clock whose pendulum was gone avisiting.

"Meg, I wish you'd go and see the Hummels. You know Mother told us not to forget them," said Beth, ten days after Mrs. March's departure.

"I'm too tired to go this afternoon," replied Meg.

"Can't you, Jo?" asked Beth.

"Too stormy for me," said Jo, who had caught a bad cold through neglect to cover her shorn head enough.

"I thought your cold was almost well."

"It's well enough for me to go out with Laurie but not well enough to go to the Hummels'," said Jo laughing.

"Why don't you go yourself?" asked Meg.

"I *have* been every day, but the baby is sick and I don't know what to do for it. It gets sicker and sicker, and I think you or Hannah ought to go." Beth spoke earnestly and Meg promised she would go tomorrow.

"My head aches so I thought some of you would go to-day," said Beth.

"Amy will be in presently and she will go," suggested Meg.

An hour passed and Amy did not come, so Beth quietly put on her hood, filled her basket with things for the poor children, and went out into the chilly air. It was late when she came back, and no one saw her creep upstairs and shut herself into her mother's room. Half an hour after Jo went to "Mother's closet" for something, and there found Beth sitting on the medicine chest looking very grave, her eyes red and a camphor bottle in her hand.

"Christopher Columbus! What's the matter?" cried Jo as Beth put out her hand as if to warn her off, saying quickly, "You've had the scarlet fever, haven't you?"

"Years ago, when Meg did. Why?"

"Then I'll tell you. Oh, Jo, the baby's dead."

"What baby?"

"Mrs. Hummel's. It died in my lap before she got home," Beth sobbed.

"My poor dear, how dreadful for you! I ought to have gone," said Jo, taking her sister in her arms. "Don't cry, dear. What did you do?"

"I just sat and held it till Mrs. Hummel came with the doctor. He said it was dead. 'Scarlet fever, ma'am. Ought to have called me before,' he said crossly. It was very sad and I cried with them till he turned 'round, all of a sudden, and told me to go home and take belladonna right away or I'd have the fever."

"Oh Beth," cried Jo, hugging her close, "if you should be sick I never could forgive myself. What *shall* we do?"

"Don't be frightened. I guess I sha'n't have it badly. I looked in Mother's book and saw that it begins with headache, sore throat and queer feelings like mine, so I did take some belladonna and I feel better," said Beth, laying her cold hands on her hot forehead.

"If Mother was only at home!" exclaimed Jo. "I'll call Hannah. She knows all about sickness."

"Now I'll tell you what we'll do," said Hannah, when she had examined and questioned Beth. "We will have Dr. Bangs. Then we'll send Amy off to Aunt March's, and one of you girls can stay at home and amuse Beth for a day or two."

"I shall stay, of course. I'm oldest," began Meg, looking anxious.

"*I* shall, because it's my fault she is sick. I told Mother I'd do the errands and I haven't," said Jo decidedly.

"Which will you have, Beth?" asked Hannah.

"Jo, please," and Beth leaned her head against her sister.

"I'll go and tell Amy," said Meg.

Amy rebelled outright and declared passionately that she had rather have the fever than go to Aunt March. Laurie walked into the parlor to find Amy sobbing. She told her story, expecting to be consoled, but Laurie only put his hands in his pockets and walked about the room whistling softly. Presently he sat down beside her and said, "Now be a sensible little woman and do as they say. Hear what a jolly plan I've got. You go to Aunt March's and I'll come and take you out every day, driving or walking, and we'll have capital times. Won't that be better than moping here?"

"But it's dull at Aunt March's and she is so cross," said Amy.

"It won't be dull with me popping in every day to tell you how Beth is, and take you out gallivanting."

"Well—I guess—I will," said Amy slowly.

"Good girl! Call Meg and tell her you'll give in," said Laurie.

Meg and Jo came running down, and Amy, feeling self-sacrificing, promised to go if the doctor said Beth was going to be ill. Dr. Bangs came, said Beth had symptoms of the fever, but thought she would have it lightly, though he looked sober over the Hummel story. Amy was ordered off at once, and departed in state with Jo and Laurie as escort.

Beth did have the fever and was much sicker than anyone but Hannah and the doctor suspected. The girls knew nothing about illness, and Mr. Laurence was not allowed to see her, so Hannah had everything her own way. Meg stayed at home, lest she should infect the Kings, and kept house, feeling very anxious and a little guilty when she wrote letters in which no mention was made of Beth's illness. She could not think it right to deceive her mother, but she had been bidden to mind Hannah, who wouldn't hear of her being told.

Jo devoted herself to Beth day and night, not a hard task, for Beth was very patient and bore her pain uncomplainingly. But there came a time when she did not know the familiar faces around her and called imploringly for her mother. Then Jo grew frightened, Meg begged to be allowed to write the truth, and even Hannah said she would think of it, though there was no danger yet. A letter from Washington added to their trouble, for Mr. March had had a relapse and could not think of coming home for a long while.

How dark the days seemed now, how sad and lonely the house, and how heavy were the hearts of the sisters as they worked and waited while the shadow of death hovered over the once happy home! Laurie haunted the house like a restless ghost, and Mr. Laurence locked the grand piano because he could not bear to be reminded of the young neighbor who used to make the twilight pleasant for him. Everyone missed Beth. The milkman, baker, grocer and butcher inquired how she did. Poor Mrs. Hummel came to beg pardon for her thoughtlessness, and the neighbors sent all sorts of comforts and good wishes. Even those who knew her best were surprised to find how many friends shy little Beth had made.

The first of December was a wintry day indeed to them, for a bitter wind blew and snow fell fast. When Dr. Bangs came that morning, he looked long at Beth, held the hot hand in both his own a minute, and laid it gently down, saying in a low tone to Hannah, "If Mrs. March *can* leave her husband, she'd better be sent for."

Hannah nodded without speaking, and Jo ran to the parlor, threw on her things and rushed out into the storm. She was soon back, and while taking off her cloak, Laurie came in with a letter saying that Mr. March was mending again. Jo read it thankfully but her face was so full of misery that Laurie asked quickly, "What is it? Is Beth worse?"

"I've sent for Mother," said Jo, tugging at her rubber boots.

"Good for you! Did you do it on your own responsibility?" asked Laurie, as he seated her in a chair and took off the boots for her.

"No. The doctor told us to."

"Oh Jo, it's not so bad as that?" cried Laurie, startled.

"Yes, it is." As the tears streamed fast down poor Jo's cheeks, she stretched out her hand as if groping in the dark. Laurie took it, whispering as well as he could with a lump in his throat, "I'm here. Hold on to me, Jo dear!"

She could not speak, but she did hold on and the warm grasp of the friendly human hand comforted her heart and seemed to lead her nearer to the divine arm which alone could uphold her in her trouble. Soon she dried her tears and looked up gratefully. "Thank you, Teddy. I'm better now. I don't feel so forlorn and will try to bear it if it comes."

"Keep hoping for the best. That will help you, Jo. Soon your mother will be here and then everything will be right."

"I'm so glad Father is better. Now she won't feel so bad about leaving him."

"Tonight I'll give you something that will warm the cockles of your heart," said Laurie, beaming at her.

"What is it?" cried Jo, forgetting her woes.

"I telegraphed to your mother yesterday and Brooke answered she'd come at once. She'll be here tonight and everything will be all right. Aren't you glad I did it?" Laurie spoke very fast, for he had kept his plot a secret for fear of disappointing the girls or harming Beth. Jo grew white, flew out of her chair, and electrified him by throwing her arms about his neck, crying joyfully, "Oh Laurie! Oh Mother! I *am* so glad!" She laughed hysterically and trembled, and clung to her friend as if she was bewildered by the news.

Laurie, though amazed, behaved with presence of mind. He patted her back soothingly and, finding that she was recovering, followed it up by a bashful kiss or two which brought Jo around at once. Holding on to the banisters she put him gently away, saying breathlessly, "Oh, don't! I didn't mean to. It was dreadful of me. But you were such a dear to go and do it in spite of Hannah that I couldn't help flying at you. Tell me all about it."

"Why, I got fidgety and so did Grandpa. We thought Hannah was overdoing the authority business and your mother ought to know. She'd never forgive us if Beth—well, if anything happened, you know. So I got Grandpa to say it was high time we did something, and off I pelted to the office yesterday. Your mother will come, I know, and the late train is in at 2:00 A.M. I shall go for her, and you've only got to bottle up your rapture and keep Beth quiet till that blessed lady gets here."

"You're an angel. How shall I ever thank you?"

"Fly at me again. I rather like it," said Laurie, looking mischievous.

"Don't tease, but go home and rest. You'll be up half the night. Bless you, Teddy, bless you!"

The doctor had been in to say that some change would probably take place about midnight, at which time he would return. So Hannah lay down on the sofa at the bed's foot and fell fast asleep. Mr. Laurence marched to and fro in the parlor. Laurie lay on the rug staring into the fire with the thoughtful look which made his black eyes beautifully soft and clear.

The girls never forgot that night, for no sleep came to them as they kept their watch. The clock struck twelve and they fancied a change passed over Beth's wan face. The house was still as death, and nothing but the wailing of the wind broke the deep hush. Weary Hannah slept on, and no one but the sisters saw the pale shadow which seemed to fall upon the little bed. An hour went by and nothing happened except Laurie's quiet departure for the station. Another hour. Still no one came, and anxious fears of delay in the storm, or accidents by the way, or, worst of all, a great grief at Washington, haunted the girls.

It was past two when Jo, who stood at the window thinking how dreary the world looked in its winding-sheet of snow, heard a movement by the bed. Turning quickly, she saw Meg kneeling before their mother's easy-chair with her face hidden. A dreadful fear passed coldly over Jo as she thought, "Beth is dead and Meg is afraid to tell me."

She was back at her post in an instant and to her excited eyes a great change seemed to have taken place. The fever flush and the look of pain were gone, and the beloved little face looked so pale and peaceful in its utter repose, that Jo felt no desire to weep or to lament. Leaning low over this dearest of sisters, she kissed the damp forehead with her heart on her lips, and softly whispered, "Good-by, my Beth, good-by!"

As if waked by the stir, Hannah started out of her sleep, hurried to the bed, looked at Beth, felt her hands, listened at her lips, and then, throwing her apron over her head, exclaimed under her breath, "The fever's turned. She's sleepin' nat'ral. Her skin's damp and she breathes easy. Praise be given! Oh, my goodness me!"

Before the girls could believe the happy truth, the doctor

came to confirm it. He smiled and said, "I think the little girl will pull through. Keep the house quiet. Let her sleep and when she wakes, give her—"

What they were to give, neither girl heard, for they crept into the dark hall and sitting on the stairs held each other close, with hearts too full for words. When they went back, they found Beth lying as she used to do with her cheek pillowed on her hand, the dreadful pallor gone, and breathing quietly as if just fallen asleep.

"If Mother would only come now!" said Jo, as the winter night began to wane.

"See," said Meg, coming up with a half-opened white rose, "I thought this would hardly be ready to lay in Beth's hand tomorrow if she—went away from us. But it has blossomed in the night, and now I mean to put it in my vase here, so that when the darling wakes the first thing she sees will be the rose and Mother's face."

Never had the sun risen so beautifully, and never had the world seemed so lovely as it did to the heavy eyes of Meg and Jo, as they looked out in the early morning when their long sad vigil was done.

"It looks like a fairy world," said Meg.

"Hark!" cried Jo, starting to her feet

There was a sound of bells at the door below, a cry from Hannah, and then Laurie's voice saying in a joyful whisper, "Girls, she's come! She's come!"

Chapter 16

AMY'S WILL

WHILE these things were happening at home, Amy was having hard times at Aunt March's. Finding the child more docile and amiable than her sister, the old lady felt it her

duty to try and counteract as far as possible the bad effects
of home freedom and indulgence. So she taught Amy as she
herself had been taught sixty years ago, a process which
made Amy feel like a fly in the web of a very strict spider.

She had to wash the cups every morning, and polish the
old-fashioned spoons, the fat silver teapot and the glasses
until they shone. Then she must dust the room. All the fur-

niture had claw legs and much carving. Then Polly must be
fed, the lapdog combed, and a dozen trips upstairs and
down, for the old lady was lame and seldom left her big
chair. After her lessons, she was allowed an hour for play.

Laurie came every day and wheeled Aunt March until
Amy was allowed to go out with him. They walked and
rode, and had capital times. After dinner, she had to read
aloud, and sit still while the old lady slept. Then patchwork
or towels appeared, and Amy sewed until dusk, when she
was allowed to amuse herself until tea time. The evenings were the worst of all, for Aunt March told long stories
of her youth.

If it had not been for Laurie, and old Esther the maid, Amy could never have got through that dreadful time. The parrot alone was enough to drive her distracted, for he pulled her hair and called her names before company. Mop, the dog, was a fat cross beast, who snarled and yelped at her. The cook was bad-tempered, the old coachman deaf, and Esther the only one who ever took any notice of her.

Esther was a Frenchwoman who had lived with Madame, as she called her mistress, for many years. Her real name was Estelle, but Aunt March had ordered her to change it and she obeyed, on condition that she was never asked to change her religion. She took a fancy to Mademoiselle, and amused her with odd stories of her life in France. She also allowed her to roam about the great house and examine the pretty things stored in the big wardrobes and ancient chests. Amy's chief delight was an Indian cabinet, full of queer drawers and secret places, in which were kept all sorts of ornaments. On velvet cushions in the jewel cases reposed the garnet set which Aunt March wore when she came out forty years ago; the pearls her father gave her on her wedding day; her diamonds, the jet mourning rings and pins, Uncle March's big watch, and, in a box all by itself, her wedding ring.

"Which would Mademoiselle choose if she had her will?" asked Esther.

"I like the diamonds best, but there is no necklace and I am fond of necklaces. I should choose this," replied Amy, looking with admiration at a string of gold and ebony beads, from which hung a heavy cross.

"I too covet that but not as a necklace. To me it is a rosary and I should use it like a good Catholic to pray with," said Esther.

"You seem to take a great deal of comfort in your prayers, Esther."

"If Mademoiselle was a Catholic, she would find true comfort. But as that is not to be, it would be well if you went apart each day, to meditate and pray, as did the good mistress whom I served before Madame. She had a little chapel and in it found solace for much trouble."

"Would it be right for me to do so too?" asked Amy, who in her loneliness felt the need of help and found she was apt to forget her little book, now that Beth was not there to remind her of it.

"It would be excellent and charming. I shall gladly arrange the little dressing room for you if you like it. Say nothing to Madame, but when she sleeps go you and sit alone a while to think good thoughts and pray the dear God to preserve your sister."

Amy liked the idea and gave her leave to arrange the closet. "I wish I knew where all these pretty things would go when Aunt March dies," she said, as she slowly replaced the rosary.

"To you and your sisters. Madame confides in me. I witnessed her will and it is to be so," whispered Esther, smiling.

"How nice! But I wish she'd let us have them now," said Amy.

"It is too soon yet for the young ladies to wear these things. The first one who is affianced will have the pearls, and I have a fancy the little turquoise ring will be given to you when you go."

"Do you think so? Oh, I'll be a lamb if I can only have that lovely ring! I do like Aunt March after all," Amy said, delighted.

From that day she was a model of obedience. Esther fitted up the closet with a little table, placed a footstool before it, and over it a picture taken from one of the shutup rooms. It was a valuable copy of one of the famous pictures of the world, and Amy's beauty-loving eyes never tired of looking up at the sweet face of the divine mother, while tender thoughts of her own were busy. On the table she laid her little Testament and hymn book, kept a vase always full of the best flowers Laurie brought her, and came every day to "sit alone, thinking good thoughts, and praying the dear God to preserve her sister." Esther had given her a rosary of black beads with a silver cross, but Amy hung it up and did not use it, feeling doubtful as to its fitness for Protestant prayers.

The little girl was sincere in all this, for she felt the need of some kind hand to hold, and she instinctively turned to the strong and tender Friend, whose fatherly love most closely surrounds His little children. But Amy was a young pilgrim and just now her burden seemed very heavy. She tried to keep cheerful and be satisfied with doing right, though no one saw or praised her for it. In her first effort at being very, very good, she decided to make her will, as Aunt March had done, so that if she *did* fall ill and die, her possessions might be justly divided. It cost her a pang even to think of giving up the little treasures which to her were as precious as Aunt's jewels.

During one of her play hours she wrote out the important document as well as she could, with some help from Esther as to certain legal terms, and when the good-natured Frenchwoman had signed her name Amy felt relieved, and laid it by to show Laurie whom she wanted as a second witness. As it was a rainy day, she went upstairs to amuse herself, and took Polly with her for company. In one of the large rooms there was a wardrobe full of old-fashioned costumes. She put on one and paraded up and down before the long mirror, sweeping her train with a rustle which delighted her. So busy was she that she did not hear Laurie's ring, nor see him peeping in at her, as she gravely promenaded to and fro, flirting her fan and tossing her head, on which she wore a great pink turban, contrasting oddly with her blue brocade dress and yellow quilted petticoat.

Having with difficulty restrained an explosion of merriment, Laurie tapped and was graciously received. "Sit down and rest while I put these things away. Then I want to consult you about a very serious matter," said Amy, removing the pink mountain from her head. After she shut the wardrobe, she took a paper out of her pocket. "I want you to read that, please, and tell me if it is legal and right. I felt that I ought to do it, for life is uncertain and I don't want any ill-feeling over my tomb."

Laurie bit his lips and read the document with praise-worthy gravity, considering the spelling.

MY LAST WILL AND TESTAMENT

I, Amy Curtis March, being in my sane mind, do give and bequeethe, all my earthly property—viz. to wit:—namely

To my father, my best pictures, sketches, maps, and works of art, including frames. Also my $100, to do what he likes with.

To my mother, all my clothes, except the blue apron with pockets—also my likeness, and my medal, with much love.

To my dear sister Margaret, I give my turquoise ring (if I get it), also my green box with the dove on it, also my piece of real lace for her neck, and my sketch of her as a memorial to her "little girl."

To Jo I leave my breastpin, the one mended with sealing wax, also my bronze inkstand—she lost the cover—and my most precious plaster rabbit, because I am sorry I burned up her story.

To Beth (if she lives after me) I give my dolls and the little bureau, my fan, my linen collars and my new slippers if she can wear them being thin when she gets well. And I herewith also leave her my regret that I ever made fun of old Joanna.

To my friend and neighbor Theodore Laurence I bequeethe my paper marshay portfolio, my clay model of a horse though he did say it hadn't any neck. Also in return for his great kindness in the hour of affliction any one of my artistic works he likes, Noter Dame is the best.

To our venerable benefactor Mr. Laurence I leave my purple box with a looking glass in the cover which will be nice for his pens and remind him of the departed girl who thanks him for his favors to her family, specially Beth.

I wish my favorite playmate Kitty Bryant to have the blue silk apron and my gold-bead ring with a kiss.

To Hannah I give the bandbox she wanted and all the

patchwork I leave hoping she "will remember me, when it you see."

And now having disposed of my most valuable property I hope all will be satisfied and not blame the dead. I forgive everyone, and trust we may all meet when the trump shall sound. Amen.

To this will and testiment I set my hand and seal on this 20th day of Nov. Anni Domino 1861.

> Amy Curtis March

Witnesses: { Estelle Valnor

Theodore Laurence

The last name was written in pencil and Amy explained that he was to rewrite it in ink, and seal it up for her properly.

"What put it into your head? Did anyone tell you about Beth's giving away her things?" asked Laurie soberly, as Amy laid a bit of red tape with sealing wax and a taper before him.

She explained, then asked anxiously, "What about Beth?"

"I'm sorry I spoke, but as I did, I'll tell you. She felt so ill one day that she told Jo she wanted to give her piano to Meg, her cats to you, and the poor old doll to Jo, who would love it for her sake. She was sorry she had so little to give, and left locks of hair to the rest of us, and her best love to Grandpa. *She* never thought of a will."

Laurie was signing and sealing as he spoke, and did not look up until a great tear dropped on the paper. Amy's face was full of trouble but she only said, "Don't people put sort of postscripts to their wills sometimes?"

"Yes. Codicils they call them."

"Put one in mine then—that I wish *all* my curls cut off and given round to my friends. I forgot it, but I want it done though it will spoil my looks."

Laurie added it, smiling at Amy's last and greatest sacrifice. Then he amused her for an hour and was much inter-

ested in all her trials. But when he came to go, Amy held
him back to whisper with trembling lips, "Is there really
any danger about Beth?"

"I'm afraid there is, but we must hope for the best so
don't cry, dear," and Laurie put his arm about her with a
brotherly gesture which was very comforting.

When he had gone, she went to her chapel and sitting in
the twilight prayed for Beth, with tears and an aching heart,
feeling that a million turquoise rings would not console her
for the loss of her gentle little sister.

Chapter 17

CONFIDENTIAL

WHEN Beth woke from her long healing sleep, the first ob-
jects on which her eyes fell were the little rose and her
mother's face. Too weak to wonder at anything, she only
smiled and slept again. The girls waited on their mother, for
she would not unclasp the thin hand which clung to hers
even in sleep.

Meg and Jo fed their mother like dutiful young storks,
while they listened to her whispered account of Father's
state, Mr. Brooke's promise to stay and nurse him, the de-
lays which the storm occasioned on the homeward journey,
and the unspeakable comfort Laurie's hopeful face had given
her when she arrived, worn out with fatigue, anxiety and
cold.

Laurie posted off to comfort Amy and told his story so
well that Aunt March actually sniffed herself and never once
said, "I told you so." Amy dried her tears quickly, and would
gladly have gone out to enjoy the bright wintry weather,
but discovering that Laurie was dropping with sleep in spite
of manful efforts to conceal the fact, she persuaded him to

rest on the sofa while she wrote a note to her mother. She was a long time about it, and when she returned he was stretched out with both arms under his head, sound asleep, while Aunt March had pulled the curtains.

After a while they began to think he was not going to wake until night, but he was effectually roused by Amy's cry of joy at sight of her mother. Later, they sat alone together in the chapel, to which her mother did not object when its purpose was explained to her. "On the contrary, I like it very much, dear," she said, looking from the dusty rosary to the well-worn little book and the lovely picture with its garland of evergreen. "It is an excellent plan to have some place where we can go to be quiet when things vex or grieve us. There are a good many hard times in this life, but we can always bear them if we ask help in the right way. I think my little girl is learning this?"

"Yes, Mother. And when I go home I mean to have a corner of the big closet to put my books and the copy of that picture which I've tried to make. The woman's face is not good—it's too beautiful for me to draw—but the baby is done better and I love it very much. I like to think He was a little child once, for then I don't seem so far away, and that helps me."

As Amy pointed to the smiling Christ Child on His mother's knee, Mrs. March saw something on the lifted hand that made her smile. Amy understood the look and added gravely: "I wanted to speak to you about this but I forgot it. Aunt gave me the ring today. She called me to her and kissed me, and put it on my finger and said I was a credit to her, and she'd like to keep me always. She gave that funny guard to keep the turquoise on, as it's too big. I'd like to wear them, Mother. Can I?"

"They are very pretty but I think you're rather too young for such ornaments, Amy," said Mrs. March, looking at the plump little hand, with the band of sky-blue stones on the forefinger and the quaint guard, formed of two tiny gold hands clasped together.

"I'll try not to be vain," said Amy. "I want to wear it to remind me not to be selfish. Beth isn't selfish, so I'm going to try and be like Beth. May I try this way?"

"Yes, though I have more faith in the corner of the big closet. Wear your ring, dear, and do your best. Now I must go back to Beth. We will soon have you home again, little daughter."

That evening, while Meg was writing to her father to report the traveler's safe arrival, Jo slipped upstairs into Beth's room.

"What is it, dearie?" asked Mrs. March, holding out her hand.

"I want to tell you something, Mother."

"About Meg?"

"How quickly you guessed," said Jo, settling herself on the floor at her mother's feet. "Last summer Meg left a pair of gloves over at the Laurences', and only one was returned. We forgot all about it till Teddy told me that Mr. Brooke had it. He kept it in his waistcoat pocket, and once it fell out and Teddy joked him about it, and Mr. Brooke owned that he liked Meg but didn't dare say so, she was so young and he so poor."

"Do you think Meg cares for him?" asked Mrs. March with an anxious look.

"Mercy me! I don't know anything about love and such nonsense!" cried Jo. "In novels, girls show it by blushing, growing thin and acting like fools. Meg eats and drinks and sleeps like a sensible creature, and only blushes a bit when Teddy jokes about lovers."

"Then you fancy that Meg is *not* interested in John?"

"Who?" cried Jo, staring.

"Mr. Brooke. I call him John now. We fell in to the way of doing so at the hospital and he likes it."

"Oh, dear! I know you'll take his part. He's been good to Father and you won't send him away but let Meg marry him, if she wants to."

"My dear, don't get angry, and I will tell you how it happened. John went with me at Mr. Laurence's request and was so devoted to poor Father that we couldn't help getting fond of him. He was perfectly open and honorable about Meg, for he told us he loved her but would earn a comfortable home before he asked her to marry him. He only wanted our leave to love her and work for her, and the right to make her love him if he could. He is a truly excellent young man and we could not refuse to listen to him, but I will not consent to Meg's engaging herself so young. Jo, I don't wish you to say anything to Meg yet. When John comes back and I see them together, I can judge better of her feelings toward him," Mrs. March sighed, and Jo looked up with an air of relief.

"You don't like it, Mother? I'm glad of it. Let's send him about his business and not tell Meg a word of it, but be all happy together as we always have been."

"I did wrong to sigh, Jo. It is natural and right you should all go to homes of your own, in time, but I do want to keep my girls as long as I can. I am sorry this happened so soon, for Meg is only seventeen and it will be some years before John can make a home for her. Your father and I have agreed that she shall not bind herself in any way nor be married before twenty. If she and John love one another, they can wait and test the love by doing so. She is conscientious and I have no fear of her treating him unkindly. My pretty, tender-hearted girl! I hope things will go happily with her."

Chapter 18

LAURIE MAKES MISCHIEF

JO'S FACE was a study next day, for the secret rather weighed upon her and she found it hard not to look mysterious and important. Meg observed it, but did not trouble herself to make inquiries, for she had learned that the best way to manage Jo was by the law of contraries, so she felt sure of being told everything if she did not ask. She was rather surprised, therefore, when the silence remained unbroken and Jo assumed a patronizing air, which decidedly aggravated Meg, who in turn assumed an air of dignified reserve and devoted herself to her mother. This left Jo to her own devices, for Mrs. March had taken her place as nurse, and bade her rest and amuse herself. Amy being gone, Laurie was her only refuge. Much as she enjoyed his society, she rather dreaded him just then, for he was an incorrigible tease and she feared he would coax her secret from her.

She was quite right. The mischief-loving lad no sooner suspected a mystery than he set himself to find it out. He wheedled, bribed, ridiculed, threatened, and scolded. He affected indifference that he might surprise the truth from her; declared he knew, then that he didn't care. At last, by dint of perseverance, he satisfied himself that it concerned Meg and Mr. Brooke. Indignant that he was not taken into his tutor's confidence, he set his wits to work to devise some proper retaliation.

"Here's a note to you, Meg, all sealed up. How odd! Teddy never seals mine," said Jo next day, as she distributed the contents of the little post office.

Mrs. March and Jo were deep in their own affairs, when a

sound from Meg made them look up to see her staring at the note with a frightened face.

"My child, what is it?" cried her mother.

"It's all a mistake. He didn't send it. Oh Jo, how could you do it?" and Meg hid her face in her hands, crying.

"Me! I've done nothing! What's she talking about?" cried Jo.

Meg's mild eyes kindled with anger as she pulled a crumpled note from her pocket and threw it at Jo, saying reproachfully, "You wrote it and that bad boy helped you. How could you be so rude, so mean and cruel to us both?"

Jo hardly heard her, for she and her mother were reading the note which was written in a peculiar hand:

> *My dearest Margaret,—*
> *I can no longer restrain my passion and must know my fate before I return. I dare not tell your parents yet, but I think they would consent if they knew that we adored one another. Mr. Laurence will help me to some good place, and then, my sweet girl, you will make me happy. I implore you to say nothing to your family yet, but to send one word of hope through Laurie to*
> *Your devoted John*

"Oh, the villain! That's the way he meant to pay me for keeping my word to Mother. I'll give him a hearty scolding and bring him over to beg pardon," cried Jo.

But her mother held her back, saying with a look she seldom wore, "Stop, Jo! You must clear yourself first. You have played so many pranks that I am afraid you have had a hand in this."

"On my word, Mother, I haven't! I never saw that note before and don't know anything about it, as true as I live!" said Jo, so earnestly that they believed her. "If I *had* taken a part in it I'd have done it better than this and have written a sensible note. I should think you'd have known Mr.

Brooke wouldn't write such stuff as that," she added, scorn-fully tossing down the paper.

"It's like his writing," faltered Meg, comparing it with the note in her hand.

"Oh Meg, you didn't answer it?" cried Mrs. March quickly.

"Yes I did!" and Meg hid her face again, overcome with shame.

"Do let me bring that wicked boy over to explain and be lectured. I can't rest till I get hold of him," and Jo made for the door again.

"Hush! Let me manage this, for it is worse than I thought. Margaret, tell me the whole story," commanded Mrs. March, sitting down by Meg yet keeping hold of Jo lest she should fly off.

"I received the first letter from Laurie who didn't look as if he knew anything about it," began Meg without looking up. "I was worried at first and meant to tell you. Then I remembered how you liked Mr. Brooke, so I thought you wouldn't mind if I kept my little secret for a few days. I'm so silly that I liked to think no one knew. While I was de-ciding what to say, I felt like the girls in books who have such things to do. Forgive me, Mother. I'm paid for my silliness now. I never can look him in the face again."

"What did you say to him?" asked Mrs. March.

"I only said I was too young to do anything about it yet, that I didn't wish to have secrets from you, and he must speak to Father. I was very grateful for his kindness and would be his friend but nothing more for a long while."

Mrs. March smiled as if well pleased and Jo clapped her hands, exclaiming with a laugh, "Tell on, Meg! What did he say to that?"

"He writes in a different way entirely, telling me that he never sent any love letter at all, and is very sorry that my roguish sister Jo should take such liberties with our names. It's very kind and respectful but think how dreadful for me!" Meg looked in despair.

Jo tramped about the room, calling Laurie names. All of a sudden she stopped, caught up the two notes, and after looking at them closely said decidedly, "I don't believe Brooke ever saw either of these letters. Teddy wrote both and keeps yours to crow over me with, because I wouldn't tell him my secret."

"Don't have any secrets, Jo. Tell it to Mother and keep out of trouble as I should have done," said Meg warningly.

"Bless you, child! Mother told me."

"That will do, Jo. I'll comfort Meg while you go and get Laurie. I shall sift the matter to the bottom and put a stop to such pranks at once."

Away ran Jo, and Mrs. March gently told Meg Mr. Brooke's real feelings. "Now dear, what are your own? Do you love him enough to wait till he can make a home for you, or will you keep yourself quite free for the present?"

"I've been so scared and worried," answered Meg. "If John doesn't know anything about this nonsense, don't tell him, and make Jo and Laurie hold their tongues. I won't be made a fool of."

The instant Laurie's step was heard in the hall, Meg fled into the study, and Mrs. March received the culprit alone. Jo had not told him why he was wanted, fearing he wouldn't come, but he knew the minute he saw Mrs. March's face, and stood twirling his hat with a guilty air which convicted him at once. Jo was dismissed, but chose to march up and down the hall like a sentinel. The sound of voices in the parlor rose and fell for half an hour, but what happened during that interview the girls never knew.

When they were called in, Laurie was standing by their mother with such a penitent face that Jo forgave him on the spot but did not think it wise to betray the fact. Meg received his humble apology and was much comforted by the assurance that Brooke knew nothing of the joke. "I'll never tell him to my dying day. Wild horses sha'n't drag it out of me. So you'll forgive me, Meg, and I'll do anything to show how out-and-out sorry I am," he added, looking ashamed.

"I'll try, but it was a very ungentlemanly thing to do. I didn't think you could be so sly and malicious, Laurie," replied Meg.

"It was altogether abominable and I don't deserve to be spoken to for a month, but you will, won't you?" and Laurie folded his hands together with an imploring gesture.

Meg pardoned him, and Mrs. March's grave face relaxed. Everyone thought the matter ended and the little cloud blown over, but the mischief was done, for though others forgot it, Meg remembered.

Chapter 19

PLEASANT MEADOWS

PEACEFUL WEEKS followed. The invalids improved rapidly and Mr. March began to talk of returning early in the new year. Beth was soon able to lie on the study sofa all day. As Christmas approached, the usual mysteries began to haunt the house, and Jo frequently convulsed the family by proposing absurd ceremonies in honor of this unusually merry Christmas.

Several days of unusually mild weather ushered in a splendid Christmas Day. Mr. March wrote that he should soon be with them. Beth felt uncommonly well that morning, and dressed in her mother's gift, a soft crimson merino wrapper, was borne in triumph to the window to behold the offering of Jo and Laurie.

Like elves, they had worked by night, and in the garden stood a stately snow maiden crowned with holly, a basket of fruit in one hand and a great roll of new music in the other, a rainbow of an afghan around her chilly shoulders, and a Christmas carol issuing from her lips on a pink paper streamer. How Beth laughed when she saw it! Laurie ran up and down to bring in the gifts, and Jo made ridiculous speeches as she presented them.

"I'm so full of happiness that if Father was only here I couldn't hold one drop more," said Beth, as Jo carried her off to the study to rest after the excitement.

"So am I," added Jo, slapping the pocket wherein reposed the long-desired *Undine and Sintram.*

"I'm sure I am," echoed Amy, poring over the engraved copy of the Madonna and Child in a pretty frame.

"Of course I am!" cried Meg, smoothing the silvery folds of her first silk dress, for Mr. Laurence had insisted on giving it.

"How can I be otherwise?" said Mrs. March gratefully, as her eyes went from her husband's letter to Beth's smiling face, and her hand caressed the brooch made of gray and golden, chestnut and dark brown hair, which the girls had just fastened on her breast.

Half an hour later, Laurie opened the parlor door and popped his head in very quietly. He might just as well have turned a somersault and uttered a warwhoop, for his face was so full of suppressed excitement and his voice so treacherously joyful, that everyone jumped up, though he only said in a queer breathless voice, "Here's another Christmas present for the March family."

Before the words were well out of his mouth, in his place appeared a tall man muffled up to the eyes, leaning on the arm of another tall man who tried to say something and couldn't. There was a general stampede and for several minutes everybody seemed to lose their wits, for the strangest things were done and no one said a word. Mr. March became invisible in the embrace of four pairs of loving arms. Jo disgraced herself by nearly fainting and had to be doctored by Laurie in the china closet. Mr. Brooke kissed Meg by mistake, as he somewhat incoherently explained. Amy, the dignified, tumbled over a stool and never stopping to get up hugged and cried over her father's boots in the most touching manner. Mrs. March was the first to recover herself, and held up her hand with a warning, "Hush! Remember Beth!"

But it was too late. The study door flew open, the little red wrapper appeared on the threshold, joy put strength into the feeble limbs, and Beth ran straight into her father's arms.

A hearty laugh set everybody straight again, for Hannah was discovered behind the door, sobbing over the fat turkey which she had forgotten to put down when she rushed up from the kitchen. As the laugh subsided, Mrs. March began to thank Mr. Brooke for his faithful care of her husband, at which Mr. Brooke suddenly remembered that Mr. March needed rest, and seizing Laurie he promptly retired. Then the two invalids were ordered to repose, which they did by both sitting in one big chair and talking hard.

There never was such a Christmas dinner. The fat turkey was a sight to behold, stuffed, browned and decorated, and so was the plum pudding. Mr. Laurence and his grandson dined with them, also Mr. Brooke, at whom Jo glowered, to Laurie's amazement. Two easy-chairs stood side by side at the head of the table, in which sat Beth and her father. They drank healths, told stories, sang, and had a thoroughly good time. A sleigh ride had been planned but the girls would not leave their father, so the guests departed early, and as twilight gathered the happy family sat together around the fire.

"Just a year ago we were groaning over the dismal Christmas we expected to have, do you remember?" asked Jo, breaking a short pause.

"Rather a pleasant year," said Meg, smiling at the fire.

"I think it's been a pretty hard one," observed Amy.

"I'm glad it's over because we've got you back," whispered Beth, who sat on her father's knee.

"Rather a rough road for you to travel, my little pilgrims, but you have got on bravely and I think the burdens are in a fair way to tumble off soon," said Mr. March looking around at the four young faces.

"How do you know?" asked Jo. "Did Mother tell you?"

"Not much. I've made several discoveries today."

"Oh, tell us what they are!" cried Meg who sat beside him.

"Here is one." Taking up the hand which lay on the arm of the chair, he pointed to the roughened forefinger, a burn on the back, and two or three hard spots on the palm. "I remember a time when this hand was white and smooth and your first care was to keep it so. It was pretty then but to me it is much prettier now. A burnt offering has been made of vanity. Meg, my dear, I'm proud to shake this good, industrious little hand."

"What about Jo? Please say something nice, for she has been so very, very good to me," said Beth in her father's ear.

He laughed, and looked across at the tall girl who sat opposite. "In spite of the curly crop I don't see the 'son Jo' whom I left a year ago," said Mr. March. "I see a young lady who pins her collars straight, laces her boots neatly, and neither whistles, talks slang, nor lies on the rug as she used to do. Her face is rather thin and pale, but I like to look at it, for it has grown gentler and her voice is lower. She doesn't bounce but moves quietly. I rather miss my wild girl, but if I get a strong, helpful woman in her place, I shall feel quite satisfied. In all Washington I couldn't find anything beautiful enough to be bought with the five-and-twenty dollars which my good girl sent me."

Jo's eyes were dim for a minute and her face grew rosy in the firelight.

"Now Beth," said Amy, longing for her turn but ready to wait.

"There's so little of her, I'm afraid she will slip away altogether, though she is not so shy as she used to be," began their father cheerfully. Recollecting how nearly he had lost her, he held her close, saying tenderly with her cheek against his own, "I've got you safe, my Beth, and I'll keep you so, please God."

After a minute's silence he looked down at Amy, who sat on the cricket at his feet, and said with a caress of the shining hair: "I observed that Amy took drumsticks at dinner, ran errands for her mother all afternoon, gave Meg her place tonight, and has waited on everyone with patience and good humor. I also observe that she does not fret much nor look in the glass, and has not even mentioned a pretty ring which she wears, so I conclude that she has learned to think of other people more and of herself less, and has decided to try and mold her character as carefully as she molds her little clay figures. I am glad of this, for though I should be very proud of a graceful statue made by her, I shall be infinitely prouder of a lovable daughter with a talent for making life beautiful to herself and others."

"What are you thinking of, Beth?" asked Jo, when Amy had thanked her father and told him about her ring.

"I read in *Pilgrim's Progress* today how, after many troubles, Christian and Hopeful came to a pleasant green meadow where lilies bloomed all the year round, and there

they rested happily, as we do now, before they went on
to their journey's end," answered Beth, adding as she slipped
out of her father's arms and went slowly to the piano, "It's
singing time now, and I want to be in my old place. I'll try
to sing the song of the shepherd boy which the Pilgrims
heard. I made the music for Father, because he likes the
verses."

Beth softly touched the keys, and in the sweet voice they
had never thought to hear again sang to her own accom-
paniment the quaint hymn.

Chapter 20

AUNT MARCH SETTLES THE QUESTION

MOTHER and daughters hovered about Mr. March the
next day, neglecting everything to look at, wait upon, and
listen to the new invalid who sat propped up in a big chair
by Beth's sofa. Mr. and Mrs. March looked at one another
with an anxious expression as their eyes followed Meg. Jo
was seen to shake her fist at Mr. Brooke's umbrella which
had been left in the hall. Meg was absent-minded, shy and
silent, started when the bell rang, and colored when John's
name was mentioned.

Amy said, "Everyone seemed waiting for something, and
couldn't settle down," and Beth innocently wondered why
their neighbors didn't run over as usual. Laurie went by in
the afternoon, and seeing Meg at the window fell down on
one knee in the snow, beat his breast, tore his hair and
clasped his hands imploringly. When Meg told him to behave himself and go away, he wrung imaginary tears out of
his handkerchief and staggered around the corner in despair.

"What does the goose mean?" said Meg laughing.

"He's showing you how your John will go on by and by. Touching, isn't it?" answered Jo scornfully.

"Don't say *my John*, it isn't proper or true," but Meg's voice lingered over the words. "There isn't to be anything said. We are all to be friendly and go on as before."

"We can't, for something *has* been said. I do wish it was all settled. I hate to wait, so if you mean ever to do it, make haste and have it over quickly," said Jo pettishly.

"*I* can't say or do anything till he speaks, and he won't because Father said I was too young," began Meg, bending over her work with a queer little smile.

"If he did speak, you wouldn't know what to say but would cry or blush instead of giving a good decided 'No.'"

"I'm not so weak as you think. I know just what I should say, for I've planned it all so I needn't be taken unawares."

"Would you mind telling me what you'd say?" asked Jo respectfully.

"Oh, I should merely say, quite calmly and decidedly, 'Thank you, Mr. Brooke, you are very kind, but I agree with Father that I am too young to enter into any engagement at present, so please say no more but let us be friends as we were.'"

"Hum! That's stiff and cool enough. I don't believe you'll ever say it. You'll give in, rather than hurt his feelings."

"No I won't. I shall tell him I've made up my mind and shall walk out of the room with dignity."

Meg rose as she spoke and was just going to rehearse the dignified exit, when a step in the hall made her fly into her seat and began to sew as if her life depended on it. Jo smothered a laugh at the sudden change, and when someone gave a modest tap, opened the door.

"Good afternoon. I came to get my umbrella, that is, to see how your father finds himself today," said Mr. Brooke, getting a trifle confused as his eyes went from one telltale face to the other.

"It's very well, he's in the rack, I'll get him, and tell it you are here," and having jumbled her father and the umbrella well together in her reply, Jo slipped out of the room to give Meg a chance to make her speech. But the instant she vanished Meg began to sidle towards the door, murmuring, "Mother will like to see you. Pray sit down and I'll call her."

"Don't go. Are you afraid of me, Margaret?" and Mr. Brooke looked so hurt that Meg thought she must have done something very rude.

She blushed up to the little curls on her forehead, for he had never called her Margaret before and she was surprised to find how natural and sweet it seemed to hear him say it. Anxious to appear friendly and at her ease, she put out her hand with a confiding gesture and said gratefully, "How can I be afraid when you have been so kind to Father? I only wish I could thank you for it."

"Shall I tell you how?" asked Mr. Brooke, holding the small hand fast in both his own and looking down at Meg with so much love in the brown eyes that her heart began to flutter.

"Oh no, please don't, I'd rather not," she said, trying to withdraw her hand and looking frightened in spite of her denial.

"I won't trouble you. I only want to know if you care for me a little, Meg. I love you so much, dear," added Mr. Brooke tenderly.

This was the moment for the calm proper speech, but Meg didn't make it. She forgot every word of it, hung her head and answered "I don't know" so softly John had to stoop down to catch the reply.

He seemed to think it was worth the trouble, for he smiled to himself as if quite satisfied, pressed the plump hand gratefully, and said in his most persuasive tone, "Will you try to find out? I want to know *so* much, for I can't go to work with my heart until I learn whether I am to have my reward in the end or not."

"I'm too young," faltered Meg, wondering why she was so fluttered yet rather enjoying it.

"I'll wait, and in the meantime you could be learning to like me. Would it be a very hard lesson, dear?"

"Not if I chose to learn it but—"

"Please choose to learn, Meg. I love to teach and this is easier than German," broke in John, getting possession of the other hand so that she had no way of hiding her face as he bent to look into it. His tone was properly beseeching, but stealing a shy look at him Meg saw that his eyes were merry as well as tender, and that he wore the satisfied smile of one who had no doubt of his success. This nettled her. Following a capricious impulse, she withdrew her hand and said petulantly, "I *don't* choose. Please go away and let me be!"

Poor Mr. Brooke looked as if his lovely castle in the air was tumbling about his ears. "Do you really mean that?" he asked anxiously.

"Yes I do. I don't want to be worried about such things. Father says I needn't. It's too soon and I'd rather not."

"Mayn't I hope you'll change your mind by and by? I'll wait. Don't play with me, Meg. I didn't think that of you."

"Don't think of me at all. I'd rather you wouldn't," said Meg.

Mr. Brooke was grave and pale now, but he stood looking at her so wistfully, so tenderly, that she found her heart relenting in spite of herself. At this interesting moment, Aunt March came hobbling in. The old lady couldn't resist her longing to see her nephew, for she had met Laurie and heard of Mr. March's arrival. The family were in the back part of the house and she had made her way in quietly, hoping to surprise them. She did surprise two of them so much that Meg started as if she had seen a ghost, and Mr. Brooke vanished into the study.

"Bless me, what's all this?" cried the old lady with a rap of her cane as she glanced from the pale young gentleman to the scarlet young lady.

"It's Father's friend. I'm *so* surprised to see you!" stammered Meg.

"That's evident," returned Aunt March, sitting down. "But what is Father's friend saying to make you look like a peony? There's mischief going on and I insist upon knowing what it is." Another rap.

"We were merely talking. Mr. Brooke came for his umbrella," began Meg, wishing that both were safely out of the house.

"Brooke? That boy's tutor? Ah! I understand now. I know all about it. Jo blundered into a wrong message in one of your father's letters and I made her tell me. You haven't gone and accepted him, child?" cried Aunt March, looking scandalized.

"Hush! He'll hear. Sha'n't I call Mother?" said Meg. troubled.

"Not yet. I've something to say to you, and I must free my mind at once. Tell me, do you mean to marry this Cook? If you do, not one penny of my money ever goes to you. Remember that, and be a sensible girl," said the old lady impressively.

Now Aunt March possessed in perfection the art of rousing the spirit of opposition in the gentlest people, and enjoyed doing it. If she had begged Meg to accept John Brooke, she would probably have declared she couldn't think of it, but as she was peremptorily ordered not to like him, she immediately made up her mind that she would. Inclination as well as perversity made the decision easy, and being already much excited, Meg opposed the old lady with unusual spirit.

"I shall marry whom I please, Aunt March, and you can leave your money to anyone you like," she said, nodding her head with a resolute air.

"Highty tighty! Is that the way you take my advice, miss? You'll be sorry when you've tried love in a cottage and found it a failure."

"It can't be worse than some people find in big houses," retorted Meg.

Aunt March put on her glasses and took a look at the

girl, for she did not know her in this new mood. She made a fresh start, "Now Meg, my dear, be reasonable and take my advice. I mean it kindly, and I don't want you to spoil your whole life by making a mistake at the beginning. You ought to marry well and help your family."

"Father and Mother don't think so. They like John though he *is* poor."

"Your parents have no more worldly wisdom than two babies."

"I'm glad of it," cried Meg stoutly.

"This Rook is poor and hasn't any rich relations, has he?"

"No, but he has many warm friends."

"You can't live on friends. He hasn't any business, has he?"

"Not yet. Mr. Laurence is going to help him."

"That won't last long. So you intend to marry a man without money, position or business, when you might be comfortable by minding me. I thought you had more sense, Meg."

"I couldn't do better if I waited half my life! John is good and wise. He's got heaps of talent, he's willing to work, and sure to get on, he's so energetic and brave. Everyone likes and respects him, and I'm proud to think he cares for me, though I'm young and silly," said Meg, looking prettier than ever in her earnestness.

"He knows *you* have rich relations, child. That's the secret of his liking, I suspect."

"Aunt March, how dare you say such a thing! John is above such meanness and I won't listen to you a minute if you talk so," cried Meg indignantly, forgetting everything but the injustice of the old lady's suspicions. "My John wouldn't marry for money any more than I would. We are willing to work and we mean to wait. I'm not afaid of being poor, for I've been happy so far and I know I shall be with him, because he loves me and I—" Meg stopped there, remembering all of a sudden that she hadn't made up her mind, and that she had told "her John" to go away and that he might be overhearing her inconsistent remarks.

Aunt March was very angry for she had set her heart on having her pretty niece make a fine match, and something in the girl's happy young face made the lonely old woman feel both sad and sour. "Well, I wash my hands of the whole affair! You are a wilful child, and you've lost more than you know by this piece of folly. I'm disappointed in you. Don't expect anything from me when you are married. Your Mr. Brook's friends must take care of you. I'm done with you forever."

And slamming the door in Meg's face, Aunt March drove off in high dudgeon. She seemed to take all the girl's courage with her, for when left alone Meg stood a moment, undecided whether to laugh or cry. Before she could make up her mind, she was taken possession of by Mr. Brooke, who said all in one breath, "I couldn't help hearing, Meg. Thank you for defending me, and Aunt March for proving that you *do* care for me a little."

"I didn't know how much till she abused you," began Meg.

"And I needn't go away but may stay and be happy, may I, dear?"

Here was another fine chance to make the crushing speech and the stately exit, but Meg never thought of doing either, and disgraced herself forever in Jo's eyes by meekly whispering, "Yes, John," and hiding her face on Mr. Brooke's waistcoat.

Fifteen minutes after Aunt March's departure, Jo came softly downstairs, paused an instant at the parlor door, and hearing no sound, nodded and smiled with a satisfied expression, saying to herself, "She has sent him away as we planned and that affair is settled. I'll go and hear the fun and have a good laugh over it."

Poor Jo was transfixed upon the threshold by a spectacle which held her there staring with her mouth nearly as wide open as her eyes. Going in to praise a strongminded sister, it was a shock to behold John sitting serenely on the sofa with the strongminded sister on his knee, wearing an expression of abject submission. Jo gave a sort of gasp, as if a cold shower had suddenly fallen on her, for such an unexpected turning of the tables actually took her breath away. At the odd sound, the lovers turned and saw her. Meg jumped up, looking both proud and shy, but "that man," as Jo called him, actually laughed and said coolly, as he kissed the astonished newcomer, "Sister Jo, congratulate me!"

That was adding insult to injury, and Jo vanished without a word. Running upstairs, she startled the invalids by exclaiming tragically, as she burst into the room, "Oh *do* somebody go down quickly! John Brooke is acting dreadfully and Meg likes it!"

Mr. and Mrs. March left the room with speed, and casting herself on the bed, Jo cried and scolded as she told the awful news to Beth and Amy. The girls, however, considered it a most interesting event, and Jo got little comfort from them, so she went up to the garret.

Nobody ever knew what went on in the parlor that afternoon, but a great deal of talking was done, and quiet Mr. Brooke astonished his friends by the eloquence and spirit with which he pleaded his suit, told his plans, and persuaded them to arrange everything just as he wanted it.

The tea bell rang before he had finished describing the paradise which he meant to earn for Meg, and he proudly took her in to supper, both looking so happy that Jo hadn't the heart to be dismal. Amy was impressed by John's devotion and Meg's dignity, Beth beamed on them from a distance, while Mr. and Mrs. March surveyed the young couple with satisfaction.

"You can't say nothing pleasant ever happens now, can you, Meg?" said Amy.

"No, I'm sure I can't. How much has happened since I said that! It seems a year ago," answered Meg.

"The joys come close upon the sorrows this time and I rather think the changes have begun," said Mrs. March. "In most families there comes now and then a year full of events. This has been such a year, but it ends well after all."

"Hope the next will end better," muttered Jo.

"I hope the third year from this *will* end better. I mean it shall, if I live to work out my plans," said Mr. Brooke, smiling at Meg.

"Doesn't it seem very long to wait?" asked Amy.

"I've got so much to learn before I shall be ready, it seems a short time to me," answered Meg, with a sweet gravity in her face.

"You have only to wait, *I* am to do the work," said John, beginning his labors by picking up Meg's napkin with an expression which caused Jo to shake her head.

The front door banged and Laurie came prancing in, bearing a great bridal-looking bouquet for "Mrs. John Brooke."

Jo's eyes went slowly around the room. The prospect was a pleasant one. Father and Mother sat together, quietly reliving the first chapter of the romance which for them began some twenty years ago. Amy was drawing the lovers, who sat apart in a beautiful world of their own. Beth lay on her sofa talking cheerily with Mr. Laurence. Jo lounged in her favorite low seat, with the grave quiet look which best became her. And Laurie, leaning on the back of her chair, his chin on a level with her curly head, smiled with his friendliest aspect and nodded at her in the long glass which reflected them both.

PART II

Chapter 21

GOSSIP

THE NEXT three years brought few changes to the quiet family. The war ended, and Mr. March was safely at home, with his books and the small parish which found in him a minister by nature as by grace, a quiet studious man, rich in the wisdom that is better than learning, the charity which calls all mankind brother.

John Brooke did his duty manfully for a year, was wounded and sent home and not allowed to return. Resigned to his discharge, he devoted himself to getting well, preparing for business, and earning a home for Meg. With the good sense and sturdy independence that characterized him, he refused Mr. Laurence's more generous offers, and accepted the place of bookkeeper, feeling better satisfied to begin with an honestly earned salary than by running risks with borrowed money.

Meg spent the time in working as well as waiting, growing wise in housewifely arts, and prettier than ever. When she and John sat together in the twilight, talking over their small plans, the future grew beautiful and bright.

Jo never went back to Aunt March, for the old lady took such a fancy to Amy that she bribed her with the offer of drawing lessons. Jo devoted herself to literature and Beth, who remained delicate long after the fever was a thing of the past. As long as *The Spread Eagle* paid her a dollar a column for her "rubbish," as she called it, Jo felt herself a woman of means and spun her little romances diligently.

Laurie, having dutifully gone to college to please his grandfather, was now getting through it in the easiest possible manner to please himself. A universal favorite, thanks to money, manners, much talent and the kindest heart that ever got its owner into scrapes by trying to get other people out of them, he frolicked and flirted, hazed and was hazed, talked slang, and more than once came perilously near suspension and expulsion. But as high spirits and the love of fun were the causes of these pranks, he always managed to save himself by frank confession, honorable atonement, or the irresistible power of persuasion which he possessed. The "men of my class" were heroes in the eyes of the girls, who never wearied of the exploits of "our fellows." Amy especially enjoyed this high honor and became quite a belle among them. They all liked Jo immensely but never fell in love with her.

The Dovecote was the name of the little brown house Mr. Brooke had prepared for Meg's first home. Laurie had christened it. It was a tiny house, with a little garden behind, and a lawn about as big as a handkerchief in front. Here Meg meant to have a fountain, shrubbery and a profusion of lovely flowers, though at present the fountain was represented by a weatherbeaten urn, the shrubbery consisted of several young larches, undecided whether to live or die, and the profusion of flowers was merely hinted by regiments of sticks, to show where seeds were planted.

But inside it was altogether charming, and the happy bride saw no fault from garret to cellar. There were no marble-topped tables, long mirrors, or lace curtains in the little parlor, but simple furniture, plenty of books, a fine picture or two, a stand of flowers in the bay window, and scattered all about the pretty gifts which came from friendly hands.

Everything was done at last, even to Amy's arranging different colored soaps to match the different colored rooms, and Beth's setting the table for the first meal.

"Are you satisfied? Does it seem like home, and do you

feel as if you should be happy here?" asked Mrs. March, as she and her daughter went through the new kingdom arm in arm.

"Yes, Mother, perfectly satisfied, thanks to you all and *so* happy that I can't talk about it," answered Meg.

They went upstairs, and Meg looked into her well-stocked linen closet. "I like this room most of all in my baby house," she said.

Beth was there, exulting over the goodly array. They all laughed as Meg spoke, for the linen closet was a joke. Having said that if Meg married "that Brooke" she shouldn't have a cent of her money, Aunt March was in a quandary when time had appeased her wrath and made her repent her vow. She never broke her word, and was much exercised in her mind how to get around it. At last she devised a plan. Mrs. Carrol, Florence's mamma, was ordered to buy, have made and marked, a generous supply of house and table linen and send it as her present, all of which was faithfully done. But the secret leaked out and was greatly enjoyed by the family, for Aunt March tried to look utterly unconscious, and insisted that she could give nothing but the old-fashioned pearls, long promised to the first bride.

They all went down to meet Laurie, whose weekly visit was an important event in their quiet lives. A tall, broad-shouldered young fellow, with a cropped head, a felt basin of a hat, and a flyaway coat, came tramping down the road at a great pace, walked over the low fence without stopping to open the gate, straight up to Mrs. March with both hands out and a hearty, "Here I am, Mother! Yes, it's all right."

The last words were in answer to the look the elder lady gave him; a kindly questioning look which the handsome eyes met so frankly that the little ceremony closed as usual with a kiss.

"For Mrs. John Brooke with the maker's compliments." As Laurie spoke he delivered a brown paper parcel to Meg.

"Undo the bundle, Meg," said Beth, eyeing it with curiosity.

"It's a useful thing to have in the house in case of fire or thieves," observed Laurie, as a watchman's rattle appeared amid laughter.

"Any time when John is away and you get frightened, Mrs. Meg, just swing that out of the front window and it will rouse the neighborhood in a jiffy. Nice thing, isn't it?" and Laurie gave them a sample of its powers that made them cover their ears.

"Teddy, I want to talk seriously to you about tomorrow," began Jo, as she and Laurie strolled away together. "You *must* promise to behave and not cut up and spoil our plans."

"I promise. I say, Jo, how is Grandpa this week? Pretty amiable?"

"Very. Why? Have you got into a scrape and want to know how he'll take it?" asked Jo rather sharply.

"Now Jo, do you think I'd look your mother in the face and say 'All right' if it wasn't?" Laurie stopped short with an injured air. "I only want some money."

"You spend a great deal, Teddy."

"Bless you, *I* don't spend it. It spends itself somehow."

"You are so generous and kindhearted that you let people borrow and can't say no to anyone. We heard about Henshaw and all you did for him. If you always spent money in that way, no one would blame you," said Jo warmly.

"Oh, he made a mountain out of a molehill. You wouldn't have let that fine fellow work himself to death just for the want of a little help, when he is worth a dozen of us lazy chaps, would you?"

"Of course not. But I don't see the use of your having seventeen waistcoats, endless neckties, and a new hat every time you come home. I thought you'd got over the dandy period."

Laurie laughed so heartily that the felt basin fell off and Jo walked on it. He folded up the maltreated hat and stuffed it into his pocket.

"I won't lecture any more if you'll *only* let your hair grow. I'm not aristocratic but I do object to being seen with a person who looks like a young prizefighter," observed Jo severely.

"This unassuming style promotes study," returned Laurie. "By the way, Jo, I think that little Parker is really getting desperate about Amy. He talks of her constantly and writes poetry. He'd better nip his little passion in the bud, hadn't he?"

"Of course he had. We don't want any more marrying in this family for years to come."

"It's a fast age. You'll go next, Jo, and we'll be left lamenting."

"Don't be alarmed. Nobody will want me."

"You won't give anyone a chance," said Laurie, with a sidelong glance and a little more color than before in his sunburned face: "You won't show the soft side of your character, and if a fellow gets a peep at it by accident and can't help showing that he likes it, you throw cold water over him and get so thorny no one dares touch or look at you."

"I don't like that sort of thing." Jo looked ready to fling cold water on the slightest provocation. "I'm too busy to be worried with nonsense. Now don't say any more about it. Meg's wedding has turned all our heads."

Laurie gave a long low whistle, and as they parted at the gate said, 'Mark my words, Jo, you'll go next."

Chapter 22

THE FIRST WEDDING

THE June roses over the porch were awake bright and early on that morning. Meg looked very like a rose herself. Neither silk, nor orange flowers would she have. "I don't want to look strange or fixed up today," she said. "I don't

want a fashionable wedding but only those about me whom
I love, and to them I wish to look and be my familiar self."

So she made her wedding gown herself. Her sisters
braided her pretty hair, and the only ornaments she wore
were the lilies of the valley which John liked best of all the
flowers that grew.

"You *do* look just like our own dear Meg, only so very
sweet and lovely that I should hug you if it wouldn't crum-
ple your dress," cried Amy, surveying her with delight when
all was done.

"Then I am satisfied. But please hug and kiss me, every
one, and don't mind my dress. I want a great many crumples
of this sort put into it today." And Meg opened her arms to
her sisters.

"Now I'm going to tie John's cravat for him, and then stay
a few minutes with Father quietly in the study."

Meg ran downstairs, and the younger sisters gave themselves the finishing touches. They all looked their best. Jo's
angles had softened. She had learned to carry herself with
ease if not grace. The curly crop had lengthened into a thick
coil, more becoming to the small head atop of the tall
figure. There was fresh color in her brown cheeks, a soft
shine to her eyes.

Beth had grown slender, pale, and quieter than ever. The
beautiful kind eyes were larger, and in them lay an expression that saddened one, the shadow of pain.

Amy was considered the flower of the family, for at
sixteen she had the air and bearing of a woman—not beautiful but possessed of indescribable charm. One saw it in
the lines of her figure, the motion of her hands, the flow of
her dress. Her nose still afflicted her, for it never would
grow Grecian. So did her mouth, being too wide, and having a decided chin. These offending features gave character to her whole face but she never could see it, and consoled herself with her fair complexion, keen blue eyes, and
curls, more golden and abundant than ever.

All three wore suits of thin silver gray—their best gowns

for the summer—with blush roses in hair and bosom. All three looked just what they were, fresh-faced, happy-hearted girls.

There were to be no ceremonious performances. Everything was to be as natural and homelike as possible. So when Aunt March arrived, she was scandalized to see the bride come running to welcome and lead her in, to find the bridegroom fastening a garland that had fallen, and to catch a glimpse of the paternal minister.

"Upon my word, here's a state of things!" cried the old lady, taking the seat of honor prepared for her, and settling the folds of her lavender moire with a great rustle. "You oughtn't to be seen till the last minute, child."

"I'm not a show, Aunty, and no one is coming to stare at me, to criticize my dress or count the cost of my luncheon. I'm too happy to care what anyone says of things, and I'm going to have my little wedding just as I like it. John, dear, here's your hammer."

Mr. Brooke didn't even say thank you, but as he stooped for the unromantic tool, he kissed his little bride behind the folding door with a look that made Aunt March whisk out her handkerchief.

A crash, a cry, and a laugh from Laurie, accompanied by "Jupiter Ammon! Jo's upset the cake again!" caused a momentary flurry, which was hardly over when a flock of cousins arrived.

"Don't let that young giant near me. He worries me worse than mosquitoes," whispered Aunt March to Amy, as the rooms filled and Laurie's black head towered above the rest.

"He has promised to be very good today, and he *can* be perfectly elegant if he likes," returned Amy, gliding away to warn Laurie.

There was no bridal procession, but a sudden silence fell on the room as Mr. March and the young pair took their places under the green arch. Mother and sisters gathered close, the fatherly voice broke more than once, which only seemed to make the service more beautiful and solemn. The bridgegroom's hand trembled visibly and no one heard his replies, but Meg looked straight up into her husband's eyes and said, "I will!" with such tender trust in her own face and voice that Aunt March sniffed audibly.

Jo didn't cry though she was very near it once, and was

only saved from a demonstration by the consciousness that Laurie was staring fixedly at her, with a comical mixture of merriment and emotion in his wicked black eyes. Beth kept her face hidden on her mother's shoulder, but Amy stood like a graceful statue with a ray of sunshine touching her forehead and the flower in her hair.

The minute she was married, Meg cried, "The first kiss for Marmee!" During the next fifteen minutes she looked more like a rose than ever, for everyone availed themselves of their privileges to the fullest extent, from Mr. Laurence to old Hannah who, adorned with a headdress fearfully and wonderfully made, fell upon her in the hall crying with a sob and a chuckle, "Bless you, dearie, a hundred times! The cake ain't hurt a mite and everything looks real lovely."

Everybody cleared up after that and said something brilliant, or tried to. There was no display of gifts, for they were already in the little house, nor was there an elaborate breakfast but a lunch of cake and fruit, dressed with flowers. After lunch, people strolled about, through house and garden. Meg and John happened to be standing together in the middle of the grass plot, when Laurie was seized with an inspiration which put the finishing touch to this unfashionable wedding.

"All the married people take hands and dance around the new-made husband and wife, as the Germans do, while we bachelors and spinsters prance in couples outside!" cried Laurie, promenading down the path with Amy with such infectious spirit and skill that everyone else followed their example. Mr. and Mrs. March, Aunt and Uncle Carrol, began it. Others rapidly joined in. Even Sallie Moffat after a moment's hesitation threw her train over her arm and whisked Ned into the ring. But the crowning joke was Mr. Laurence and Aunt March, for when the stately old gentleman chasséed solemnly up to the old lady, she just tucked her cane under her arm and hopped briskly away to join hands with the rest and dance about the bridal pair, while the young folks pervaded the garden like butterflies on a midsummer day. Want of breath brought the impromptu ball to a close and then people began to go.

"I wish you well, my dear, I heartily wish you well, but I think you'll be sorry for it," said Aunt March to Meg, adding to the bridegroom, as he led her to the carriage, "You've got a treasure, young man. See that you deserve it."

"Laurie, my lad, if you ever want to indulge in this sort of thing, get one of those girls to help you and I shall be perfectly satisfied," said Mr. Laurence, settling himself in his easychair.

"I'll do my best to gratify you, sir," was Laurie's dutiful reply, as he carefully unpinned the posy Jo had put in his buttonhole.

The little house was not far away, and the only bridal journey Meg had was the quiet walk with John from the old home to the new. When she came down, looking like a pretty Quakeress in her dove-colored suit and straw bonnet tied with white, they all gathered about her to say good-by.

They stood watching her, with faces full of love and hope and tender pride, as she walked away, leaning on her husband's arm, with her hands full of flowers and the June sunshine brightening her happy face. So Meg's married life began.

Chapter 23

ARTISTIC ATTEMPTS

IT TAKES people a long time to learn the difference between talent and genius, especially ambitious young men and women. Amy was learning this distinction through much tribulation, for mistaking enthusiasm for inspiration she attempted every branch of art with youthful audacity. For a long time there was a lull in the "mudpie" business and she devoted herself to the finest pen-and-ink drawing, in which she showed such taste and skill that her graceful handiwork proved both pleasant and profitable. But overstrained eyes soon caused pen and ink to be laid aside, and Amy fell to painting with oils. An artist friend fitted her out with his castoff palettes, brushes and colors, and she daubed away, producing pastoral and marine views such as were never seen on land or sea. Swarthy boys and dark-eyed Madonnas suggested Murillo; oily brown shadows of faces with a lurid streak in the wrong place meant Rembrandt; buxom ladies and dropsical infants, Rubens; and Turner appeared in tempests of blue thunder, orange lightning, brown rain, and purple clouds, with a tomato-colored splash in the middle which might be the sun or a buoy, a sailor's shirt or a king's robe.

Charcoal portraits came next, and the entire family hung in a row, looking as wild and crocky as if just evoked from a coal bin. A return to clay and plaster followed, and ghostly casts of her acquaintances haunted corners of the house, or tumbled off closet shelves onto people's heads. Then she undertook to cast her own pretty foot, and one day the family was alarmed by an unearthly bumping and screaming. Running to the rescue, they found the young enthusiast hopping wildly about the shed with her foot held fast in a panful of plaster which had hardened with unexpected rapidity. With much difficulty and some danger she was dug out, for Jo was so overcome with laughter that her knife cut the poor foot.

After this Amy subsided, until a mania for sketching from nature set her to haunting river, field and wood for picturesque studies. She caught endless colds sitting on damp grass. She sacrificed her complexion floating on the river in the midsummer sun. Meanwhile, she was learning, doing and enjoying other things, for she had resolved to be an attractive and accomplished woman even if she never became a great artist. Here she succeeded better. Everybody liked her for among her gifts was tact. One of her weaknesses was a desire to move in "our best society," without being quite sure what the best really was. Money, position, fashionable accomplishments and elegant manners were most desirable things in her eyes.

"I want to ask a favor of you, Mamma," Amy said one day.

"Well, little girl, what is it?" replied her mother, in whose eyes the stately young lady still remained the baby.

"Our drawing class breaks up next week, and before the girls separate for the summer, I want to ask them out here for a day. They are wild to see the river and sketch the broken bridge. They have been very kind and I am grateful, for they are all rich, yet they never made any difference."

"Why should they?" and Mrs. March put the question with what the girls called her Maria Theresa air.

"You know as well as I that it *does* make a difference with nearly everyone, so don't ruffle up like a dear, motherly hen."

Mrs. March laughed and asked, "Well, what is your plan?"

"I should like to ask the girls out to lunch next week, to take them a drive to the places they want to see, a row on the river, perhaps, and make a little artistic fete for them."

"That looks feasible. What do you want for lunch? Cake, sandwiches, fruit and coffee will be all that is necessary, I suppose?"

"Oh dear, no! We must have cold tongue and chicken, French chocolate and ice cream besides. The girls are used to such things."

"How many young ladies are there?" asked her mother.

"Twelve or fourteen, but I dare say they won't all come."

"Bless me, child, you will have to charter an omnibus."

"Why, Mother, how *can* you think of such a thing? Not more than six or eight will probably come, so I shall hire a beach wagon, and borrow Mr. Laurence's cherry-bounce." (Hannah's pronunciation of *charàbanc*.)

"All this will be expensive, Amy."

"Not very. I've calculated the cost and I'll pay for it myself."

"Don't you think, dear, that as these girls are used to such things, and the best we can do will be nothing new, that some simpler plan would be pleasanter to them as a change if nothing more, and much better for us than buying or borrowing what we don't need?"

"If I can't have it as I like, I don't care to have it at all. I know I can carry it out perfectly well, if you and the girls will help. I don't see why I can't if I'm willing to pay for it," said Amy, with the decision which opposition was apt to change into obstinacy.

"Very well, Amy. If your heart is set on it, and you see your way through without too great an outlay of money time and temper, I'll say no more. Talk it over with the girls and whichever way you decide, I'll do my best to help you."

"Thanks, Mother, you are always *so* kind," and away went Amy to lay her plan before her sisters.

Meg agreed at once and promised her aid, gladly offering anything she possessed, but Jo frowned on the whole project. "Why in the world should you spend your money, worry your family, and turn the house upside down for a parcel of girls who don't care a sixpence for you? I thought you had too much pride."

"The girls do care for me and I for them," returned Amy indignantly, "and there's a great deal of kindness and sense and talent among them. You don't care to make people like you, to go into good society, and cultivate your manners and tastes. I do, and I mean to make the most of every chance that comes."

Much against her will, Jo at length consented to help her sister through what she regarded as "a nonsensical business." The invitations were sent, nearly all accepted, and the following Monday was set apart for the grand event. Hannah was out of humor because her week's work was deranged. This hitch in the mainspring of the domestic machinery had a bad effect on the whole concern. Hannah's cooking didn't turn out well—the chicken was tough, the tongue too salt, and the chocolate wouldn't froth properly. Then the cake and ice cost more than Amy expected, so did the wagon; and various other expenses which seemed trifling at the outset, counted up rather alarmingly afterward. Beth got a cold and went to bed, Meg had an unusual number of callers to keep her at home, and Jo was in a divided state of mind.

"If it hadn't been for Mother I never should have got through," Amy declared afterward.

If it was not fair on Monday, the young ladies were to come on Tuesday, an arrangement which aggravated Jo and Hannah to the last degree. On Monday morning the weather was in that undecided state which is more exasperating than a steady pour. Amy was up at dawn, hustling people out of their beds and through their breakfasts that the house might be got in order. She arranged chairs over the worn places in the parlor carpet, covered stains on the walls with pictures framed in ivy, and filled empty corners with homemade statuary.

The lunch looked charming, and as she surveyed it, Amy sincerely hoped it would taste well and that the borrowed glass, china and silver would get safely home again. The carriages were promised, Meg and Mother were all ready to do the honors, Beth was able to help Hannah behind the scenes, and Jo had engaged to be as lively and amiable as an absent mind and an aching head would allow. As she wearily dressed, Amy cheered herself with anticipation of the happy moment when, lunch safely over, she should drive away with her friends for an afternoon of artistic delights.

Then came two hours of suspense. A smart shower at eleven had evidently quenched the enthusiasm of the young ladies who were to arrive at twelve, for nobody came. At two the exhausted family sat down in a blaze of sunshine to consume the perishable portions of the feast.

"No doubt about the weather today. They will certainly come, so we must fly around and be ready for them," said Amy as the sun woke her next morning.

"I can't get any lobsters, so you will have to do without salad today," said Mr. March coming in half an hour later.

"Use the chicken, then. The toughness won't matter in a salad," advised his wife.

"Hannah left it on the kitchen table a minute and the kittens got it. I'm very sorry, Amy," added Beth.

"Then I *must* have a lobster for tongue alone won't do," said Amy.

"Shall I rush into town and demand one?" asked Jo.

"You'd come bringing it home under your arm without any paper, just to try me. I'll go myself," answered Amy.

Shrouded in a thick veil and armed with a genteel traveling basket, she departed. After some delay, the object of her desire was procured, likewise a bottle of dressing. As the omnibus contained only one other passenger, a sleepy old lady, Amy pocketed her veil and beguiled the tedium of the way by trying to find out where all her money had gone to. So busy was she with her card full of refractory figures that she did not observe a newcomer, who entered without stopping the vehicle, until a masculine voice said, "Good morning, Miss March," and looking up she beheld one of Laurie's most elegant college friends. Fervently hoping that he would get out before she did, Amy ignored the basket at her feet, and congratulating herself that she had on her new traveling dress, returned the young man's greeting with her usual spirit.

They got on excellently, for Amy's chief care was soon set at rest by learning that the gentleman would leave first, and she was chatting away in a peculiarly lofty strain, when the old lady got out. In stumbling to the door, she upset the basket, and the lobster in all its vulgar size and brilliancy was revealed.

"By Jove, she's forgotten her dinner!" cried the youth, poking the scarlet monster into its place with his cane and preparing to hand out the basket after the old lady.

"Please don't—it's—it's mine," murmured Amy, with a face nearly as red as her fish.

"Oh, really, I beg pardon. It's an uncommonly fine one, isn't it?" said Tudor with great presence of mind.

Amy recovered herself in a breath, set her basket boldly on the seat, and said laughing, "Don't you wish you were to have some of the salad he's to make, and to see the charming young ladies who are to eat it?"

Now that was tact, for the lobster was instantly surrounded by a halo of pleasing reminiscences, and curiosity about "the charming young ladies" diverted his mind from the comical mishap.

"I suppose he'll laugh and joke over it with Laurie but I sha'n't see them," thought Amy, as Tudor bowed and departed.

She did not mention this meeting at home, though she discovered the upset had sent rivulets of dressing down the skirt of her new dress, but went through with the preparations which now seemed more irksome than before. At twelve o'clock all was ready again, so Amy ordered the "cherry-bounce" and drove away in state to meet her guests.

"There's the rumble, they're coming! I'll go into the porch to meet them," and Mrs. March suited the action to word. But after one glance, she retired with an indescribable expression, for looking quite lost in the big carriage sat Amy and one young lady.

"Run, Beth, and help Hannah clear half the things off the table," cried Jo, hurrying away to the lower regions. "It will be too absurd to put a luncheon for twelve before a single girl."

In came Amy, quite calm and delightfully cordial to the one guest who had kept her promise. The rest of the family played their parts equally well, and Miss Elliott found them a most hilarious set, for it was impossible to control entirely the merriment which possessed them. The remodeled lunch being gaily partaken of, the studio and garden visited and art discussed with enthusiasm, Amy ordered a buggy and drove her friend quietly about the neighborhood until sunset.

As she came walking in, looking very tired but as composed as ever, she observed that every vestige of the unfortunate fete had disappeared.

"You've had a lovely afternoon for your drive, dear," said her mother, as respectfully as if the whole twelve had come.

"Miss Elliott is a very sweet girl and seemed to enjoy herself, I thought," observed Beth with unusual warmth.

"Could you spare me some of your cake? I really need some, I have so much company and I can't make such delicious stuff as yours," asked Meg soberly.

"Take it all. I'm the only one here who likes sweet things and it will mold before I can dispose of it," answered Amy, thinking with a sigh of the generous store she had laid in.

"It's a pity Laurie isn't here to help us," began Jo, as they sat down to ice cream and salad for the second time in two days.

A warning look from her mother checked any further remarks, and the whole family ate in heroic silence, until Mr. March mildly observed, "Salad was one of the favorite dishes of the ancients, and Evelyn—" here a general explosion of laughter cut short the "history of sallets," to the great surprise of the learned gentleman.

"Bundle everything into a basket and give it away," cried Amy, wiping her eyes. "I'm sick of the sight of this, and there's no reason you should all die of a surfeit because I've been a fool."

"I thought I should have died when I saw you two girls rattling about in the what-you-call-it, and Mother waiting in state to receive the throng," sighed Jo, quite spent with laughter.

"I'm very sorry you were disappointed, dear, but we all did our best to satisfy you," said Mrs. March in a tone full of regret.

"I *am* satisfied. I've done what I undertook and it's not my fault that it failed. I comfort myself with that," said Amy with a little quiver in her voice. "I thank you all very much for helping me and I'll thank you still more if you won't allude to it for a month."

No one did for several months, but the word *fete* always produced a general smile, and Laurie's birthday gift to Amy was a tiny coral lobster in the shape of a charm for her watch guard.

Chapter 24

LITERARY LESSONS

FORTUNE suddenly smiled on Jo and dropped a good luck penny in her path. Every few weeks she would shut herself up in her room, put on her scribbling suit, and "fall into a vortex," as she expressed it, writing away at her novel with all her heart and soul, for until that was finished she could find no peace. When the writing fit came on, she gave herself up to it with entire abandon, and day and night were all too short. It usually lasted a week or two, and then she emerged from her "vortex," hungry, sleepy, cross or despondent.

She was just recovering from one of these attacks when she was prevailed on to escort Miss Crocker to a lecture, and in return for her virtue was rewarded with a new idea. It was a People's Course, and the lecture was on the pyramids. They were early, and while Miss Crocker set the heel of her stocking, Jo amused herself by examining the faces of the people who occupied the seat with them. On her right, her only neighbor was a studious-looking lad absorbed in a newspaper. It was a pictorial sheet, and Jo saw a lurid illustration. Pausing to turn a page, the lad saw her looking, and with boyish good nature offered her half his paper, saying, "Want to read it? That's a first-rate story."

Jo accepted it with a smile and soon found herself involved in the usual labyrinth of love, mystery and murder.

"Prime, isn't it?" asked the boy, as her eye read the last paragraph.

"I think you and I could do as well if we tried," returned Jo.

"I should think I was pretty lucky if I could. She makes a

good living out of such stories, they say," and he pointed to the name under the title of the tale.

"Do you know her?" asked Jo with sudden interest.

"No, but I read all her pieces. She knows just what folks like and gets paid well for writing it."

Here the lecture began but Jo heard very little of it. She covertly took down the address of the paper, resolving to try for the hundred-dollar prize offered in its columns for a sensational story. By the time the lecture ended and the audience awoke, she had built up a splendid fortune for herself and was already deep in her story, being unable to decide whether the duel should come before the elopment or after the murder.

She said nothing of her plan at home but fell to work the next day. Her story was as full of desperation and despair as her limited acquaintance with those uncomfortable emotions enabled her to make it, and having located it in Lisbon she wound up with an earthquake. The manuscript was privately dispatched accompanied by a note, modestly saying that if the tale didn't get the prize, she would be very glad to receive any sum it might be considered worth.

Six weeks is a long time to wait, and Jo was just beginning to give up all hope of ever seeing her manuscript again, when a letter arrived which almost took her breath away, for on opening it a check for a hundred dollars fell into her lap. For a minute she stared at it as if it had been a snake, then she read her letter and began to cry. Jo valued the letter more than the money because it was encouraging.

A prouder young woman was seldom seen than she, when she electrified the family by appearing before them with the letter in one hand, the check in the other, announcing she had won the prize. Of course there was a great jubilee, and when the story came everyone read and praised it, though her father shook his head and said, "You can do better than this, Jo. Aim at the highest and never mind the money."

"*I* think the money is the best part of it. What *will* you do with such a fortune?" asked Amy, regarding the magic slip of paper with a reverential eye.

"Send Beth and Mother to the seaside for a month or two," answered Jo promptly.

"Oh, how splendid! No, I can't do it, dear, it would be so selfish," cried Beth.

"Ah, but you shall go, I've set my heart on it. That's what I tried for and that's why I succeeded."

To the seaside they went, after much discussion. So Jo was satisfied with the investment of her prize money and fell to work with a cheery spirit bent on earning more of those delightful checks. She did earn several that year. "The Duke's Daughter" paid the butcher's bill, "A Phantom Hand" put down a new carpet, and "The Curse of the Coventrys" proved the blessing of the Marches for groceries and gowns.

Little notice was taken of her stories, but they found a market and encouraged by this fact she copied her novel for the fourth time and submitted it with fear and trembling to three publishers. She at last disposed of it on condition that she would cut it down one-third, and omit all the parts which she particularly admired.

With Spartan firmness the young authoress laid her first-born on her table and chopped it up ruthlessly. Then to complete the ruin she cut it one-third, and confidently sent the story out into the busy world. It was printed and she got three hundred dollars for it; likewise plenty of praise and blame, both so much greater than she expected that she was thrown into a state of bewilderment from which it took her some time to recover.

Chapter 25

DOMESTIC EXPERIENCES

LIKE MOST other young matrons, Meg began her married life with the determination to be a model housekeeper, John should find home a paradise, he should always see a smiling face, should fare sumptuously every day, and never know the loss of a button. She brought so much love and energy to the work that she could not but succeed in spite of some obstacles. She was too tired sometimes even to smile. She soon learned to wonder where buttons went and to shake her head over the carelessness of men. They were very happy, even after they discovered that they couldn't live on love alone. The little house ceased to be a glorified bower but it became a home, and the young couple soon felt it was a change for the better.

Fired with a housewifely wish to see her storeroom stocked with homemade preserves, she undertook to put up her own currant jelly. John was requested to order home a dozen or so of the little pots and an extra quantity of sugar, for their currants were ripe and were to be attended to at once. Home came four dozen delightful little pots, half a barrel of sugar, and a small boy to pick the currants for her. With her pretty hair tucked into a little cap, arms bared to the elbow, and a checked apron which had a coquettish look in spite of the bib, the young housewife fell to work feeling no doubts about her success. The array of pots rather amazed her at first, but John was so fond of jelly and the nice little jars would look so well on the top shelf, that Meg resolved to fill them all.

Meg spent a long day picking, boiling, straining and fussing over her jelly. She did her best—she reboiled, re-sugared and re-strained—but that dreadful stuff wouldn't jell. She longed to run home, bib and all, and ask her mother to lend a hand, but John and she had agreed that they would never annoy anyone with their private worries or quarrels. They had laughed over the idea of that last. So Meg wrestled all that hot summer day, and at five o'clock sat down in her topsy-turvy kitchen and wept.

Now in the first flush of the new life she had often said, "My husband shall always feel free to bring a friend home whenever he likes. I shall always be prepared—a neat house, a cheerful wife, and a good dinner. John dear, never stop to ask my leave, invite whom you please, and be sure of a welcome from me."

How charming that was, to be sure! John glowed with pride to hear her say it, but although they had had company from time to time, it never happened to be unexpected. If John had not forgotten all about the jelly, it really would have been unpardonable in him to choose that day, of all the days in the year, to bring a friend home to dinner unexpectedly. Congratulating himself that a handsome repast would be ready, and indulging in pleasant anticipations of the charming effect it would produce when his pretty wife came running out to meet him he escorted his friend to his mansion with the irrepressible satisfaction of a young host and husband.

When John reached the Dovecote, he discovered that the front door, usually hospitably open, was now not only shut but locked, and yesterday's mud still adorned the steps. The parlor windows were closed and curtained, and no pretty wife or brighteyed hostess smiling a shy welcome as she greeted her guest. Not a soul appeared but a boy asleep under the currant bushes.

"I'm afraid something has happened. Step into the garden, Scott, while I look up Mrs. Brooke," said John, alarmed at the silence.

Around the house he hurried, led by a pungent smell of burned sugar, and Mr. Scott strolled after him with a queer look on his face. He paused discreetly at a distance when

Brooke disappeared, but he could both see and hear, and being a bachelor enjoyed it. Confusion and despair reigned in the kitchen. Jelly trickled from pot to pot, was on the floor, and burned gaily on the stove. Lotty, the little maid, calmly ate bread and currant wine, for the jelly was liquid. Mrs. Brooke, with her apron over her head, sat sobbing dismally.

"My dearest girl, what is the matter?" cried John, rushing in with visions of scalded hands, sudden news of affliction, and secret consternation at the thought of the guest in the garden.

"Oh John, I am so tired and hot and cross and worried! I've been at it till I'm all worn out. Do come and help me or I shall die!" and the exhausted housewife cast herself upon his breast, giving him a sweet welcome in every sense of the word, for her pinafore had been baptized at the same time as the floor.

"What worries you, dear? Has anything dreadful happened?" asked the anxious John, tenderly kissing the crown of the little cap.

"Yes," sobbed Meg. "The jelly won't jell and I don't know what to do?"

John Brooke laughed then as he never dared to laugh afterward, and the derisive Scott smiled involuntarily as he heard the hearty peal, which put the finishing stroke to poor Meg's woe.

"Is that all? Fling it out the window and don't bother any more about it. I'll buy you quarts, but for heaven's sake don't have hysterics, for I've brought Jack Scott home to dinner and—"

John got no further, for Meg clasped her hands with a tragic gesture as she fell into a chair, exclaiming in a tone of mingled indignation, reproach and dismay: "A man to dinner and everything in a mess! John Brooke, how *could* you do such a thing?"

"Hush! He's in the garden. I forgot the confounded jelly," said John

"You ought to have sent word or told me this morning, and you ought to have remembered how busy I was," continued Meg.

"I didn't know it this morning and there was no time to send word, for I met him on the way out. I never thought of asking leave, when you have always told me to do as I liked. I never tried it before and hang me if I ever do again!" added John.

"I should hope not! Take him away at once. I can't see him, and there isn't any dinner. I hadn't time to cook anything. I meant to dine at Mother's. I'm sorry, but I was *so* busy," and Meg's tears began again.

John was a mild man, but after a long day's work to come home tired and hungry, to find a chaotic house, an empty table, and a cross wife was not exactly conducive to repose of mind or manner. He restrained himself, however, and the little squall would have blown over but for one unlucky word.

"It's a scrape, I acknowledge, but if you will lend a hand, we'll pull through and have a good time yet. Just give us cold meat, and bread and cheese. We won't ask for jelly." He meant it for a good-natured joke but that one word sealed his fate. The last atom of Meg's patience vanished as she spoke.

"You must get yourself out of the scrape as you can. Take that Scott up to Mother's and tell him I'm away, sick, dead —anything. I won't see him and you two can laugh at me and my jelly as much as you like. You won't have anything else here." Having delivered her defiance all in one breath, Meg fled to her own room.

What they did in her absence she never knew, but when Meg descended Lotty reported that they had eaten "a much, and greatly laughed, and the master bid her throw away all the sweet stuff and hide the pots."

Meg longed to tell Mother, but a sense of shame at her own shortcomings, of loyalty to John, restrained her. After clearing up, she dressed herself prettily, and sat down to wait for John to come and be forgiven. Unfortunately, John didn't come, not seeing the matter in that light. He had carried it off as a good joke with Scott, excused his wife as well as he could, and played the host so hospitably that his friend enjoyed the impromptu dinner and promised to come again. But John was angry, though he did not show it. He felt that Meg had got him into a scrape and then deserted him. But when he strolled home, after seeing Scott off, a milder mood came over him.

"Poor little thing," he thought. "I was hard on her when she tried so to please me. She was wrong, of course, but then she was young. I must be patient and teach her." He hoped she had not gone home, for he hated gossip and interference. He was ruffled at the mere thought of it, and then the fear that Meg would cry herself sick softened his heart and sent him on at a quicker pace, resolving to be calm and kind, but firm, quite firm, and show her where she had failed in her duty.

Meg likewise resolved to be calm and kind but firm, and show him his duty. She longed to run to meet him and beg pardon, and be kissed and comforted as she was sure of being, but she did nothing of the sort. When she saw John coming, she began to hum as she rocked and sewed. John, feeling that his dignity demanded the first apology, made none. He came leisurely in and laid himself on the sofa with the singularly relevant remark, "We're going to have a new moon, my dear."

"I've no objection," was Meg's equally soothing remark. Conversation languished. John unfolded his paper and wrapped himself in it. Meg sewed as if new rosettes for her slippers were among the necessaries of life. Neither spoke; both felt uncomfortable.

"Oh dear," thought Meg, "married life is very trying and does need infinite patience, as well as love, as Mother says." The word *Mother* suggested other maternal counsels, given long ago and received with unbelieving protests.

"John is a good man but he has his faults, and you must

learn to see and bear with them, remembering your own. He is very decided but never will be obstinate if you reason kindly, not oppose impatiently. He is very accurate and particular about the truth, a good trait though you call him fussy. Never deceive him by look or word, Meg, and he will give you the confidence you deserve, the support you need. He has a temper not like ours—one flash and then all over— but the white still anger that is seldom stirred, but once kindled is hard to quench. Be careful, very careful, not to wake this anger against yourself, for peace and happiness depend on keeping his respect. Watch yourself, be the first to ask pardon if you both err, and guard against the little piques, misunderstandings and hasty words that often pave the way for bitter sorrow and regret."

These words came back to Meg as she sat sewing in the sunset, especially the last. This was the first serious disagreement. Her own hasty speeches sounded both silly and unkind as she recalled them, and her own anger looked childish now. She put down her work and went slowly across the room, for pride was hard to swallow. She stood by him but he did not turn his head. Stooping down, she softly kissed her husband on the forehead. John had her on his knee in a minute, saying tenderly, "It was too bad to laugh at the poor little jelly pots. Forgive me, dear. I never will again!"

Later, Meg had Mr. Scott to dinner by special invitation, and served him up a pleasant feast without a cooked wife for the first course. She was so gay and gracious, and made everything go off so charmingly, that Mr. Scott told John he was a happy fellow, and shook his head over the hardships of bachelorhood all the way home.

So the year rolled round, and at midsummer, Laurie came sneaking into the kitchen of the Dovecote one Saturday with an excited face. He was received with the clash of cymbals, for Hannah clapped her hands with a saucepan in one hand and the cover in the other.

"How's the little mamma? Where is everybody? Why

didn't you tell me before I came home?" began Laurie in a loud whisper.

"Happy as a queen, the dear! Now you go into the parlor and I'll send 'em down to you," and Hannah vanished, chuckling.

Presently Jo appeared, proudly bearing a flannel bundle on a large pillow. Her face was sober but her eyes twinkled. There was an odd sound in her voice as she said invitingly, "Shut your eyes and hold out your arms."

Laurie backed into a corner and put his hands behind him with an imploring gesture. "No thank you, I'd rather not. I shall drop it or smash it, as sure as fate."

"Then you sha'n't see your nevvy," said Jo decidedly.

"I will, I will! Only you must be responsible for damages," and Laurie shut his eyes while something was put into his arms. A peal of laughter from Jo, Amy, Mrs. March, Hannah, and John caused him to open them the next minute, to find himself invested with two babies instead of one. No wonder they laughed for he stood and stared wildly with such dismay that Jo sat down on the floor and screamed.

"Twins, by Jupiter!" was all he said for a minute. Then turning to the women with an appealing look he added, "Take 'em quick, somebody! I'm going to laugh and I shall drop 'em."

John rescued his babies and marched up and down with one on each arm, as if already initiated into the mysteries of baby-tending, while Laurie laughed until the tears ran down his cheeks.

"It's the best joke of the season, isn't it? I wouldn't have you told, for I set my heart on surprising you," said Jo when she got her breath.

"I never was more staggered in my life. Isn't it fun? Are they boys? What are you going to name them? Let's have another look. Hold me up, Jo, for upon my life it's one too many for me," returned Laurie, regarding the infants with the air of a big Newfoundland looking at a pair of kittens.

"Boy and girl. Aren't they beauties?" said the proud papa beaming.

"Most remarkable I ever saw. Which is which?" Laurie asked.

"Amy put a blue ribbon on the boy and a pink on the girl, French fashion, so you can always tell. Besides, one has blue eyes and one brown. Kiss them, Uncle Teddy," said wicked Jo.

Laurie screwed up his face and obeyed with a gingerly peck at each little cheek that produced another laugh and made the babies squeal. "There, I knew they didn't like it! That's the boy. See him kick. He hits out with his fists like a good one. Now then, young Brooke, pitch into a man of your own size, will you?" cried Laurie, delighted with a poke in the face from a tiny fist, flapping aimlessly about.

"He's to be named John Laurence, and the girl Margaret, after mother and grandmother. We shall call her Daisy, so as not to have two Megs, and I suppose the mannie will be Jack unless we find a better name," said Amy.

"Name him Demijohn and call him Demi for short," said Laurie.

"Daisy and Demi, just the thing. I knew Teddy would do it," cried Jo, clapping her hands.

And the babies were Daisy and Demi to the end of the chapter.

Chapter 26

CALLS

"COME JO, it's time."

"For what?"

"You don't mean to say you have forgotten that you promised to make half a dozen calls with me today?"

"I've done a good many rash and foolish things in my life, but I don't think I ever was mad enough to say I'd make six calls in one day."

"Yes you did. It was a bargain between us. I was to finish the crayon of Beth for you, and you were to go with me, if it was fair."

"There are clouds in the east. It's not fair and I don't go."

"Now that's shirking. It's a lovely day. Come do your duty."

Jo hated formal calls and never made any until Amy compelled her. But there was no escape, so she gave in, and took up her hat and gloves.

"Jo March, you don't intend to make calls in that state, I hope!" cried Amy, surveying her with amazement.

"Why not? I'm neat and cool and comfortable. It's a warm day."

"Oh dear!" sighed Amy. "I'll do anything for you, Jo, if you'll only dress yourself nicely and come and help me do the civil. You can talk so well, look so aristocratic in your best things and behave so beautifully that I'm proud of you."

"You're an artful little puss to flatter your cross old sister in that way. Well, I'll go if I must and do my best."

"Put on your best things. Do your hair the pretty way. Take your light gloves and the embroidered handkerchief. We'll stop at Meg's and borrow her white sunshade and you can have my dove-colored one."

Jo rustled into her new organdy and squeezed her hands into tight gloves with three buttons and a tassel, as the last touch of elegance.

"Turn around slowly and let me get a careful view," commanded Amy.

Jo revolved and Amy gave a touch here and there, then observed graciously, "Yes, you'll do. Your white bonnet with the rose is ravishing. Hold back your shoulders and carry your hands easily, no matter if your gloves do pinch. Is the point of my mantle in the middle?"

"You are a thing of beauty and a joy forever," said Jo. "Am I to drag my best dress through the dust or loop it up, please ma'am?"

"Hold it up when you walk but drop it in the house. The sweeping style suits you best and you must learn to trail your skirts gracefully. You haven't half buttoned one cuff. Do it at once. You'll never look finished if you are not careful about the little details."

Jo sighed and proceeded to burst the buttons off her glove in doing up her cuff, but at last both were ready and sailed away.

"Now Jo dear, the Chesters consider themselves very elegant people, so I want you to put on your best deportment. Don't make any of your abrupt remarks or do anything odd, will you? Just be calm, cool and quiet for fifteen minutes," said Amy as they approached the first place.

"Let me see. Calm, cool and quiet. Yes, I think I can promise that."

Amy looked relieved but naughty Jo took her at her word. In vain Mrs. Chester alluded to her charming novel, and the Misses Chester introduced parties, picnics, the opera and the fashions. Each and all were answered by a smile, a bow, and a demure "Yes" or "No" with the chill on. In vain Amy telegraphed the word "Talk," tried to draw her out, and administered covert pokes with her foot. Jo sat as if blandly unconscious of it all.

"What a haughty, uninteresting creature that oldest Miss March is!" was the unfortunately audible remark of one of the ladies as the door closed upon their guests. Jo laughed noiselessly but Amy looked disgusted at the failure of her instructions.

"How could you mistake me so? I merely meant you to be properly dignified and composed, not a stone. Try to be sociable at the Lambs', gossip as the other girls do, and be interested in dress and flirtations."

"I'll be agreeable. I'll gossip and giggle. I can do it, for I have May Chester as a model and I'll improve upon her."

Amy felt anxious, as well she might, for when Jo turned freakish there was no knowing where she would stop. Amy's face was a study when she saw her sister skim into the next drawing room, kiss all the young ladies with effusion, beam graciously upon the young gentlemen, and join in the chat with spirit. Amy was taken possession of by Mrs. Lamb, with whom she was a favorite, while three delightful young gentlemen hovered near, waiting for a pause to rescue her. She was powerless to check Jo, who seemed possessed by a spirit of mischief and talked away as volubly as the old lady. A knot of heads gathered about her, and Amy strained her ears to hear, for broken sentences filled her with alarm, and peals of laughter made her wild to share the fun. One may imagine her suffering on overhearing fragments of this sort of conversation, "She rides splendidly. Who taught her?"

"No one. She used to practice mounting, holding the reins, and sitting straight, on an old saddle in a tree. Now she rides anything, for she doesn't know what fear is, and the stableman lets her have horses cheap, because she trains them to carry ladies so well. She has such a passion for it, I often tell her if everything else fails she can be a horse-breaker and get her living so."

At this awful speech Amy contained herself with difficulty, but what could she do? The old lady was in the middle of her story and long before it was done Jo was off again.

One of the young ladies asked Jo where she got the pretty hat she wore to the picnic, and Jo answered, "Oh, Amy painted it. You can't buy those soft shades, so we paint ours any color we like."

"We read a story of yours and enjoyed it very much," observed the elder Miss Lamb, wishing to compliment the literary lady.

Any mention of her works always had a bad effect on Jo, who either looked offended or changed the subject with a brusque remark, as now. "Sorry you could find nothing better to read. I write that rubbish because it sells and ordinary people like it. Are you going to New York this winter?"

As Miss Lamb had enjoyed the story, this speech was not grateful. The minute it was made, Jo saw her mistake, but fearing to make the matter worse, suddenly remembered it was for her to make the first move toward departure, and did so with an abruptness that left three people with half-finished sentences in their mouths.

"Amy, we *must* go. Good-by dear. Do come and see us. We are *pining* for a visit. I don't dare ask *you*, Mr. Lamb, but if you *should* come, I don't think I shall have the heart to send you away." Jo said this with such a droll imitation of May Chester's gushing style that Amy got out of the room as rapidly as possible.

"Didn't I do that well?" asked Jo with a satisfied air.

"Nothing could have been worse," was Amy's crushing reply. "What possessed you to tell those stories about my saddle, and the hats and all the rest of it?"

"Why it's funny, and amuses people. They know we are poor, so it's no use pretending we have things as fine as they do."

"You needn't tell them all our little shifts and expose our poverty."

Jo looked abashed. "How shall I behave here?" she asked, as they approached the third mansion.

"Just as you please. I wash my hands of you," Amy said shortly.

"Then I'll enjoy myself. The boys are at home, and we'll have a comfortable time. Elegance has a bad effect upon my constitution," said Jo.

An enthusiastic welcome from three big boys and several pretty children soothed Jo's ruffled feelings. Leaving Amy to entertain the hostess and Mr. Tudor, who happened to be calling, Jo devoted herself to the young folks and found the change refreshing. Amy enjoyed herself to her heart's content. Mr. Tudor's uncle had married an English lady who was third cousin to a living lord, and Amy regarded the whole family with great respect. But even the satisfaction of talking with a distant connection of the British nobility did not render Amy forgetful of time. When the proper number of minutes had passed, she reluctantly tore herself from this aristocratic society and looked about for Jo.

Her sister was sitting on the grass with an encampment of boys about her, and a dirty-footed dog reposing on the skirt of her state dress, as she related one of Laurie's pranks to her admiring audience. One small child was poking turtles with Amy's cherished parasol, a second was eating ginger-bread over Jo's best bonnet, and a third played ball with her gloves. All were enjoying themselves.

"Capital boys, aren't they? I feel quite young and brisk again after that," said Jo, strolling along with her hands behind her, partly from habit, partly to conceal the bespattered parasol.

"Why do you always avoid Mr. Tudor?" asked Amy, wisely refraining from any comment on Jo's dilapidated appearance.

"Don't like him. He puts on airs, snubs his sisters, worries his father, and doesn't speak respectfully of his mother. Laurie says he is fast, and I don't consider him a desirable acquaintance."

"You might treat him civilly, at least. You gave him a cool nod, and just now you bowed and smiled to Tommy Chamberlain, whose father keeps a grocery store. If you had reversed the nod and bow, it would have been right," said Amy reprovingly.

"No it wouldn't," returned perverse Jo. "I neither like, respect nor admire Tudor, though his grandfather's uncle's nephew's niece *was* third cousin to a lord. Tommy is poor and bashful, and good and very clever. I think well of him and like to show that I do."

"It's no use trying to argue with you," began Amy.

"Not the least, my dear," interrupted Jo. "Let us drop a card here, as the Kings are evidently out, for which I am deeply grateful."

The family card case having done its duty, the girls

walked on. Jo uttered another thanksgiving at the fifth house when they were told the young ladies were engaged.

"Now let us go home and never mind Aunt March today. We can run down there any time, and it's really a pity to trail through the dust in our best bibs and tuckers, when we are tired and cross."

"Speak for yourself. Aunt likes to have us pay her the compliment of coming in style and making a formal call. It's a little thing to do, but it gives her pleasure. Let me take the crumbs off your bonnet."

"What a good girl you are, Amy!" said Jo, with a repentant glance from her own damaged costume to that of her sister, which was fresh and spotless still.

They found Aunt Carrol with the old lady, both absorbed in some very interesting subject; but they dropped it as the girls came in with a conscious look which betrayed that they had been talking about their nieces. Jo was not in a good humor and the perverse fit returned, but Amy, who had virtuously done her duty, kept her temper and pleased everybody, was in a most angelic frame of mind. This amiable spirit was felt at once, and both the aunts "my deared" her affectionately.

"Are you going to help about the fair, dear?" asked Mrs. Carrol, as Amy sat down beside her with a confiding air.

"Yes Aunt. Mrs. Chester asked me if I would, and I offered to tend a table as I have nothing but my time to give."

"I'm not," put in Jo decidedly. "I hate to be patronized and the Chesters think it's a great favor to allow us to help with their fair. I wonder you consented, Amy. They only want you to work."

"I am willing to work. I think it very kind of them to let me share the labor and the fun. Patronage does not trouble me when it is well meant."

"Quite right and proper. I like your grateful spirit, my dear," observed Aunt March, looking over her spectacles at Jo. If Jo had only known what a great happiness was wavering in the balance for one of them, she would have turned dovelike in a minute. By her next speech Jo deprived herself of several years of pleasure and received a timely lesson in the art of holding her tongue.

"I don't like favors. They oppress and make me feel like a slave. I'd rather do everything for myself and be perfectly independent."

"Ahem!" coughed Aunt Carrol softly, with a look at Aunt March.

"I told you so," said Aunt March, with a decided nod to Aunt Carrol.

Mercifully unconscious of what she had done, Jo sat with her nose in the air and a revolutionary aspect which was anything but inviting.

"Do you speak French, dear?" asked Mrs. Carrol, her hand on Amy's.

"Pretty well, thanks to Aunt March who lets Esther talk to me as often as I like," replied Amy gratefully, which caused the old lady to smile.

"How are you about languages?" asked Mrs. Carrol of Jo.

"Don't know a word. Can't bear French, i.'s such a slippery, silly sort of languages," was the brusque reply.

Another look passed between the ladies, and Aunt March said to Amy, "You are quite strong and well now, dear, I believe? Eyes don't trouble you any more, do they?"

"Not at all, thank you, ma'am. I'm very well and mean to do great things next winter so that I may be ready for Rome, whenever that joyful time arrives."

"Good girl! You deserve to go and I'm sure you will someday," said Aunt March, with an approving pat on the head as Amy picked up her ball for her.

"*Crosspatch, draw the latch, sit by the fire and spin,*" squalled Polly, bending down from his perch on the back of her chair to peep into Jo's face.

"Most observing bird," said the old lady.

"Come and take a walk, my dear?" cried Polly.

"Thank you, I will. Come, Amy," and Jo brought the visit

to an end, feeling more strongly than ever that calls did have a bad effect on her constitution. She shook hands in a gentlemanly manner, but Amy kissed both the aunts and the girls departed, leaving behind them the impression of shadow and sunshine, which impression caused Aunt March to say, as they vanished, "You'd better do it, Mary. I'll supply the money," and Aunt Carrol to reply decidedly, "I certainly will, if her father and mother consent."

Chapter 27

CONSEQUENCES

MRS. CHESTER'S FAIR was so select that it was considered a great honor by the young ladies of the neighborhood to be invited to take a table, and everyone was much interested in the matter. Amy was asked but Jo was not. Amy's talent and taste were duly complimented by the offer of the art table. Everything went smoothly until the day before the fair opened. Then there occurred one of the little skirmishes which it is almost impossible to avoid when some five-and-twenty women try to work together.

May Chester was rather jealous of Amy because the latter was a greater favorite than herself. Amy's dainty pen-and-ink work entirely eclipsed May's painted vases; the all-conquering Tudor had danced four times with Amy at a late party and only once with May; and there was a rumor which some obliging gossip had whispered to her that the March girls had made fun of her at the Lambs'. All the blame of this should have fallen on Jo, for her naughty imitation had been too lifelike to escape detection, and the Lambs had permitted the joke to escape. No hint of this had reached the culprits, however, and Amy's dismay can be imagined when, the very evening before the fair as she was putting the last touches to her pretty table, Mrs. Chester, who resented the supposed ridicule of her daughter, said in a bland tone but with a cold look:

"I find, dear, that there is some feeling among the young ladies about my giving this table to anyone but my girls. As this is the most prominent and some say the most attractive table of all, it is thought best for them to take this place. I'm sorry, but I know you are too sincerely interested in the cause to mind. You shall have another table if you like."

Amy felt that there was something behind this, and said quietly showing she felt hurt, "Perhaps you had rather I took no table at all?"

"Now my dear, don't have any ill-feeling, I beg. It's merely a matter of expediency, you see. My girls will naturally take the lead and this table is considered their proper place. Wouldn't you like the flower table? The little girls undertook it but they are discouraged. You could make a charming thing of it."

"Especially to gentlemen," added May, with a look which enlightened Amy. She colored angrily but answered with unexpected amiability, "It shall be as you please, Mrs. Chester. I'll give up my place here at once and attend to the flowers, if you like."

"You can put your own things on your own table if you prefer," began May, feeling a little consciencestricken as she looked at the pretty racks, the painted shells and quaint illuminations that Amy had so carefully made and so gracefully arranged. She meant it kindly but Amy mistook her meaning, and said quickly, "Oh certainly, if they are in your way," and sweeping her contributions into her apron, she walked off.

"Now she's mad. Oh, dear, I wish I hadn't asked you to speak, Mamma," said May disconsolately.

"Girls' quarrels are soon over," returned her mother, feeling a trifle ashamed of her own part in this one.

The little girls hailed Amy and her treasures with delight, and she fell to work. But everything seemed against her. It was late and she was tired, and everyone was too busy with their own affairs to help her. The evergreen arch wouldn't stay firm but threatened to tumble down; her best tile got a splash of water; she bruised her hands with hammering, and got cold working in a draft.

There was great indignation at home when she told her story that evening. Her mother said it was a shame but told her she had done right. Beth declared she wouldn't go to the fair at all, and Jo demanded why she didn't take all her pretty things and leave those mean people to get on without her.

"Because they are mean is no reason why I should be. I hate such things and though I think I've a right to be hurt, I don't intend to show it. They will feel that more than angry speeches or actions, won't they Marmee?"

"That's the right spirit, my dear," said her mother.

In spite of various natural temptations to resent and retaliate, Amy adhered to her resolution all the next day. As she arranged her table that morning, while the little girls were in an anteroom filling the baskets, she took up her pet production—a little book, the antique cover of which her father had found among his treasures and in which, on leaves of vellum, she had beautifully illuminated different texts. As she turned the pages, her eye fell on a verse framed in a brilliant scroll work of scarlet, blue and gold, with little spirits of good will helping one another up and down among the thorns and flowers—*Thou shalt love thy neighbor as thyself.*

"I ought but I don't," thought Amy, as her eyes went from the bright page to May's discontented face behind the big vases that could not hide the vacancies her pretty work had once filled. A group of girls was standing about May's table. They dropped their voices but Amy knew they were speaking of her, hearing one side of the story and judging accordingly. She heard May say sorrowfully: "It's too bad, for there is no time to make other things and I don't want to fill up with odds and ends."

"I daresay she'd put them back if you asked her," suggested someone.

"How could I after all the fuss?" began May, but Amy's voice came across the hall, "You may have them and welcome, if you want them. I was just thinking I'd offer to put them back, for they belong to your table rather than mine. Here they are. Please take them."

As she spoke, Amy returned her contribution with a nod and a smile, and hurried away again, feeling that it was easier to do a friendly thing than it was to stay and be thanked for it.

"Now I call that lovely of her," cried one girl.

May's answer was inaudible, but another girl added with a disagreeable laugh, "Very lovely, for she knew she wouldn't sell them at her own table."

For a minute Amy was sorry she had done it, but presently her spirits began to rise and her table to blossom under her skillful hands. It was a long day and a hard one to Amy, as she sat behind her table, often quite alone.

The art table *was* the most attractive in the room. There was a crowd about it all day long. Amy often looked wistfully across, longing to be there where she felt at home and happy, instead of in a corner with nothing to do. She did not go home until night, and then she looked so pale and quiet that they knew the day had been hard. Jo hinted darkly that the tables were about to be turned.

"Don't do anything rude, Jo. I won't have any fuss made so let it all pass," begged Amy, as she departed early, hoping to find a reinforcement of flowers to refresh her table.

"I merely intend to make myself entrancingly agreeable to everyone I know, and to keep them in your corner as long as possible. Teddy and his boys will lend a hand and we'll have a good time yet," returned Jo, leaning over the gate to watch for Laurie.

Presently the familiar tramp was heard in the dusk and she ran out to meet him. "Is that my boy?"

"As sure as this is my girl!" and Laurie tucked her hand in his arm.

"Oh Teddy, such doings!" and Jo told Amy's wrongs with sisterly zeal.

"A flock of our fellows are going to drive over by-and-by, and I'll be hanged if I don't make them buy every flower she's got and camp before her table afterward," said Laurie with warmth.

"The flowers are not at all nice, Amy says, and the fresh ones may not arrive in time. I don't wish to be unjust or suspicious but I shouldn't wonder if they never came at all," observed Jo in disgust.

"Didn't Hayes give you the best out of our gardens?"

"I didn't know that. He forgot, I suppose, and as your grandpa was poorly, I didn't like to ask."

"Now Jo, how could you think there was any need of asking! They are just as much yours as mine. Didn't we always go halves in everything?" began Laurie in the tone that always made Jo turn thorny.

"Gracious, I hope not! Half of some of your things wouldn't suit me at all. But we mustn't stand here. I've got to help Amy, so if you'll be so kind as to let Hayes take flowers up to the hall, I'll bless you forever."

"Couldn't you do it now?" asked Laurie.

Jo shut the gate in his face, saying "Go away, Teddy. I'm busy."

Thanks to the conspirators the tables were turned that night, for Hayes sent up a wilderness of flowers, with a lovely basket arranged in his best manner for a centerpiece. People not only came but stayed, admiring Amy's taste and apparently enjoying themselves. Laurie and his friends gallantly bought up the bouquets, camped before the table, and made that corner the liveliest spot in the room. Amy was in her element.

Jo circulated about the hall, picking up various bits of gossip which enlightened her on the Chester change of base.

She reproached herself for her share of the ill-feeling, and resolved to exonerate Amy as soon as possible. She also discovered what Amy had done about the things in the morning. As she passed the art table she glanced over it for her sister's things, but saw no signs of them. "Tucked away out of sight," thought Jo, hotly resentful.

"Good evening, Miss Jo. How does Amy get on?" asked May, with a conciliatory air.

"She has sold everything she had that was worth selling and now she is enjoying herself. The flower table is always attractive, you know, 'especially to gentlemen.'" Jo couldn't resist the little slap, but May took it so meekly she regretted it a minute after. "Is Amy's illumination anywhere about? I took a fancy to buy that for Father," said Jo, anxious to learn the fate of her sister's work.

"Everything of Amy's sold long ago. I took care that the right people saw them and they made a nice sum."

Much gratified, Jo rushed back to tell the good news, and Amy looked both touched and surprised.

"Now gentlemen, I want you to go and do your duty by the other tables as generously as you have by mine, especially the art table," she said, ordering out "Teddy's Own," as the girls called them.

"'Charge, Chester, charge!' is the motto for that table," said Jo.

"To hear is to obey, but March is fairer far than May," said little Parker, making a frantic effort to be both witty and tender and getting promptly quenched by Laurie who said, "Very well, my son, for a small boy!"

"Buy the vases," whispered Amy to Laurie.

To May's great delight, Mr. Laurence not only bought the vases, but pervaded the hall with one under each arm. The other gentlemen wandered about with wax flowers, painted fans, and filigree portfolios.

Aunt Carrol was there, heard the story, looked pleased and said something to Mrs. March. The fair was pronounced a success, and when May bade Amy good night she gave her an affectionate kiss and a look which said "Forgive and forget," which satisfied Amy.

A week later a letter came from Aunt Carrol, and Mrs. March's face was illuminated to such a degree when she read it that Jo and Beth, who were with her, demanded what the glad tidings were.

"Aunt Carrol is going abroad next month and wants—"

"Me to go with her!" burst in Jo, flying out of her chair.

"No dear, not you. It's Amy."

"Oh Mother! She's too young. It's my turn first. I've wanted it so long—it would do me so much good, I *must* go."

"I'm afraid it's impossible, Jo. Aunt says Amy, decidedly, and it is not for us to dictate when she offers such a favor."

"It's always so. Amy has all the fun and I have all the work. It isn't fair, oh it isn't fair!" cried Jo passionately.

"I'm afraid it is partly your own fault, dear. When Aunt spoke to me the other day, she regretted your blunt manners and too independent spirit. Here she writes, as if quoting something you had said: 'Planned at first to ask Jo, but as "favors burden her" and she "hates French," I think I won't venture to invite her. Amy is more docile, will make a good companion for Flo, and receive gratefully any help the trip may give her.' "

"Oh my tongue, my abominable tongue! Why can't I learn to keep it quiet?" groaned Jo, remembering.

When she had heard the explanation of the quoted phrases, Mrs. March said sorrowfully, "I wish you could have gone, but there is no hope of it this time, so don't sadden Amy's pleasure by reproaches or regrets."

"I'll try," said Jo, winking hard as she knelt down to pick up the basket she had joyfully upset. "I'll take a leaf out of her book and try not only to seem glad but to be so and not grudge her one minute of happiness. But it won't be easy for it is a dreadful disappointment."

"Jo dear, I'm very selfish but I couldn't spare you, and I'm glad you are not going yet," whispered Beth, embracing her basket and all.

By the time Amy came in, Jo was able to take her part in the family jubilation. The young lady herself received the news as tidings of great joy, went about in a solemn sort of rapture, and began to sort her colors and pack her pencils that evening, leaving such trifles as clothes, money and passports to those less absorbed in art.

"It isn't a mere pleasure trip to me, girls," she said impressively. "It will decide my career, for if I have any genius, I shall find it out in Rome and will do something to prove it."

"Suppose you haven't?" asked Jo.

"Then I shall come home and teach drawing for my living," replied the aspirant for fame with philosophic composure.

"No you won't. You hate hard work. You'll marry some rich man and come home to sit in the lap of luxury all your days," said Jo.

"Your predictions sometimes come to pass but I don't believe that one will. I'm sure I wish it would, for if I can't be an artist myself, I should like to be able to help those who are," said Amy, smiling.

There was not much time for preparation and the house was in a ferment until Amy was off. Jo bore up very well until the last flutter of blue ribbon vanished, when she retired to the garret and cried until she couldn't cry any more. Amy likewise bore up stoutly until the steamer sailed. Then just as the gangway was about to be withdrawn it suddenly came over her that a whole ocean was soon to roll between her and those who loved her best. She clung to Laurie, the last lingerer, saying with a sob, "Oh, take care of them for me, and if anything should happen—"

"I will, dear, I will. And if anything happens I'll come and comfort you," whispered Laurie, little dreaming he would be called on to keep his word.

Chapter 28

TENDER TROUBLES

"JO, I'm anxious about Beth."

"Why, Mother, she has seemed unusually well lately."

"It's not her health that troubles me now. It's her spirits. I'm sure there is something on her mind and I want you to discover what it is."

"What makes you think so, Mother?"

"She sits alone a good deal and doesn't talk to her father as much as she used to. When she sings, the songs are always sad ones, and now and then I see a look in her face that I don't understand. This isn't like Beth, and it worries me."

"Have you asked her about it?"

"I have tried once or twice, but she either evaded my questions, or looked so distressed that I stopped. I never force my children's confidence and I seldom have to wait for it long."

After sewing thoughtfully for a minute Jo said, "I think she is growing up, and so begins to dream dreams, and have hopes and fears without knowing why or being able to explain them. Beth's eighteen but we don't realize it, and treat her like a child."

"So she is. Dear heart, how fast you do grow up," returned her mother with a sigh and a smile.

While apparently absorbed in her own affairs, Jo watched Beth, and finally settled on what seemed to explain the change in her. She was affecting to write busily one Saturday afternoon when she and Beth were alone together, yet as she scribbled she kept her eye on her sister, who seemed unusually quiet. Sitting at the window, Beth's work often dropped into her lap, and she leaned her head on her hand dejectedly. Suddenly someone passed below, whistling, and a voice called out, "All serene! Coming in tonight."

Beth started, leaned forward, smiled and nodded, watched the passer-by until his quick tramp died away. Then she said softly, as if to herself, "How strong and well and happy that dear boy looks."

"Hum!" said Jo, still intent on her sister's face, for the bright color faded as quickly as it came, the smile vanished, and presently a tear lay shining on the window ledge. Beth whisked it off and glanced apprehensively at Jo, but she was scratching away on *Olympia's Oath*. The instant Beth turned, Jo began her watch again, saw Beth's hand go quietly to her eyes more than once, and in her half-averted face read a tender sorrow that made her own eyes fill. Fearing to betray herself, she slipped away.

"Mercy on me, Beth loves Laurie!" she said, sitting down in her own room, pale with the shock of the discovery which she believed she had just made. "I never dreamed of such a thing. What *will* Mother say? I wonder if he—" There Jo stopped and turned scarlet with a sudden thought. "If he shouldn't love back again, how dreadful it would be. He must. I'll make him!" and she shook her head threateningly at the picture of the mischievous-looking boy laughing at her from the wall.

Then she sighed and fell into a reverie from which she did not wake until the early twilight sent her down to take new observations, which only confirmed her suspicion. Though Laurie flirted with Amy and joked with Jo, his manner to Beth had always been peculiarly kind and gentle, but so was everybody's. Therefore no one thought of imagining that he cared more for her than for the others. Indeed, a general impression had prevailed in the family of late that "our boy" was getting fonder than ever of Jo.

When Laurie first went to college, he fell in love about once a month, but these small flames were as brief as ardent, did no damage, and much amused Jo who took great inter-

est in the alternations of hope, despair and resignation which
were confided to her in their weekly conferences. But there
came a time when Laurie ceased to worship at many shrines,
hinted darkly at one all-absorbing passion, and indulged
occasionally in Byronic fits of gloom. Then he avoided the
tender subject altogether, wrote philosophical notes to Jo,
turned studious, and gave out that he was intending to grad-
uate in a blaze of glory.

Things were in this state when the grand discovery was
made, and Jo watched Laurie that night as she had never
done before. If she had not got the new idea into her head,
she would have seen nothing unusual in the fact that Beth
was very quiet, and Laurie very kind to her. But having
given the rein to her lively fancy, it galloped away with her.
As usual, Beth lay on the sofa and Laurie sat in a low chair
close by, amusing her with all sorts of gossip. But that evening Jo fancied that Beth's eyes rested on the lively dark
face beside her with peculiar pleasure, and that she listened
with intense interest to an account of some exciting cricket
match. She also fancied that she saw a certain increase of
gentleness in Laurie's manner.

"Who knows? Stranger things have happened," thought
Jo, as she fussed about the room. "She will make quite an
angel of him, and he will make life delightfully easy and
pleasant for the dear, if they only love each other. I don't
see how he can help it, and I do believe he would if the
rest of us were out of the way."

As everyone was out of the way but herself, Jo began to
feel that she ought to dispose of herself with all speed. But
where should she go? She sat down on the old sofa to settle
that point. The sofa was long, broad, well-cushioned and
low; also a trifle shabby. All the girls loved it, for it was
a family refuge and one corner had always been Jo's favorite lounging place. Among its many pillows was a hard,
round one, covered with a knobby button at each end. This
was her especial property, used as a weapon of defense, a
barricade, or a stern preventive of too much slumber.

Laurie knew this pillow well and had cause to regard it with deep aversion, having been unmercifully pummelled with it in former days when romping was allowed, and now frequently debarred by it from taking the seat he most coveted, next to Jo in the sofa corner. If the sausage, as they called it, stood on end it was a sign that he might approach and repose, but if it lay flat across the sofa, woe to the man, woman or child who dared disturb it! That evening Jo forgot to barricade her corner and had not been in her seat five minutes before a massive form appeared beside her, and with both arms spread over the sofa back and both long legs stretched out before him, sighed with satisfaction.

Jo slammed down the pillow but it was too late. There was no room for it, and coasting on to the floor it disappeared mysteriously.

"Come, Jo, don't be thorny. Do you hate your boy and want to fire pillows at him?"

"How many bouquets have you sent Miss Randal this week?" Jo asked sternly.

"Not one, upon my word. She's engaged. Now then."

"I'm glad of it. That's one of your extravagances, sending flowers to girls for whom you don't care two pins," continued Jo reprovingly.

"Sensible girls for whom I do care whole papers of pins won't let me send them flowers, so what can I do?"

"Mother doesn't approve of flirting, even in fun, and you do flirt desperately, Teddy."

"I'd give anything if I could answer 'So do you.' As I can't, I'll merely say that I don't see any harm if all parties understand it's play."

"Well, it does look pleasant but I can't learn how it's done."

"I'm glad you can't flirt. It's really refreshing to see a sensible, straightforward girl who can be jolly and kind without making a fool of herself. We fellows don't like flirts though we may act as if we did sometimes. The pretty modest girls are never talked about except respectfully among gentlemen."

Jo knew that "young Laurence" was regarded as most eligible by worldly mammas and was much smiled on by their daughters, so she watched him rather jealously, fearing he would be spoiled, and rejoiced more than she confessed to find that he still believed in modest girls. Returning suddenly to her admonitory tone, she said dropping her voice, "Teddy, devote yourself to one of the pretty modest girls whom you do respect."

"You really advise it?" and Laurie looked at her with an odd mixture of anxiety and merriment in his face.

"Yes I do, but you'd better wait till you are through college, and be fitting yourself for the place meantime. You're not half good enough for—well, whoever the modest girl may be," and Jo looked queer, for a name had almost escaped her.

"That I'm not!" acquiesced Laurie, with an expression of humility quite new to him, as he dropped his eyes.

"Mercy on us, this will never do," thought Jo, adding aloud, "Go and sing to me. I'm dying for some music and always like yours."

The minute it was well *Up with the bonnets of bonnie Dundee,* she slipped away to return no more until the young gentleman had departed.

Jo lay long awake that night, and was just dropping off when the sound of a stifled sob made her fly to Beth's bedside with the anxious inquiry, "What is it, dear?"

"I thought you were asleep," sobbed Beth.

"Is it the old pain, my precious?"

"No, it's a new one but I can bear it," and Beth tried to check her tears.

"Tell me all about it, and let me cure it as I often did the other."

"You can't. There is no cure." There Beth's voice gave way and clinging to her sister she cried so despairingly that Jo was frightened.

"Where is it? Shall I call Mother?"

"No, no, don't call her, don't tell her. I shall be better soon. Lie down here and 'poor' my head. I'll be quiet and go to sleep."

Jo obeyed, but as her hand went softly to and fro across Beth's hot forehead and wet eyelids, she asked, "Does anything trouble you, dearie?"

"Yes Jo," after a long pause.

"Wouldn't it comfort you to tell me what it is?"

"Not now. Not yet."

"Then I won't ask, but remember, Bethy, that Mother and Jo are always glad to hear and help you if they can."

"I know it. I'll tell you by-and-by."

Cheek to cheek they fell asleep, and on the morrow Beth seemed quite herself. But Jo had made up her mind, and after pondering over a project for some days, she confided it to her mother. "I want to go away somewhere this winter for a change," she began, as they sat along together.

"Why, Jo?" and her mother looked up quickly.

With her eyes on her work Jo answered soberly, "I want something new. I feel restless and anxious to be seeing, doing and learning more than I am. I'd like to hop a little way and try my wings."

"Where will you hop?"

"To New York. I had a bright idea yesterday. You know Mrs. Kirke wrote to you for some young person to teach her children and sew. It's rather hard to find just the thing but I think I should suit if I tried."

"My dear, go out to service in that great boarding house!" and Mrs. March looked surprised but not displeased.

"It's not exactly going out to service, for Mrs. Kirke is your friend and would make things pleasant for me, I know. Her family is separate from the rest and no one knows me there. Don't care if they do. It's honest work and I'm not ashamed of it."

"Nor I, but your writing?"

"All the better for the change. I shall see and hear new things, and get new ideas."

"I have no doubt of it, but are these your only reasons for going?"

"No, Mother."

"May I know the others?"

Jo said slowly, with sudden color in her cheeks, "It may be vain and wrong to say it but—I'm afraid—Laurie is getting too fond of me."

"Then you don't care for him in the way it is evident he begins to care for you?" and Mrs. March looked anxious.

"Mercy, no! I love the dear boy as I always have, and am immensely proud of him, but as for anything more, it's out of the question."

"I'm glad of that, Jo."

"Why, please?"

"Because, dear, I don't think you suited to one another. As friends you are very happy and your frequent quarrels soon blow over, but you are too much alike and too fond of freedom, not to mention hot tempers and strong wills, to get on happily together in a relation which needs infinite patience and forbearance as well as love."

"That's just the feeling I had, though I couldn't express it. I'm glad you think he is only beginning to care for me. It would trouble me to make him unhappy, for I couldn't fall in love with the dear old fellow merely out of gratitude, could I?"

"You are sure of his feeling for you?"

The color deepened in Jo's cheeks as she answered, "I'm afraid it is so, Mother. He hasn't said anything but he looks a great deal. I think I had better go away before it comes to anything."

"I agree with you, and if it can be managed you shall go."

Jo looked relieved, and after a pause said smiling, "How Mrs. Moffat would wonder at your want of management, if she knew, and how she will rejoice that Annie still may hope."

"Ah, Jo, mothers may differ in their management but the hope is the same in all—the desire to see their children happy. Meg is so, and I am content with her success. You I leave to enjoy your liberty till you tire of it, for only then will you find that there is something sweeter. Amy is my chief care now, but her good sense will help her. For Beth I indulge no hopes except that she may be well. By the way, she seems brighter this last day or two. Have you spoken to her?"

"Yes. She owned she had a trouble and promised to tell me by-and-by. I said no more for I think I know it," and Jo told her little story.

Mrs. March shook her head and did not take so romantic a view of the case, but looked grave and repeated her opinion that for Laurie's sake Jo should go away for a time.

"Let us say nothing about it to him till the plan is settled," Jo said. "Then I'll run away before he can collect his wits and be tragical. Beth must think I'm going to please myself, as I am, for I can't talk about Laurie to her. But she can comfort him after I'm gone and so cure him of this romantic notion."

The plan was talked over in a family council and agreed on. Mrs. Kirke gladly accepted Jo and promised to make a pleasant home for her. The teaching would render her independent and such leisure as she got might be made profitable by writing, while the new scenes and society would be both useful and agreeable. Jo liked the prospect and was eager to be gone. When all was settled, with fear and trembling she told Laurie, but to her surprise he took it very quietly. Jo was relieved and made her preparations with a lightened heart.

"One thing I leave to your especial care," she said to Beth the night before she left.

"You mean your papers?" asked Beth.

"No, my boy. Be very good to him, won't you?"

"Of course I will, but I can't fill your place and he'll miss you sadly."

"It won't hurt him, so remember I leave him in your charge."

"I'll do my best for your sake," promised Beth, wondering why Jo looked at her so queerly.

When Laurie said good-by he whispered significantly, "It won't do a bit of good, Jo. My eye is on you, so mind what you do or I'll come and bring you home."

Chapter 29

JO'S JOURNAL

New York, November

DEAR MARMEE AND BETH,—

I'm going to write you a regular volume, for I've got heaps to tell. Mrs. Kirke welcomed me so kindly I felt at home at once, even in that big house full of strangers. She gave me a funny little sky parlor, all she had, but there is a stove in

it, and a nice table in a sunny window, so I can sit here and
write whenever I like. The nursery where I am to teach and
sew is a pleasant room next Mrs. Kirke's private parlor, and
the two little girls are pretty children. They took a fancy to
me after telling them *The Seven Bad Pigs.*

As I went downstairs, I saw something I liked. The flights
are very long in this tall house, and as I stood waiting at
the head of the third one for a little servant girl to lumber
up, I saw a gentleman come along behind her, take the
heavy hod of coal out of her hand, carry it all the way up,
put it down at a door nearby, and walk away saying with a
kind nod and a foreign accent, "It goes better so. The little
back is too young to haf such heaviness."

When I mentioned it to Mrs. K. that evening, she laughed
and said, "That must have been Professor Bhaer. He's always
doing things of that sort." It seems he is from Berlin, very
learned and good but poor as a churchmouse, and gives lessons to support himself and two little orphan nephews whom
he is educating here. Mrs. K. lends him her parlor for some
of his scholars. There is a glass door between it and the
nursery, and I mean to peep at him and then I'll tell you
how he looks. He's almost forty so it's no harm, Marmee.

Tuesday Eve.
After luncheon I went to my needlework. The parlor door
opened and shut, and someone began to hum *Kennst du das
land.* I couldn't resist the temptation, and lifting one end of
the curtain before the glass door I peeped in. Professor Bhaer
was there, and while he arranged his books I took a good
look at him. A regular German, rather stout, with brown hair
tumbled all over his head, a bushy beard, good nose, the
kindest eyes I ever saw, and a splendid big voice. His clothes
were rusty, his hands were large and he hadn't a really
handsome feature in his face except his beautiful teeth. Yet
I liked him for he had a fine head, his linen was very nice,
and he looked like a gentleman, though two buttons were
off his coat and there was a patch on one shoe.

I went down to dinner, and at the very bottom of the table was the Professor, shouting answers to the questions of a very inquisitive deaf old gentleman on one side, and talking philosophy with a Frenchman on the other. He had a great appetite and shoveled in his dinner in a manner which would have horrified Amy, but I didn't mind for I like to see folks eat with a relish, as Hannah says.

Thursday

Yesterday was a quiet day, spent in teaching, sewing and writing up in my little room. I was introduced to the Professor. Tina, the child of the Frenchwoman who does the fine ironing in the laundry here, has lost her heart to Mr. Bhaer and follows him about the house like a dog, which delights him as he is very fond of children, though a "bacheldore." Kitty and Minnie Kirke likewise regard him with affection, and tell about the plays he invents, the presents he brings, and the splendid tales he tells.

I was in our parlor last evening when Mr. Bhaer came in with some newspapers for Mrs. Kirke. She wasn't there, but Minnie, who is a little old woman, introduced me very prettily. "This is Mamma's friend, Miss March."

"Yes, and she's jolly and we like her lots," added Kitty.

We both bowed, and then we laughed, for the prim introduction and the blunt addition were a comical contrast.

"Ah, yes, I hear these naughty ones go to vex you, Mees Marsch. If so again, call at me and I come," he said with a threatening frown that delighted the little wretches.

I promised I would, and he departed. But it seems as if I was doomed to see a good deal of him, for today as I passed his door on my way out by accident I knocked against it with my umbrella. It flew open, and there he stood in his dressing gown with a big blue sock on one hand and a darning needle in the other. He didn't seem at all ashamed of it. I explained and hurried on, laughing all the way downstairs, but it was a little pathetic to think of the poor man having to mend his own clothes.

Forward Amy's letters as soon as you can spare them. My small news will sound very flat after her splendors, but you will like them, I know. Is Teddy studying so hard that he can't find time to write to his friends? Take good care of him for me, Beth. Heaps of love to everyone.

From your faithful,

Jo

P.S. On reading over my letter it strikes me as rather Bhaery, but I am always interested in odd people, and I really had nothing else to write about.

December

My Precious Betsey,—

As this is to be a scribble-scrabble letter, I direct it to you, for it may amuse you. The little girls are not so interesting to me as Tina and the boys, but I do my duty by them and they are fond of me. Franz and Emil, Professor Bhaer's nephews, are jolly little lads, and on pleasant days they all go to walk, like a seminary with the Professor and myself to keep order.

We are very good friends now and I've begun to take lessons in German. I really couldn't help it, and it all came about in such a droll way that I must tell you. One day as I passed Mr. Bhaer's room, Mrs. Kirke called to me.

"Did you ever see such a den, my dear? Come and help me put these books to rights, for I've turned everything upside down trying to discover what he has done with the six new handkerchiefs I gave him not long ago."

I went in and while we worked I looked about me. Books and papers everywhere; a ragged bird without any tail chirped on one window seat, and a box of white mice adorned the other; half-finished boats and bits of string lay among the manuscripts; dirty little boots stood drying before the fire; and traces of the dearly beloved boys, for whom he makes a slave of himself, were to be seen all over the room. We found three of the handkerchiefs—one over the birdcage, one covered with ink, and a third burned brown, having been used as a holder.

"Such a man!" laughed Mrs. K. "I suppose the others are torn up to rig ships or make kite tails. I agreed to do his washing and mending but he forgets to give out his things, and I forget to look them over."

"Let me mend them," said I. "I don't mind it and he needn't know. I'd like to—he's so kind about bringing my letters and lending books."

So I have got his things in order, and knit heels into two pairs of the socks, for they were boggled out of shape with his queer darns. I hoped he wouldn't find out, but one day last week he caught me at it.

"So!" he said, as I stared like a goose. "You peep at me, I peep at you, and that is not bad. But see, I am not pleasanting when I say, haf you a wish for German?"

"Yes, but you are too busy. I am too stupid to learn," I blundered.

"Prut! We will make the time and we fail not to find the sense. At efening I shall gif a little lesson with much gladness, for look you, Miss Marsch, I haf this debt to pay," and he pointed to my work. "These so kind ladies think I am a stupid old fellow and will not opserve that my sock-heels go not in holes any more and that my buttons grow out new. Ah, but I haf an eye and I see much. I haf a heart and I feel the thanks for this. Come, a little lesson then and now, or no more good fairy works for me and mine."

Of course I couldn't say anything after that, and I made the bargain and we began. I took four lessons and then I stuck fast in a grammatical bog. The Professor was very patient with me and we got on better, and now I read my lessons pretty well.

I'm glad Laurie seems so happy and busy that he has given up smoking and lets his hair grow. Do your best, only don't make a saint of him. I'm afraid I couldn't like him without a spice of human naughtiness. Read him bits of my letters. I haven't time to write much.

January
A Happy New Year to you all, my dearest family, which
of course includes Mr. L and a young man by the name of
Teddy. I can't tell you how much I enjoyed your Christmas
bundle, for I didn't get it till night and had given up hoping. The things were just what I wanted, and I'll read carefully the books Father has marked. Thank you all, heaps and
heaps!

Speaking of books reminds me that I'm getting rich in that
line, for on New Year's Day Mr. Bhaer gave me a fine Shake-
speare. It is one he values much and I've often admired it,
so you may imagine how I felt when he brought it down
and showed me my name in it, *from my friend Friedrich
Bhaer.*

"You say often you wish a library. Here I gif you one, for
it is many books in one. Read him well and he will help you
much, for the study of character in this book will help you
to read it in the world and paint it with your pen."

I thanked him as well as I could and talk now about "my
library" as if I had a hundred books. Not having much
money, or knowing what he'd like, I got several little things
and put them about the room where he would find them
unexpectedly. They were useful, pretty or funny—a little
vase for his flower, and a holder for his blower, so that he
needn't burn up what Amy calls his *mouchoirs.* I made it
like those Beth invented, a big butterfly with a fat body,
black-and-yellow wings, worsted feelers and bead eyes. It
took his fancy immensely, and he put it on his mantelpiece.
Poor as he is, he didn't forget a servant or a child in the
house, and not a soul here forgot him. I was so glad of that.

I had a very happy New Year. I'm cheerful all the time
now, work with a will, and take more interest in other people than I used to. Bless you all! Ever your loving

Jo

Chapter 30

A FRIEND

THOUGH very happy in the social atmosphere about her, and very busy with the daily work that earned her bread, Jo still found time for literary labors. She saw that money conferred power. Money and power, therefore, she resolved to have, not to be used for herself alone, but for those whom she loved more than self. The dream of filling home with comforts, giving Beth everything she wanted, from strawberries in winter to an organ in her bedroom; going abroad herself, and always having *more* than enough, so that she might indulge in the luxury of charity, had been Jo's for years.

She took to writing sensation stories. She concocted a thrilling tale, and boldly carried it herself to Mr. Dashwood, editor of *The Weekly Volcano*. She dressed herself in her best, and trying to persuade herself that she was neither excited nor nervous, bravely climbed two pairs of dark and dirty stairs to find herself in a disorderly room, a cloud of cigar smoke, and the presence of three gentlemen sitting with their heels rather higher than their hats, which none of them took the trouble to remove on her appearance. Somewhat daunted by this reception, Jo hesitated on the threshold, murmuring in much embarrassment, "Excuse me, I was looking for *The Weekly Volcano* office. I wish to see Mr. Dashwood."

Down went the highest pair of heels, up rose the smokiest gentleman, and carefully cherishing his cigar between his fingers he advanced with a nod. Feeling she must get through the matter somehow, Jo produced her manuscript, and blushing redder with each sentence said, "A friend of mine desired me to offer—a story—just as an experiment—would like your opinion—be glad to write more if this suits."

While she blushed and blundered, Mr. Dashwood had taken the manuscript and was turning over the leaves with dirty fingers, casting critical glances up and down the neat pages. "Not a first attempt, I take it?" observing that the pages were numbered and covered only one side.

"No sir. She has had some experience, and got a prize for a tale in *The Blarneystone Banner*."

"Oh, did she?" and Mr. Dashwood gave Jo a quick look which seemed to take note of everything she had on. "Well, you can leave it, if you like. I'll give you an answer next week."

Jo did not like to leave it, for Mr. Dashwood didn't suit her at all, but under the circumstances there was nothing for her to do but bow and walk away.

When she went again, Mr. Dashwood was alone, much wider awake than before, and not too deeply absorbed in a cigar to remember his manners. So the second interview was much more comfortable than the first.

"We'll take this"—editors never say *I*—"if you don't object to a few alterations. It's too long but omitting the passages I've marked will make it just the right length," he said in a businesslike tone.

Jo hardly knew her own manuscript again, so crumpled and underscored were its pages and paragraphs, but she looked at the marked passages and was surprised that the moral reflections had been stricken out.

"But sir, I thought every story should have some sort of a moral so I took care to have a few of my sinners repent."

Mr. Dashwood's editorial gravity relaxed into a smile, for Jo had forgotten her "friend" and spoken as only an author could. "People want to be amused not preached at, you know. Morals don't sell nowadays."

"You think it would do with these alterations, then?"

"Yes. It's a new plot and pretty well worked up—language good, and so on," was Mr. Dashwood's reply.

"What do you—that is, what compensation—" began Jo, not knowing exactly how to express herself.

"Oh yes, well, we give from twenty-five to thirty for things of this sort. Pay when it comes out," returned Mr. Dashwood, as if that point had escaped him.

"Very well, you can have it," said Jo, handing back the story. "Shall I tell my friend you will take another if she has one better than this?" asked Jo, unconscious of her little slip of the tongue and emboldened by her success.

"Well, we'll look at it. Can't promise to take it. Tell her to make it short and spicy, and never mind the moral. What name would your friend like to put to it?" in a careless tone.

"None at all, if you please. She doesn't wish her name to appear, and she has no *nom de plume*," said Jo, blushing in spite of herself.

"Just as she likes, of course. The tale will be out next week. Will you call for the money or shall I send it?"

"I'll call. Good morning, sir."

Following Mr. Dashwood's direction, Jo rashly took a plunge into sensational literature. Like most young scribblers she went abroad for her characters and scenery, and banditti, counts, gypsies, nuns and duchesses appeared upon her stage and played their parts with as much accuracy and spirit as could be expected. She soon became interested in her work and the little hoard she was making to take Beth to the mountains next summer grew slowly but surely as the weeks passed. One thing disturbed her satisfaction, and that was that she did not tell them at home. She had a feeling that Father and Mother would not approve, and preferred to have her own way first, and beg pardon afterward. It was easy to keep her secret, for no name appeared with her stories.

Jo soon found that her innocent experience had given her but few glimpses of the tragic world which underlies society, so regarding it in a business light she set about supplying her deficiencies with characteristic energy. Eager to find material for stories, and bent on making them original in plot if not masterly in execution, she searched newspapers for accidents, incidents and crimes; she excited the suspicions of librarians by asking for works on poisons; she studied faces in the street and characters—good, bad and indifferent—all about her.

While endowing her imaginary heroes with every perfection under the sun, Jo was discovering a live hero who interested her in spite of many human imperfections. Mr. Bhaer in one of their conversations had advised her to study simple, true and lovely characters wherever she found them as good training for a writer. Jo took him at his word, for she coolly turned around and studied him, a proceeding which would have surprised him.

Why everybody liked him was what puzzled Jo at first. He was neither rich nor great, young nor handsome, in no respect what is called fascinating, imposing or brilliant. Yet he was as attractive as a genial fire, and people seemed to gather about him as naturally as about a warm hearth. He was poor, yet always appeared to be giving something away; a stranger, yet everyone was his friend; no longer young but as happy-hearted as a boy; plain and peculiar, yet his face looked beautiful to many and his oddities were freely forgiven for his sake. Jo often watched him, trying to discover the charm.

"That's it!" said Jo to herself, when she at length discovered that genuine good will towards one's fellowmen could beautify and dignify even a stout German teacher burdened with the surname of Bhaer. Jo valued goodness highly but she respected intellect, and a little discovery which she made about the Professor added much to her regard for him. From Miss Norton, a rich maiden lady at the boarding house, Jo learned that Mr. Bhaer was an honored professor in Berlin, though only a poor language master in America.

Another and better gift than intellect was shown her in a most unexpected manner. Miss Norton had the *entrée* into literary society, and took Jo and the Professor with her one night to a select symposium held in honor of several celebrities. Jo's reverence for genius received a shock that night, and it took her some time to recover from the discovery that the great creatures were only men and women after all. Imagine her dismay on stealing a glance of timid admiration at the poet, whose lines suggested an ethereal being fed on "spirit, fire and dew," to behold him devouring his supper with an ardor which flushed his intellectual countenance. Turning as from a fallen idol, she saw the famous divine flirting openly. The young musician talked horses, and the specimen of the British nobility was very ordinary.

Before the evening was half over, Jo sat down in a corner to recover herself. Mr. Bhaer soon joined her, looking rather out of his element, and presently several of the philosophers, each mounted on his hobby, came ambling up. The conversation was miles beyond Jo's comprehension but she enjoyed it, though Kant and Hegel were unknown gods. It dawned on her gradually that the world was being picked to pieces and put together on new and infinitely better principles than before; that religion was in a fair way to be reasoned into nothingness, and intellect was to be the only god.

She looked around to see how the Professor liked it and found him looking at her with the grimmest expression she had ever seen him wear. He shook his head and beckoned her to come away, but she was fascinated and kept her seat. Mr. Bhaer bore it as long as he could, but when he was appealed to for an opinion, he blazed up with honest indignation and defended religion with all the eloquence of truth, an eloquence which made his broken English musical and his plain face beautiful. Somehow as he talked the world got right again to Jo. God was not a blind force, and immortality was not a pretty fable but a blessed fact. She felt as if she had solid ground under her feet again, and when he paused, outtalked but not one whit convinced, Jo wanted to clap her hands and thank him. As she remembered this scene, she began to see that character is a better possession than money, rank, intellect or beauty. Friedrich Bhaer was not only good but great.

This belief strengthened daily. Jo valued his esteem, she coveted his respect, she wanted to be worthy of his friendship. Just when the wish was sincerest, she came near losing everything. It all grew out of a cocked hat, for one evening the Professor came in to give Jo her lesson with a paper soldier cap on his head which Tina had put there and he had forgotten to take off. It amused Jo, and her eyes danced. The Professor didn't know what to make of her and stopped at last, to ask with an air of mild surprise, "Mees Marsch, for what do you laugh in your master's face? Haf you no respect for me?"

"How can I be respectful, sir, when you forget to take your hat off?"

The absentminded Professor gravely removed the little cocked hat, looked at it a minute and then laughed. But the lesson did not go on for a few minutes, because Mr. Bhaer caught sight of a picture on the hat. Unfolding it, he said with an air of disgust, "I wish these papers did not come in the house. They are not for children to see, nor young people to read. It is not well and I haf no patience with those who make this harm."

Jo glanced at the sheet and saw a pleasing illustration composed of a lunatic, a corpse, a villain and a viper. She did not like it, but the impulse that made her turn it over was not one of displeasure but fear, because for a minute she fancied the paper was the *Volcano*. It was not, and her panic subsided as she remembered that even if it had been, and one of her own tales in it, there would have been no name to betray her. She had betrayed herself by a look and a blush, for though an absentminded man the Professor saw a good deal more than people fancied. He knew that Jo wrote and had met her down among the newspaper offices more than once, but as she never spoke of it, he asked no questions in spite of a strong desire to see her work. Now it occurred to him that she was doing what she was ashamed to own and it troubled him.

He said gravely, "Yes, you are right to put it from you. I do not like to think that good young girls should see such things. I would more rather give my boys gun-powder to play with than this bad trash."

"All may not be bad, only silly, and if there is a demand for it, I don't see any harm in supplying it. Many very respectable people make an honest living out of what are called sensation stories," said Jo.

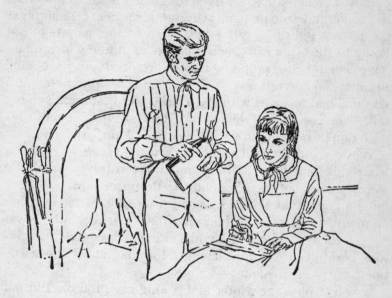

"If the respectable people knew what harm they did, they would not feel that the living *was* honest. They haf no right to put poison in the sugarplum and let the small ones eat it. No, they should think a little and sweep mud in the street before they do this thing."

Mr. Bhaer spoke warmly and walked to the fire, crumpling the paper in his hands. Jo sat still, and her cheeks burned long after the cocked hat had turned to smoke. She thought what a blaze her pile of papers upstairs would make, and her hard-earned money lay heavily on her conscience. Then she thought, "Mine are not like that. They are only silly, never bad, so I won't be worried."

As soon as she went to her room she got out her papers and carefully reread every one of her stories. The faults glared at her and filled her with dismay. "They *are* trash and will soon be worse. What *should* I do if they were seen at home or Mr. Bhaer got hold of them?"

She turned hot at the bare idea, and stuffed the whole bundle into her stove, nearly setting the chimney afire with the blaze. Jo wrote no more sensational stories, deciding that the money did not pay for her share of the sensation, but going to the other extreme she produced a tale which might have been more properly called an essay or a sermon, so intensely moral was it. She found no purchaser and was inclined to agree with Mr. Dashwood that morals didn't sell. Then she tried a child's story, but nothing came of it.

"I don't know anything! I'll wait till I do," she said.

While these internal revolutions were going on, her external life had been as busy and uneventful as usual. No words passed between her and the Professor on the subject, but he knew that she had given up writing. He helped her in many ways, proving himself a true friend, and Jo was happy, for while her pen lay idle she was learning other lessons beside German, and laying a foundation for the sensation story of her own life.

It was a pleasant winter and a long one, for she did not leave Mrs. Kirke until June. Everyone seemed sorry.

"Going home? Ah, you are happy that you haf a home to go in," Mr. Bhaer said when she told him.

"Now sir," she said warmly, "you won't forget to come and see us, if you ever travel our way, will you? I'll never forgive you if you do, for I want them all to know my friend."

"Do you? Shall I come?" he asked, looking down at her with an eager expression which she did not see.

"Yes. Come next month. Laurie graduates then and you'd enjoy commencement as something new."

"That is your best friend of whom you speak?" he said in an altered tone.

"Yes, my boy Teddy. I'm very proud of him and should like you to see him."

Jo looked up then, quite unconscious of anything but her own pleasure in the prospect of showing them to one another. Something in Mr. Bhaer's face suddenly recalled the fact that she might find Laurie more than a "best friend," and simply because she particularly wished not to look as if anything was the matter, she began to blush hoping the Professor did not see it. But he did, and his own face changed from momentary anxiety to its usual expression, as he said cordially,

"I fear I shall not make the time for that, but I wish the friend much success and you all happiness. Gott bless you!" and with that he shook hands warmly, shouldered Tina, and went away.

Early as it was, he was at the station the next morning to see Jo off, and thanks to him she began her solitary journey with the pleasant memory of a familiar face smiling its farewell, a bunch of violets to keep her company, and best of all the happy thought: "Well, the winter's gone and I've written no books, earned no fortune, but I've made a friend worth having and I'll try to keep him all my life."

Chapter 31

HEARTACHE

WHATEVER his motive might have been Laurie studied to some purpose that year, for he graduated with honor and gave the Latin oration. They were all there, his grandfather —oh, so proud!—Mr. and Mrs. March, John and Meg, Jo and Beth, and all exulted over him.

"I've got to stay for this confounded supper, but I shall be home early tomorrow. You'll come and meet me as usual, girls?" Laurie said, as he put the sisters into the carriage. He said girls, but he meant Jo, for she was the only one who kept up the old custom.

She had not the heart to refuse her boy anything and answered warmly, "I'll come, Teddy, rain or shine."

Laurie thanked her with a look that made her think in a sudden panic, "Oh dear me! I know he'll say something and then what shall I do?"

Evening meditation and morning work somewhat allayed her fears, and she set forth at the appointed time. A call at Meg's further fortified her, but when she saw a stalwart figure looming in the distance, she had a strong desire to turn and run.

His greeting was not loverlike, and Jo took heart. She always used to take his arm on these occasions. Now she did not and he made no complaint, which was a bad sign, but talked on rapidly about all sorts of subjects until they turned from the road into the little path that led homeward through the grove. Then he walked more slowly, suddenly lost his fine flow of language, and now and then a dreadful pause occurred. To rescue the conversation from one of the wells of silence into which it kept falling, Jo said hastily, "Now you must have a good long holiday!"

"I intend to."

Something in his resolute tone made Jo look up quickly to find him looking down at her with an expression that assured her the dreaded moment had come. She put her hand out with an imploring, "No, Teddy, please don't!"

"I will and you *must* hear me. It's no use, Jo, we've got to have it out and the sooner the better for both of us." He was flushed and excited.

"Say what you like, then. I'll listen," said Jo with a desperate sort of patience.

Laurie was in earnest, so he plunged into the subject with characteristic impetuosity, in a voice that would get choky now and then. "I've loved you ever since I've known you, Jo; couldn't help it, you've been so good to me. I've tried to show it but you wouldn't let me. Now I'm going to make you hear and give me an answer, for I can't go on so any longer."

"I wanted to save you this. I thought you'd understand—" began Jo, finding it harder than she expected.

"I know you did, but girls are so queer you never know what they mean. They say no when they mean yes, and drive a man out of his wits just for the fun of it."

"*I* don't. I never wanted to make you care for me so, and I went away to keep you from it, if I could."

"I thought so. It was like you but it was no use. I only loved you all the more, and I worked hard to please you. I gave up everything you didn't like, and waited and never complained, for I hoped you'd love me, though I'm not half good enough—" here there was a choke, and he cleared his "confounded throat."

"Yes you are. You're a great deal too good for me and I'm so grateful to you, and so proud and fond of you, I don't see why I can't love you as you want me to. I've tried, but I can't change the feeling and it would be a lie to say I do when I don't."

"Really truly, Jo?" He stopped short and caught both her hands with a look that she did not soon forget.

"Really truly, dear."

They were in the grove now, close by the stile, and when the last words fell reluctantly from Jo's lips, Laurie dropped her hands and turned as if to go on, but instead he laid his head down on the mossy post and stood so still that Jo was frightened.

"Oh Teddy, I'm so sorry, so desperately sorry. I could kill myself if it would do any good! I wish you wouldn't take it so hard. I can't help it. You know it's impossible for people to make themselves love other people if they don't," cried Jo remorsefully, as she softly patted his shoulder, remembering the time when he had comforted her so long ago.

"They do sometimes," said a muffled voice.

"I don't believe it's the right sort of love," was the decided answer.

There was a long pause, while a blackbird sang blithely on the willow by the river and the tall grass rustled in the wind. Presently Jo sat down on the stile and said, "Laurie, I want to tell you something."

He started, threw up his head, and cried fiercely, "Don't tell me that, Jo. I can't bear it now!"

"Tell what?" she asked, wondering at his violence.

"That you love that old man."

"What old man?" demanded Jo, thinking he must mean his grandfather.

"The devilish Professor you were always writing about. If you say you love him, I shall do something desperate."

Jo wanted to laugh but restrained herself, and said warmly, "Don't swear, Teddy! He isn't old nor anything bad, but good and kind and the best friend I've got, next to you. I haven't the least idea of loving him or anybody else."

"But you will after a while and then what will become of me?"

"You'll love someone else, like a sensible boy, and forget all this."

"I *can't* love anyone else, and I'll never forget you, Jo, never, never!" with a stamp to emphasize his words.

"What shall I do with him?" sighed Jo, finding that emotions were more unmanageable than she expected. "You haven't heard what I wanted to tell you. Sit down and listen, for indeed I want to do right and make you happy," she said, hoping to soothe him with reason.

Seeing a ray of hope in that last speech, Laurie threw himself down on the grass at her feet, leaned his arm on the lower step of the stile and looked up at her with an expectant face, his eyes full of love and longing, his lashes wet. She gently turned her head away saying, as she stroked the wavy hair which had been allowed to grow for her sake:

"I agree with Mother that you and I are not suited to

each other, because our quick tempers and strong wills would probably make us very miserable if we were so foolish as to—" Jo paused, but Laurie said rapturously, "Marry —no, we shouldn't! If you loved me, Jo, I should be a saint, for you could make me anything you like."

"No I can't. I've tried and failed, and I won't risk our happiness by such a serious experiment. We don't agree and we never shall, so we'll be good friends all our lives but we won't do anything rash."

"Yes, we will if we get the chance," muttered Laurie.

"Do be reasonable and take a sensible view," implored Jo.

"I won't be reasonable. I don't want to take what you call a sensible view. It won't help me and it only makes you harder. I don't believe you've got any heart."

"I wish I hadn't!"

Laurie thought the quiver in Jo's voice a good omen, and turning around brought all his persuasive powers to bear as he said, "Don't disappoint us, dear! Everyone expects it. Grandpa has set his heart on it, your people like it, and I can't get on without you. Say you will and let's be happy. Do, do!"

Not until months afterward did Jo understand how she had the strength of mind to hold fast to the resolution she had made when she decided she did not love her boy.

"I can't say yes truly, so I won't say it at all. You'll see that I'm right by-and-by, and thank me for it—" she began.

"I'll be hanged if I do!" Laurie bounced off the grass.

"Yes you will!" persisted Jo. "You'll get over this after a while, and find some lovely accomplished girl who will adore you and make a fine mistress for your fine house. I shouldn't. I'm homely and awkward, and odd and old, and you'd be ashamed of me, and we should quarrel. We can't help it even now, you see. And I shouldn't like elegant society and you would, and you'd hate my scribbling and I couldn't get on without it, and we should be unhappy and wish we hadn't done it!"

"Anything more?" asked Laurie, becoming impatient.

"Nothing, except that I don't believe I shall every marry."

"I know better!" broke in Laurie. "You think so now but there'll come a time when you *will* care for somebody, and you'll love him tremendously and live and die for him. I know you will. It's your way, and I shall have to stand by and see it," and the despairing lover cast his hat on the ground.

"Yes I will live and die for him, if he ever comes and makes me love him in spite of myself, and you must do the best you can!" cried Jo, losing patience with poor Teddy. "I've done my best but you won't be reasonable, and it's selfish of you to keep teasing for what I can't give. I shall always be fond of you, very fond indeed, as a friend, but I'll never marry you and the sooner you believe it the better for both of us!"

Laurie looked at her a minute as if he did not quite know what to do with himself, then turned sharply away, saying in a desperate sort of tone, "You'll be sorry some day, Jo."

"Oh, where are you going?" she cried, for his face frightened her.

"To the devil!" was the consoling answer.

For a minute Jo's heart stood still as he swung himself down the bank toward the river. Some blind instinct led him to fling hat and coat into his boat and row away with all his might. Jo drew a long breath as she watched.

"That will do him good and he'll come home in such a penitent state of mind that I sha'n't dare to see him," she said. She walked slowly home, thinking, "Now I must prepare Mr. Laurence to be very kind to my poor boy."

Sure that no one could do it so well as herself, she went straight to Mr. Laurence, told the hard story bravely through, and then broke down, crying dismally.

When Laurie came home, dead tired but quite composed, his grandfather met him as if he knew nothing. At twilight, Laurie went to the piano and began to play. The windows were open and Jo, walking in the garden with Beth, for once understood music better than her sister, for he played the *Sonata Pathétique* as he never had.

Dashing into a livelier strain, Laurie played for several minutes. In a momentary lull, Mrs. March's voice was heard calling, "Jo dear, come in. I want you." What Laurie longed to say, with a different meaning! The music ended with a broken chord in the dark.

"I can't stand this," muttered the old gentleman, and he groped his way to the piano. With a hand on either of the broad shoulders he said gently, "I know, my boy."

No answer for an instant, then Laurie asked sharply, "Who told you?"

"Jo herself."

"Then there's an end of it!" he shook off his grandfather's hands impatiently, for though grateful for sympathy, his pride couldn't bear pity.

"Not quite," returned Mr. Laurence mildly. "You won't care to stay at home just now perhaps?"

"I don't intend to run away from a girl," said Laurie.

"I'm disappointed, but the girl can't help it, and the only thing left for you to do is to go away for a time. Where will you go?"

"Anywhere. I don't care what becomes of me."

"Why not go abroad as you planned and forget it?"

"I can't."

"But you've been wild to go. I promised you should."

"Ah, but I didn't mean to go alone."

"I don't ask you to. There's someone glad to go."

"Who, sir?" Laurie stopped his pacing to listen.

"Myself."

Laurie put out his hand and said huskily, "I'm a selfish brute, but—you know—Grandfather—"

"Lord help me, yes, I do know, for I've been through it all before, once in my own young days and then with your father. Now sit down and hear my plan. There is business in London that needs looking after. I meant you should at tend to it, but I can do it better myself, and things here will get on very well with Brooke to manage them."

A restless movement from Laurie made the old man add hastily, "I don't mean to be a burden. I don't intend to gad about with you, but leave you free to go where you like. I've friends in London and Paris, and you can go to Italy, Germany and Switzerland."

Laurie sighed and said, "Just as you like sir."

When the parting came he affected high spirits, although his gaiety did not fool anybody. He got on very well until Mrs. March kissed him, with a whisper full of motherly solicitude. He hastily embraced them all around, and ran downstairs. Jo followed, to wave her hand if he looked around. He did, came back, put his arms about her. "Oh Jo, can't you?"

"Teddy dear, I wish I could!"

Laurie straightened himself, said, "It's all right, never mind," and went away without another word. He left her without a look behind him, and she knew that the boy Laurie never would come again.

Chapter 32

BETH'S SECRET

WHEN Jo came home that spring, she had been struck with the change in Beth. No one spoke of it or seemed aware of it, for it had come too gradually to startle those who saw her daily, but to eyes sharpened by absence it was plain, and a heavy weight fell on Jo's heart as she saw her sister's face. It was no paler and but little thinner than in the autumn, yet there was a strange transparent look about it. Jo said nothing at the time, and soon the first impression lost much of its power, for Beth seemed happy, no one appeared to doubt that she was better, and presently Jo for a time forgot her fear.

But when Laurie was gone the vague anxiety returned and haunted her. She had confessed her sins and been forgiven, but when she showed her savings and proposed the mountain trip, Beth had thanked her heartily but begged not to go so far away from home. A visit to the seashore would suit her better, and Jo took Beth down to the quiet place where she could let the fresh sea breezes blow a little color into her pale cheeks.

Jo wondered, and was thankful also, that her parents did not seem to see what she saw. During the quiet weeks, when the shadow grew so plain to her, she said nothing of it to those at home, believing that it would tell itself when Beth came back no better. She wondered still more if her sister really guessed the hard truth.

One day Beth told her. Jo thought she was asleep, she lay so still. It came to her more bitterly than ever that Beth was slowly drifting away from her, and her arms instinctively tightened their hold on her, as she lay on the warm rocks, her head in Jo's lap, the winds blowing over her and the sea making music at her feet.

She was aware of Beth looking up at her, as she said, "Jo dear. I'm glad you know it. I've tried to tell you but I couldn't."

There was no answer except her sister's cheek against her own, not even tears, for when most deeply moved Jo did not cry.

"I've known it for a good while, dear," Beth said trying to comfort her sister. "Now I'm used to it. It isn't hard to think of or to bear. Try to see it so, and don't be troubled about me because it's best."

"Is this what made you so unhappy in the autumn, Beth?" asked Jo, glad to know that Laurie had no part in Beth's trouble.

"Yes. I gave up hoping then but I didn't like to own it. I tried to think it was a sick fancy, but when I saw you all so well and strong, and full of happy plans, it was hard to feel I could never be like you, and then I was miserable, Jo."

"Oh Beth, and you didn't tell me! How could you bear it all alone?" Jo's heart ached to think of the struggle that must have gone on while Beth learned to say good-by to health, love and life.

"Perhaps it was wrong but I tried to do right. I wasn't sure. No one said anything and I hoped I was mistaken. It would have been selfish to frighten you all when Marmee was anxious about Meg, Amy away, and you so happy with Laurie, at least, I thought so then."

"And I thought you loved him, Beth. I went away because I couldn't."

Beth looked so amazed at the idea that Jo smiled in spite of her pain and added softly, "Then you didn't, dearie? I was afraid it was so."

"Why Jo, how could I when he was so fond of you?" asked Beth. "I do love him dearly. He is so good to me, how can I help it? But he never could be anything to me but my brother. I hope he will be, sometime."

"Not through me," said Jo decidedly. "Amy is left for him and they would suit excellently. Beth, you *must* get well."

"I want to, oh, so much! I try, but every day I lose a little and feel more sure that I shall never gain it back. It's like the tide, Jo. When it turns it goes slowly, but it can't be stopped."

"It *shall* be stopped. Your tide must not turn so soon. Nineteen is too young. Beth, I can't let you go. I'll work and pray and fight against it. I'll keep you in spite of everything. There must be ways. It can't be too late. God won't be so cruel as to take you from me," cried poor Jo rebelliously. The sisters held each other close as the first bitter wave of this great sorrow broke over them together.

By-and-by Beth said, "You'll tell them this when we go home?"

"I think they will see it without words," sighed Jo.

"Perhaps not. I've heard that the people who love best are often blindest to such things. Tell them for me. It's kinder to prepare them. You must stand by Father and Mother, won't you, Jo?"

"If I can. But Beth, I don't give up." For several minutes there was no sound but the sigh of the wind and the lapping of the tide. A white-winged gull flew by, and Beth watched it, her eyes full of sadness. A little gray-coated sand bird came tripping over the beach, and sat on a warm stone quite close to Beth, dressing its wet feathers. Beth smiled, and felt comforted, for the tiny thing reminded her of the pleasant world.

When they got home there was no need for any words, for Father and Mother saw plainly now what they had prayed to be saved from seeing. When Jo went down, after putting Beth to bed, she found her father standing, his head resting on the mantelpiece. He did not turn as she came in, but her mother stretched out her arms as if for help, and Jo went to comfort her without a word.

Chapter 33

NEW IMPRESSIONS

AT THREE O'CLOCK in the afternoon, all the fashionable world at Nice may be seen on the Promenade des Anglis. The wide walk bordered with palms, flowers and tropical shrubs, is bounded on one side by the sea, on the other by the grand drive lined with hotels and villas, while beyond lie orange groves and the hills. Many nations are represented, many languages spoken, many costumes worn. On a sunny day, the spectacle is as gay and brilliant as a carnival.

Along this walk on Christmas day, a tall young man

walked slowly, with his hands behind him and an absent expression. He look like an Italian, was dressed like an Englishman, and had the independent air of an American. Feminine eyes looked approvingly after him. The young man took little notice, except to glance now and then at some blonde girl or lady in blue. Presently the quick trot of ponies' feet made him look up, as a little carriage containing a single lady came rapidly down the street. The lady was young, blonde, and dressed in blue. He stared a minute, then woke up and waving his hat like a boy, hurried forward to meet her.

"Oh Laurie, is it really you? I thought you'd never come!" cried Amy, dropping the reins and holding out both hands.

"I was detained, but I promised to spend Christmas with you and here I am."

"How is your grandfather? When did you come? Where are you staying?"

"Very well—last night—at the Chauvain. I called at your hotel, but you were all out."

"I have so much to say I don't know where to begin! Get in and we can talk as we drive. Flo's saving up for tonight."

"What happens then? A ball?"

"A Christmas party at our hotel. You'll go with us, of course?"

"Thank you. Where now?" asked Laurie, leaning back and folding his arms, which suited Amy who preferred to drive.

"I'm going to the banker's first, for letters, and then to Castle Hill. The view is so lovely. Have you ever been there?"

Often, years ago, but I don't mind having a look at it."

"Now tell me all about yourself. The last I heard of you, your grandfather wrote that he expected you from Berlin."

"Yes, I spent a month there and then joined him in Paris, where he has settled for the winter. I go and come and we get on capitally."

"That's a sociable arrangement," said Amy, missing something in Laurie's manner though she couldn't tell what.

As she watched him, Amy felt a new sort of shyness steal over her, for he was changed and she could not find the merry-faced boy she left in the moody-looking man beside her. He was handsomer than ever, but he looked tired and spiritless, as well as older and graver. She couldn't understand it. At Avigdor's she found the precious home letters, and, giving the reins to Laurie, read them as they wound up the shady road between green hedges where tea roses bloomed.

"Beth is very poorly, Mother says. I often think I ought to go home, but they all say stay, so I do, for I shall never have another chance like this," said Amy, looking sober over one page.

"I think you are right. You could no nothing at home and it is a great comfort to them to know you are happy and enjoying so much, my dear." He drew a little nearer and looked more like his old self.

She laughed and showed him a small sketch of Jo in her scribbling suit, with the bow rampant on her cap, and the words "Genius burns!" issuing from her mouth. Laurie smiled and put it in his vest pocket, "to keep it from blowing away," and listened with interest to the letter.

"This will be a regularly merry Christmas to me, with presents in the morning, you and letters in the afternoon, and a party at night," said Amy, as they alighted among the ruins of the old fort.

After idling away an hour they drove home, and having paid his respects to Mrs. Carrol, Laurie left them, promising to return that evening.

Amy deliberately prinked that night. Time and absence had done its work on both the young people. She had seen her old friend in a new light, not as "our boy" but as a handsome and agreeable man, and she was conscious of a desire to find favor in his sight. Amy knew her good points and made the most of them.

She put on Flo's old white silk ball dress and covered it

with a cloud of fresh illusion, out of which her white shoulders and golden head emerged with an artistic effect. Her hair she had the sense to leave alone, after gathering up the thick waves and curls in a knot at the back of her head. Having no ornaments fine enough, Amy looped her fleecy skirts with rosy clusters of azalea, and framed the white shoulders in delicate green vines. She surveyed her white satin slippers with girlish satisfaction, and chasséed down the room, admiring her aristocratic feet.

"My new fan just matches my flowers, my gloves fit to a charm, and the real lace on aunt's *mouchoir* gives an air to my whole dress. If I only had a classical nose and mouth I should be perfectly happy," she said, surveying herself with a critical eye.

She looked unusually gay and graceful as she glided away, and walked up and down the long salon while waiting for Laurie. He saw her first as she stood at a distant window, her head half turned and one hand gathering up her dress. The slender white figure against the red curtains was as effective as a well-placed statue.

"Good evening, Diana!" said Laurie with a look of satisfaction.

"Good evening Apollo!" she answered, smiling back at him.

"Here are your flowers," and he handed her a delicate nosegay in a holder she had long coveted as she daily passed it in Cardiglia's window.

"How kind you are," she exclaimed gratefully, as she snapped the silver bracelet on her wrist. He buttoned her gloves for her and asked if his tie was straight, as he used to do at parties at home.

Amy took the stage that night leaning on Laurie's arm. She knew she looked well, she loved to dance, and she enjoyed a delightful sense of power. With the first burst of the band, Amy's color rose, her eyes began to sparkle and her feet to tap the floor impatiently.

"Do you care to dance?" Laurie asked tranquilly.

Her amazed look and quick "One usually does at a ball," caused Laurie to repair his error.

"I meant the first dance. May I have the honor?"

"I can give you one if I put off the Count. He dances divinely, but he will excuse me as you are an old friend," said Amy, hoping the name would have a good effect.

"Nice little boy but rather a short Pole to support *a daughter of the gods, divinely tall, and most divinely fair,*" was all the satisfaction she got, however.

They walked decorously through a cotillion, and when Amy gallopaded away with the Count, she saw Laurie sit down by her aunt with an expression of relief. That was unpardonable, and Amy took no more notice of him except a word now and then between dances. Her anger had a good effect, for she hid it under a smiling face and seemed unusually blithe and brilliant. Laurie's eyes followed her with pleasure, and before the evening was half over he had decided that "little Amy was going to make a very charming woman."

Christmas merriment made hearts happy and heels light. The musicians fiddled, tooted and banged as if they enjoyed it and everybody who could, danced, while those who couldn't admired their neighbors.

Amy's treatment of Laurie was successful, for after the little Pole relinquished her, Laurie rose with alacrity to give her his seat. When he hurried away to bring her some supper, she said to herself with a smile, "Ah, I thought that would do him good!"

Laurie felt an odd sort of pleasure in having "little Amy" order him about, for she had lost her shyness now. "Where did you learn all this sort of thing?" he asked, with a quizzical look.

"Would you kindly explain?" returned Amy, knowing perfectly well what he meant.

"Well, the general air, the style, the self-possession, the—the—" and he indicated her dress.

Amy was gratified, but demurely answered, "Foreign life

polishes one in spite of one's self. I study as well as play. As for this—" with a little gesture toward her dress—"why, tulle is cheap, posies to be had for nothing, and I am used to making the most of my things."

Amy rather regretted that last sentence, but Laurie liked her the better for it, and found himself both admiring and respecting the brave patience that made the most of opportunity, and the cheerful spirit that covered poverty with flowers. Amy did not know why he looked at her so kindly, nor why he filled up her book with his own name and devoted himself to her for the rest of the evening in the most delightful manner. But the impulse that wrought this agreeable change was the result of one of the new impressions which both of them were unconsciously giving and receiving.

Chapter 34

LAZY LAURENCE

LAURIE went to Nice intending to stay a week and remained a month. He was tired of wandering about alone, and Amy's familiar presence seemed to give a homelike charm to the foreign scenes in which she bore a part. They naturally took comfort in each other's society and were much together, riding, walking, dancing or dwadling. But while amusing themselves in the most careless fashion, they were half-consciously making discoveries and forming opinions about each other. Amy rose daily in the estimation of her friend, but he sank in hers, and each felt the truth before a word was spoken.

"I am going to Valrosa to sketch. Will you come?" asked Amy, as she joined Laurie one lovely day when he lounged in as usual about noon. "I'm going to have the little carriage.

and Baptiste can drive, so you'll have nothing to do but hold your umbrella and keep your gloves nice," she continued, with a glance at the immaculate kids.

"I'll go with pleasure," and he put out his hand for her sketch book. But she tucked it under her arm with a sharp, "Don't trouble yourself. It's no exertion to me but you don't look equal to it."

Laurie lifted his eyebrows and followed at a leisurely pace as she ran downstairs. When they got into the carriage he took the reins. The two never quarreled. Amy was too well-bred and just now Laurie was too lazy, so in a minute he peeped under her hat brim with an inquiring air. She answered with a smile, and they drove on.

Valrosa well deserved its name, for in that climate of perpetual summer, roses blossomed everywhere. They lined the avenue up to the villa on the hill. Roses covered the walls of the house, and ran riot over the balustrade of the wide terrace whence one looked down on the sunny Mediterranean and the white-walled city on its shore.

"This is a regular honeymoon paradise, isn't it? Did you ever see such roses?" asked Amy, pausing on the terrace.

"No, nor felt such thorns," returned Laurie, with his thumb in his mouth after a vain attempt to capture a solitary scarlet flower that grew just beyond his reach.

"Try lower down and pick those that have no thorns," said Amy, gathering three of the tiny cream-colored ones that starred the wall behind her. She put them in his buttonhole as a peace offering and he stood a minute looking down at them with a curious expression.

"Laurie, when are you going to your grandfather?" Amy asked presently, as she settled herself on a rustic seat.

"Very soon."

"You have said that a dozen times the last three weeks. He expects you, and you really ought to go."

"Hospitable creature! I know it."

"Then why don't you do it?"

"Natural depravity, I suppose."

"Natural indolence, you mean. It's dreadful!" Amy looked severe. "Go to sleep, if you like," she added, as Laurie composed himself for a lounge on the broad ledge of the balustrade. "I intend to work hard," and she opened her sketch book energetically.

"What delightful enthusiasm!" and Laurie leaned against a tall urn.

"What would Jo say if she saw you now?" asked Amy.

"As usual, 'Go away, Teddy, I'm busy!'" He laughed as he spoke, but the laugh was not natural and a shade passed over his face. Both tone and shadow struck Amy, for she had seen and heard them before, and now she looked up in time to catch a new expression on Laurie's face—a hard bitter look, full of pain, dissatisfaction and regret. It was gone before she could study it and the listless expression back again. She watched him for a moment with artistic pleasure, thinking how like an Italian he looked, as he lay basking in the sun.

"You look like the effigy of a young knight asleep on his tomb," she said, carefully tracing the well-cut profile.

"Wish I was!"

"That's a foolish wish unless you have spoiled your life. You are so changed, I sometimes think—" there Amy stopped with a half-timid, half-wistful look, more significant than her unfinished speech. Laurie saw and understood the affectionate anxiety which she hesitated to express, and looking straight into her eyes said, just as he used to say it to her mother, "It's all right, ma'am."

That satisfied her and set at rest the doubts that had begun to worry her lately. It also touched her, and she said in a cordial tone, "I'm glad of that! Don't stay out there in the sun. Come and lie on the grass here and let us be friendly, as Jo used to say when we got in the sofa corner and told secrets."

Laurie obediently threw himself down on the turf, and began to stick daisies into Amy's hat ribbons. "I'm all ready for secrets," he said.

"I've none to tell. You may begin."

"Haven't one to bless myself with. When do you begin your great work of art, Raphaella?" he asked.

"Never," she answered with a despondent but decided air. "Rome took all the vanity out of me. After seeing the wonders there, I gave up all my foolish hopes."

"Why should you, with so much energy and talent?"

"That's just why. Because talent isn't genius, and no amount of energy can make it so. I want to be great or nothing. I won't be a commonplace dauber, so I don't intend to try any more."

"And what are you going to do with yourself now?"

"Polish up my other talents and be an ornament to society, if I get the chance."

"Good. And here is where Fred Vaughn comes in, I fancy."

Amy preserved a discreet silence but there was a conscious look in her downcast face that made Laurie sit up and say gravely, "Now I'm going to play brother and ask questions. May I?"

"I don't promise to answer."

"Your face will if your tongue won't. I heard rumors about Fred and you last year, and it's my private opinion that if he had not been called home so suddenly and detained so long, something would have come of it."

"That's not for me to say," was Amy's prim reply, but her lips would smile and there was a sparkle in her eye.

"You are not engaged, I hope?" Laurie looked grave.

"No."

"But you will be, if he comes back and goes properly down on his knees, won't you?"

"Very likely."

"Then you are fond of old Fred?"

"I could be if I tried."

"But you don't intend to try till the proper moment? Bless my soul, what unearthly prudence! He's a good fellow, Amy, but not the man I fancied you'd like."

"He is rich, a gentleman, and has delightful manners," began Amy, trying to be dignified, but feeling a little ashamed in spite of her sincerity.

"I understand. Queens of society can't get on without money, so you mean to make a good match and start in that way? Quite right and proper, but it sounds odd from the lips of one of your mother's girls."

"True, nevertheless." A short speech but the quiet decision with which it was uttered contrasted curiously with the young speaker. Laurie felt this instinctively, and laid himself down again with a sense of disappointment he could not explain. His look and silence, as well as a certain inward self-disapproval, ruffled Amy.

"I wish you'd do me the favor to rouse yourself a little," she said sharply.

"Do it for me, there's a dear girl."

"I could if I tried."

"Try then. I give you leave," returned Laurie, who enjoyed having someone to tease.

"Flo and I have a new name for you. It's 'Lazy Laurence.'"

She thought it would annoy him, but he only folded his arms under his head. "That's not bad. Thank you."

"Do you want to know what I honestly think of you?"

"Pining to be told."

"Well, I despise you." The grave, almost sad, accent of her voice made him open his eyes and ask quickly, "Why, if you please?"

"Because with every chance for being good, useful and happy, you are faulty, lazy and miserable."

"Pray go on. It's quite interesting."

"I thought you'd find it so. Selfish people always like to talk about themselves."

"Am *I* selfish?" The question slipped out involuntarily, for the one virtue on which he prided himself was generosity.

"Yes, very selfish," continued Amy, in a calm cool voice twice as effective as an angry one. "Here you have been abroad nearly six months and done nothing but waste time and money and disappoint your friends."

"Isn't a fellow to have any pleasure after a four-year grind?"

"You don't look as if you'd had much. I said when we first met that you had improved. I take it all back, for I don't think you half so nice as when I left you at home. You have grown lazy, you like gossip, you waste your time on frivolous things. With money, talent, position, health and beauty you can find nothing to do but dawdle. Instead of being the man you might and ought to be, you are only—" she stopped.

"Saint Laurence on a gridiron," added Laurie. But the lecture began to take effect.

"I supposed you'd take it so. You men tell us we are angels, and say we can make you what we will, but the instant we honestly try to do you good, you laugh at us and won't listen." Amy spoke bitterly.

In a minute a hand came down over the page, so that she could not draw, and Laurie said, like a child, "I will be good, oh, I will be good!"

But Amy did not laugh for she was in earnest. Tapping on the outspread hand with her pencil she said, "Aren't you ashamed of a hand like that? It's as soft and white as a woman's, and looks as if it never did anything but wear gloves and pick flowers for the ladies. I'm glad to see there are no rings on it, only the little old one Jo gave you so long ago. I wish she was here to help me!"

"So do I!"

The hand vanished as suddenly as it came. Amy glanced down at him with a new thought, but he was lying with his hat over his face, as if for shade, and his mustache hid his mouth. Various hints and trifles assumed shape and significance in Amy's mind and told her what her sister had never confided. She remembered that Laurie never spoke voluntarily of Jo. She recalled the shadow on his face just now, and the little old ring, no ornament to a handsome hand. When she spoke again it was in a voice both soft and kind.

"I know I have no right to talk so to you, Laurie. If you weren't the sweetest-tempered fellow in the world you'd be angry with me. But we are all so fond and proud of you, I couldn't bear to think they should be disappointed in you at home as I have been, though perhaps they would understand the change better than I do."

"I think they would," came grimly from under the hat.

"They ought to have told me and not let me go blundering and scolding when I should have been kind and patient. I never did like that Miss Randal and now I hate her!" Artful Amy wished to be sure of her facts this time.

"Hank Miss Randal!" Laurie knocked the hat off.

"I beg pardon, I thought—" and there she paused diplomatically.

"No you didn't. You knew perfectly well I never cared for anybody but Jo," Laurie said in his old impetuous tone, turning away.

"I did think so but as they never said anything about it and you came away, I supposed I was mistaken. And Jo wouldn't be kind to you? I was sure she loved you."

"She was kind but not in the right way. And it's lucky for her she didn't love me, if I'm the good-for-nothing fellow you think me. It's her fault though, and you may tell her so." The hard bitter look came back again and it troubled Amy.

"I was wrong. I didn't know. I'm very sorry I was so cross but I wish you'd bear it better, Teddy dear."

"Don't. That's her name for me!" and Laurie put up his hand with a quick gesture to stop the words spoken in Jo's half-kind, half-reproachful tone. "Wait till you've tried it yourself," he added.

"I'd take it manfully and be respected if I couldn't be loved," said Amy, with decision.

As if suddenly shaken out of a dream, Laurie sat up and asked, "Do you think Jo would despise me as you do?"

"Yes, if she saw you now. She hates lazy people. Why don't you do something splendid and make her love you?"

"I did my best but it was no use."

"Graduating well, you mean? That was no more than you ought to have done for your grandfather's sake. It would have been shameful to fail!"

"I did fail, say what you will, for Jo wouldn't love me," began Laurie, leaning his head on his hand.

"No you didn't, and you'll say so in the end, for it did you good and proved that you could do something if you tried. If you'd only set about another task, you'd soon forget your trouble."

"That's impossible."

"Try it and see. Love Jo all your days, if you choose, but don't let it spoil you, for it's wicked to throw away gifts because you can't have the one you want."

Neither spoke for several minutes. Laurie sat turning the little ring on his finger, and Amy put the last touches to the hasty sketch. Presently she said, "How do you like that?"

He looked and then he smiled, as he could not well help doing, for it was capitally done. "How well you draw!" he said, with surprise and pleasure, adding with a half-laugh, "Yes, that's me."

"As you are. This is as you were," and Amy laid another sketch beside the one he held.

It was not nearly so well done but there was a life and spirit in it which atoned for many faults. It recalled the past so vividly that a sudden change swept over the young man's face as he looked. Only a rough sketch of Laurie taming a horse. Hat and coat were off and every line of the active figure, resolute face and commanding attitude was full of energy and meaning. Laurie said nothing but as his eyes went from one to the other Amy saw him flush and fold his lips together as if he read and accepted the little lesson she had given him.

That satisfied her, and without waiting for him to speak she said, "Don't you remember that day? I sat on the fence and drew you. I found that sketch in my portfolio the other day and kept it to show you."

"Much obliged. You've improved immensely since then and I congratulate you." Laurie rose as he spoke, returned the pictures with a smile and a bow, and looked at his watch.

They laughed and chatted all the way home but both felt ill at ease. The friendly frankness was disturbed, the sunshine had a shadow.

"Shall we see you this evening?" asked Amy as they parted.

"Unfortunately I have an engagement," and Laurie bent as if to kiss her hand in the foreign fashion. Something in his face made Amy say quickly and warmly, "No. Be yourself with me, Laurie, and part in the good old way. I'd rather have a hearty English handshake."

"Good-by, dear," and with these words, uttered in the tone she liked, Laurie left her, after a hearty handshake.

Next morning, instead of the usual call Amy received a note which made her smile at the beginning and sigh at the end:

> *My dear Mentor,—*
> *Please make my adieux to your aunt and exult within yourself, for "Lazy Laurence" has gone to his grandpa like the best of boys. A pleasant winter to you, and may the gods grant you a blissful honeymoon at Valrosa! I think Fred would be benefitted by a rouser. Tell him so, with my congratulations.*
>
> *Yours gratefully,*
Telemachus

"Good boy! I'm glad he's gone," said Amy, adding with a sigh, "Yes, I *am* glad, but how I shall miss him!"

Chapter 35

THE VALLEY OF THE SHADOW

WHEN the first bitterness was over, the family accepted the inevitable and tried to bear it cheerfully, helping one another by the increased affection which comes to bind households tenderly together in times of trouble. They put away their grief and each did his or her part toward making that last year a happy one.

The pleasantest room in the house was set apart for Beth, and in it was gathered everything that she most loved—flowers, pictures, her piano, the little work table, and the beloved pussies. Father's best books found their way there,

Mother's easychair, Jo's desk, Amy's finest sketches, and every day Meg brought her babies. John quietly set apart a little sum, that he might enjoy the pleasure of keeping the invalid supplied with the fruit she loved and longed for. Old Hannah never wearied of concocting dainty dishes to tempt a capricious appetite, dropping tears as she worked. From across the sea came little gifts and cheerful letters.

Here sat Beth, tranquil and busy as ever. The feeble fingers were never idle, and one of her pleasures was to make little things for the school children daily passing to and fro. If Beth had wanted any reward, she found it in the bright little faces always turned up to her window, with nods and smiles, and the droll little letters which came to her full of bots and gratitude.

The first few months were happy ones, and Beth often used to look around and say, "How beautiful this is!" as they all sat together in her sunny room, the babies on the floor, Mother and sisters working near, and Father reading from the wise old books which seemed rich in good and comfortable words, as applicable now as when written centuries ago.

It was well for all that this peaceful time was given them as preparation for the sad hours to come, for by-and-by Beth said the needle was "so heavy," and put it down forever. Talking wearied her, faces troubled her, and pain claimed her for its own. The thin hands stretched out beseechingly, the bitter cry "Help me, help me!" tore at their hearts. The sharp struggle of the young life with death was mercifully brief, and then the old peace returned more beautiful than ever. With the wreck of her frail body, Beth's soul grew strong. Though she said little, those about her felt that she was ready, saw that the first pilgrim called was likewise the fittest, and waited with her on the shore, trying to see the Shining Ones coming to receive her when she crossed the river.

Jo never left her for an hour since Beth had said, "I feel stronger when you are here." She slept on a couch in the room, waking often to renew the fire, to feed, lift, or wait upon the patient creature who seldom asked for anything, and "tried not to be a trouble." All day she haunted the room, jealous of any other nurse, and prouder of being chosen then than of any honor her life ever brought her.

Often when she woke, Jo found Beth reading in her well-worn little book, heard her singing softly, to beguile the sleepless nights, or saw her lean her face upon her hands while slow tears dropped through the transparent fingers. Jo would lie watching her, with thoughts too deep for tears, feeling that Beth in her simple unselfish way was trying to wean herself from the dear old life and fit herself to the life to come by sacred words of comfort, quiet prayers and the music she loved so well.

Seeing this did more for Jo than the wisest sermons, the saintliest hymns, the most fervent prayers, for with eyes made clear by many tears and a heart softened by the tenderest sorrow, she recognized the beauty of her sister's life —uneventful, unambitious, yet full of the genuine virtues which "smell sweet and blossom in the dust," the self-forgotfulness that makes the humbled on earth remembered soonest in heaven, the true success which is possible to all.

So the spring days came and went, the sky grew clearer, the earth greener, the flowers were up, and the birds came back in time to say good-by to Beth, who like a tired but trustful child clung to the hands that had led her all her life, as Father and Mother guided her tenderly through the Valley of the Shadow and gave her up to God.

As Beth had hoped, the tide went out easily, and in the dark hour before the dawn, on the bosom where she had drawn her first breath, she quietly drew her last, with no farewell but one loving look, one little sigh.

With tears and prayers and tender hands, mother and sisters made her ready for the long sleep that pain would never mar again, seeing with grateful eyes the beautiful serenity that soon replaced the pathetic patience that had wrung their hearts so long, and feeling with reverent joy that to their darling death was a benignant angel, not a phantom full of dread.

When morning came, for the first time in many months the fire was out, Jo's place was empty, and the room was very still. But a bird sang blithely on a budding bough close by, the snowdrops blossomed freshly at the window, and the spring sunshine streamed in like a benediction over the placid face on the pillow—a face so full of painless peace that those who loved it best smiled through their tears and thanked God that Beth was well at last.

Chapter 36

LEARNING TO FORGET

AMY'S LECTURE did Laurie good, though of course he did not own it until long afterward. He went back to his grandfather and was so devoted for several weeks that the old gentleman declared the climate of Nice had improved him wonderfully and he had better try it again. There was nothing Laurie would have liked better, but elephants could not have dragged him back after the scolding he had received. Laurie soon brought himself to confess that he had been selfish and lazy. Jo wouldn't love him but he might make her respect and admire him by doing something to prove a girl's "No" had not spoiled his life.

Laurie resolved to compose a requiem which should harrow Jo and melt the heart of every hearer. So he went to Vienna where he had musical friends, but he soon discovered the requiem was beyond him at present. Often in the middle of a plaintive strain he would find himself humming a dancing tune that recalled the Christmas ball at Nice.

Then he tried an opera, but again difficulties beset him.

He wanted Jo for his heroine and called on his memory for romantic visions of his love. Memory turned traitor and would only recall Jo's oddities, faults and freaks. When he looked about for another damsel to immortalize in melody, memory produced one who wore many faces but always had golden hair and floated airily before his mind's eye in a pleasing chaos of roses, white ponies and blue ribbons.

Laurie grew more and more discontented with his desultory life and began to long for some real work. He came to the conclusion that everyone who loved music was not a composer. "She is right," he said to himself. "Talent isn't genius and you can't make it so. I won't be a humbug any longer. Now what shall I do?" That was a hard question to answer.

Laurie thought that the task of forgetting his love for Jo would absorb all his powers for years, but to his great surprise he discovered it grew easier every day. He refused to believe it at first and grew angry with himself, for instead of trying to forget he found himself trying to remember. He carefully stirred up the embers of his lost love but they refused to burst into a blaze. There was only a comfortable glow that warmed him, and he was reluctantly obliged to confess that the boyish passion was subsiding into a more tranquil sentiment, leaving a brotherly affection which would last unbroken to the end.

As the word "brotherly" passed through his mind, he smiled and glanced up at the picture of Mozart. "He was a great man," he thought. "When he couldn't have one sister he took the other and was happy." The next instant he kissed the little old ring, saying, "No I won't! I haven't forgotten, I never can. I'll try again—"

Leaving his sentence unfinished, he wrote to Jo—wouldn't she let him come home and be happy? The answer came at last, and Jo decidedly wouldn't and couldn't. She was wrapped up in Beth and begged him to be happy with somebody else. In a postscript she desired him not to tell

Amy that Beth was worse. Laurie must write to her often and not let Amy feel lonely, homesick or anxious.

"So I will, poor little girl. It will be a sad going home for her, I'm afraid." But he did not write the letter that day, for in the desk he found several of Jo's letters, and three notes from Amy. Laurie gathered up all Jo's letters, put them neatly into a small drawer of the desk, slowly drew off the ring and laid it with the letters. Then he locked the drawer.

The letter went soon and was promptly answered, for Amy was homesick. The correspondence flourished, and Laurie wanted desperately to go to Nice but would not until he was asked. Amy would not ask him, for just then she was having experiences of her own.

Fred Vaughn had returned and put the question to which she had once decided to answer, "Yes, thank you," but now she said, "No, thank you," kindly but steadily. When the time came her courage failed her and she found that something more than money and position was needed to satisfy the new longing. The words "Fred is a good fellow but not at all the man I fancied you would like," and Laurie's face as he uttered them, kept returning to her as her own did when she said in look if not in words, "I shall marry for money." It troubled her to remember that now, and she wished she could take it back.

Amy never lectured now. She asked Laurie's opinion on all subjects. She was interested in everything he did, made him charming little presents, and sent two letters a week, full of lively gossip, sisterly confidences, and captivating sketches. She grew pale and pensive that spring and went sketching alone a good deal. She sat for hours with her hands folded on the terrace at Valrosa, or absently sketched any fancy that occurred to her—a stalwart knight carved on a tomb, a young man asleep in the grass, or a curly-haired girl promenading down a ballroom on the arm of a tall gentleman.

Her aunt thought that she regretted her answer to Fred,

and Amy let her think what she liked, taking care that Laurie should know Fred had gone to Egypt. That was all, but he understood it.

While these changes were going on abroad, trouble had come at home, but the letter telling that Beth was failing never reached Amy and when the next found her, the grass was green above her sister. The sad news met her at Vevey, for the heat had driven them from Nice in May and they traveled slowly to Switzerland by way of Genoa and the Italian lakes. She bore it very well and submitted to the family decree that she had better stay and let absence soften her sorrow. But her heart was heavy and she longed to be at home. Every day she looked wistfully across the lake, waiting for Laurie to come and comfort her.

He did come very soon, for the same mail brought letters to them both, but he was in Germany and it took some days to reach him. The minute he read it he packed his knapsack and was off to keep his promise, with a heart full of joy and sorrow, hope and suspense. He knew Vevey well, and as soon as the boat touched the little quay he hurried along the shore to La Tour, where the Carrols were living. The The garçon was in despair that the whole family had gone to take a promenade on the lake, but no, the blonde mademoiselle might be in the chateau garden.

A pleasant old garden on the borders of the lovely lake, with chestnuts rustling overhead, ivy climbing everywhere, and the black shadow of the tower falling far across the sunny water. At one corner of the wide low wall was a seat, and here Amy often came to read or work. She was sitting, leaning her head on her hand, with a homesick heart and heavy eyes, thinking of Beth and wondering why Laurie did not come. She did not hear him cross the courtyard nor see him pause in the archway that led from the subterranean path into the garden.

He stood a minute, looking at her with new eyes, seeing what no one had ever seen before—the tender side of Amy's character. Everything about her mutely suggested love and sorrow—the blotted letters in her lap, the black ribbon that tied up her hair, the womanly pain and patience in her face. Even the little ebony cross at her throat seemed pathetic to Laurie, for he had given it to her.

The minute she looked up and saw him, she ran to him, exclaiming in a tone of unmistakable love and longing, "Oh Laurie, Laurie, I knew you'd come to me!"

Everything was said and settled then. As they stood together silent for a moment, with the dark head bent down protectingly over the light one, Amy felt that no one could comfort and sustain her so well as Laurie, and Laurie decided that Amy was the only woman in the world who could fill Jo's place and make him happy. He did not tell her so, but she was not disappointed, for both felt the truth and were satisfied.

While she dried her tears, Laurie gathered up the scattered papers. "It was a surprise to look up and see you when I began to fear you wouldn't come," she said.

"I came the minute I heard. I wish I could say something to comfort you for the loss of dear little Beth but I can only feel and—" He could not get any further for he turned bashful all of a sudden and did not know what to say. He gave her hand a sympathetic squeeze.

"Beth is well and happy and I mustn't wish her back," she said, "but I dread going home much as I long to see them all. You needn't go right back need you?"

"Not if you want me, dear."

"I do, so much. Aunt and Flo are kind, but you are one of the family."

"Come and walk with me. The wind is too chilly for you to sit still," he said, in the half-caressing, half-commanding way that Amy liked. He tied on her hat, drew her arm through his and began to pace up and down the sunny walk, under the new-leaved chestnuts.

The quaint old garden had sheltered many pairs of lovers and it seemed expressly made for them. For an hour they walked and talked or rested on the wall, and when an unromantic dinner bell warned them, Amy felt as if she left her burden of loneliness and sorrow behind in the garden.

At Nice, Laurie had lounged and Amy had scolded. At Vevey, Laurie was never idle, but always walking, riding, boating or studying, while Amy admired everything he did. In spite of the new sorrow, it was a happy time, so happy that Laurie could not bear to disturb it by a word. It took him a little while to recover from his surprise at the rapid cure of his first, and as he had firmly believed his last and only, love. He consoled himself with the conviction that it would have been impossible to love any other woman but Amy so soon and so well. His first wooing had been tempestuous, and he resolved his second should be as calm and simple as possible. There was hardly any need of telling Amy that he loved her. She knew it without words and had given him his answer long ago. She knew everybody would be pleased, even Jo. So Laurie let the days pass, enjoying every hour and leaving to chance the utterance of the word that would put an end to the first and sweetest part of his new romance.

He rather imagined it would take place in the chateau garden by moonlight, but it turned out exactly the reverse, for the matter was settled on the lake at noonday. They had been floating about all morning, a cloudless blue sky overhead and the bluer lake below. Amy had been dabbling her hand in the water, and when she looked up Laurie was leaning on his oars with an expression that made her say hastily, "You must be tired. Rest a little and let me row."

"I'm not tired, but you may take an oar if you like," returned Laurie.

Amy accepted an oar, for she rowed as well as she did many other things. "How well we pull together, don't we?" said Amy.

"So well that I wish we might always pull in the same boat. Will you, Amy?"

"Yes, Laurie." Then they stopped rowing, and added a

pretty little tableau of love and happiness to the dissolving views reflected in the lake.

Chapter 37

ALL ALONE

IT WAS EASY to promise self-abnegation when self was wrapped up in another, and heart and soul were purified by a sweet example. But when the helpful voice was silent, the daily lesson over, the beloved presence gone, and nothing remained but loneliness and grief, then Jo found her promise very hard to keep. How could she comfort Father and Mother when her own heart ached with a ceaseless longing for her sister? How could she make the house cheerful when all its light and warmth and beauty seemed to

have deserted it when Beth left the old home for the new. And where in the world could she find some useful, happy work to do that would take the place of the loving service which had been its own reward. She tried in a blind hopeless way to do her duty, secretly rebelling against it all the while, for it seemed unjust that her few joys should be lessened, her burdens made heavier, and life get harder and harder as she toiled along.

Poor Jo, these were dark days to her, for something like despair came over her when she thought of spending all her life in that quiet house devoted to humdrum cares, a few small pleasures and the duty that never seemed to grow any easier. "I can't do it. I wasn't meant for a life like this, and I know I shall break away and do something desperate if somebody doesn't come and help me," she said to herself when her first efforts failed and she fell into the moody, miserable state of mind which often comes when strong wills have to yield to the inevitable.

One day she went to the study, and leaning over the gray head lifted to welcome her with a smile, she said very humbly, "Father, talk to me as you did to Beth. I need it more than she did, for I'm all wrong."

"My dear, nothing can comfort me like this," he answered with a falter in his voice and both arms around her, as if he too needed help and did not fear to ask it.

Then sitting close beside him in Beth's little chair, Jo told her troubles—the resentful sorrow for her loss, the fruitless efforts that discouraged her, the want of faith that made life look so dark, and all the sad bewilderment which we call despair. She gave him entire confidence, he gave her the help she needed, and both found consolation. Happy thoughtful times there in the old study, which Jo called "the church of one member," and from which she came with fresh courage, recovered cheerfulness, and a more submissive spirit. For the parents who had taught one child to meet death without fear, were trying now to teach another to accept life.

Other helps had Jo—humble wholesome duties and delights that would not be denied their part in serving her, and which she slowly learned to see and value. Brooms and dishcloths never could be as distasteful as they once had been, for Beth's housewifely spirit seemed to linger around the little mop and the old brush. As she used them, Jo found herself humming the songs Beth used to hum and imitating Beth's orderly ways.

As they sat sewing together, Jo discovered how much improved her sister Meg was, how well she could talk, how much she knew, how happy she was in husband and children, and how much they were doing for each other.

"Why don't you write?" said her mother once, when the desponding fit overshadowed Jo. "That always used to make you happy."

"I've no heart to write, and if I had nobody cares for my things."

"We do. Write something for us and never mind the rest of the world. Try it, dear. I'm sure it would do you good and please us."

"Don't believe I can," but Jo got out her desk and began to overhaul her half-finished manuscripts.

An hour afterward her mother peeped in, and there she was scratching away, with her black pinafore on and an absorbed expression which caused Mrs. March to smile and slip away, well pleased with the success of her suggestion. Jo never knew how it happened but something got into that story that went straight to the hearts of those who read it. When her family had laughed and cried over it, her father sent it, much against her will, to one of the popular magazines and to her utter surprise it was not only paid for but others requested. Letters from several persons whose praise was honor followed the appearance of the little story, newspapers copied it, and strangers as well as friends admired it. For a small thing it was a great success, and Jo was more astonished than when her novel was commended and condemned.

"I don't understand it. What can there be in a simple story like that to make people praise it so?" she asked.

"There is truth in it, Jo. That's the secret. Humor and pathos make it alive and you have found your style at last. You wrote with no thought of fame or money and put your heart into it, my daughter. You have had the bitter and now comes the sweet. Do your best and grow as happy as we are in your success."

"If there *is* anything good or true in what I write, it isn't mine. I owe it all to you and Mother and to Beth," said Jo touched by her father's words.

When Amy and Laurie wrote of their engagement, Mrs. March feared Jo would find it difficult to rejoice, but her fears were soon set at rest. Jo looked grave at first, and took it quietly, but she was full of hopes and plans for "the children" before she read the letter twice.

"You like it, Mother?" said Jo, as they laid down the closely written sheets and looked at one another.

"Yes, I hoped it would be so ever since Amy wrote that she had refused Fred. A hint here and there in her letters made me suspect that Laurie would win the day."

"How sharp you are, Marmee. You never said a word."

"I was half afraid to put the idea into your head, lest you should write and congratulate them before the thing was settled."

"I'm not the scatterbrain I was. You may trust me."

"I was afraid it might pain you to learn that your Teddy loved anyone else. I have thought that if he came back and asked you again you might perhaps feel like giving another answer."

"No, Mother. It is better as it is. I'm glad Amy has learned to love him. But I am lonely and perhaps if Teddy had tried again I might have said yes, not because I love him any more but because I care more to be loved than when he went away."

By-and-by Jo roamed away upstairs, for it was rainy and she could not walk. A restless spirit possessed her, and the old feeling came again—a wonder why one sister should have all she asked, the other nothing. Amy's happiness woke the longing for someone "to love with heart and soul, and cling to while God let them be together."

Up in the garret stood four little wooden chests in a row, each marked with its owner's name and filled with relics of girlhood. Jo leaned her chin on the edge of hers. A bundle of old exercise books caught her eye. She drew them out, turned them over, and relived that pleasant winter at Mrs. Kirke's. When she came to a little message written by the Professor, her lips began to tremble, the books slid out of her lap, and she sat looking at the friendly words as if they took a new meaning.

Wait for me, my friend. I may be a little late but I shall surely come.

Holding the little paper as if it were a promise yet to be fulfilled, Jo laid her head down on a comfortable rag bag and cried, as the rain pattered on the roof.

Chapter 38

SURPRISES

JO was alone in the twilight, lying on the old sofa, looking at the fire and thinking. It was her favorite way of spending the hour of dusk. No one disturbed her and she used to lie there on Beth's little red pillow, planning stories, dreaming dreams, or thinking of the sister who never seemed far away. Her face looked tired and sad, for tomorrow was her birthday, and she was thinking how fast the years went by, how old she was getting and nothing to show for it. Almost twenty-five.

Suddenly Laurie's ghost seemed to stand before her, leaning over her with the look he used to wear when he felt a good deal and didn't like to show it. She lay staring up at him in startled silence until he stopped and kissed her. Then she knew him and flew up, crying joyfully, "Oh, my Teddy! Oh, my Teddy."

"Dear Jo. You are glad to see me then?"

"Glad! My blessed boy, words can't express my gladness. Where's Amy?"

"Down at Meg's. We stopped there by the way, and there was no getting my wife out of their clutches."

"Your what?" cried Jo.

"Oh, the dickens! Now I've done it," and looked guilty.

"You've gone and got married!"

"Yes, please, but I never will again," and he went down on his knees, clasping her hands, his face full of mischief, mirth and triumph.

"Get up, you ridiculous boy, and tell me all about it."

"Not a word, unless you let me come in my old place and promise not to barricade."

Jo laughed and patted the sofa invitingly. "The old pillow is up garret. So come and 'fess, Teddy."

"How good it sounds to hear you say Teddy! No one ever calls me that but you," and Laurie sat down with an air of great content.

"What does Amy call you?"

"My lord."

"That's like her. Well, you look it," and Jo's eyes betrayed that she found her boy comelier than ever.

The pillow was gone but there was a barricade, nonetheless, raised by time, absence and change of heart. Both felt it and for a minute looked at one another as if it cast a shadow over them. It was gone directly, for Laurie said, "Don't I look like a married man?"

"Not a bit and you never will. You've grown bigger and bonnier, but you are the same scapegrace as ever."

"It's no use of your going out in the cold to get Amy, for they are all coming up presently. I couldn't wait. I wanted to be the one to tell you the grand surprise."

"You spoiled your story by beginning at the wrong end. Now start right and tell me how it all happened."

"Well, we planned to come home with the Carrols a month or more ago, but they suddenly changed their minds and decided to pass another winter in Paris. But Grandpa wanted to come home. He went to please me and I couldn't let him go alone, neither could I leave Amy. Mrs. Carrol had English notions about chaperons and such nonsense, and wouldn't let Amy come with us. So I just settled the difficulty by saying, 'Let's be married and then we can do as we like.'"

"When, where, how?" asked Jo in a fever of curiosity.

"It was only taking time by the fetlock, as my wife says. Six weeks ago, at the American Consul's in Paris. A very quiet wedding, of course, for even in our happiness we didn't forget dear little Beth."

Jo put her hand in his as he said that, and Laurie gently smoothed the little red pillow which he remembered well.

"Why didn't you let us know afterward?" asked Jo.

"We wanted to surprise you. Amy had once called Valrosa a regular honeymoon home, so we went there. My faith, it was love among the roses!"

Laurie seemed to forget Jo, and she was glad, for it assured her he had forgiven and forgotten. She tried to draw away her hand but Laurie held it fast.

"Jo dear, I want to say one thing and then we'll put it by forever. As I told you in my letter, when I wrote that Amy had been so kind to me, I never shall stop loving you. But the love is altered and I have learned to see that it is better as it is. Amy and you changed places in my heart, that's all. I think it was meant to be so and would have come about naturally if I had waited, as you tried to make me, but I never could be patient. At one time I didn't know which I loved best, you or Amy, and tried to love both alike. When I saw her in Switzerland, everything seemed to clear up all at once. You both got into your right places, and I felt could honestly share my heart between sister Jo and wife Amy and love them both dearly. Will you believe it?"

"I'll believe it with all my heart. I shall miss my boy but I shall love the man as much and admire him more because he means to be what I hoped he would. We'll love and help one another all our lives."

He did not say a word but took the hand she offered him and laid his face down on it for a minute. Presently Jo said cheerfully, "I can't make it true that you children are really married. It seems only yesterday I was buttoning Amy's pinafore and pulling your hair when you teased. How time does fly!"

"As one of the children is older than yourself you needn't talk like a grandma," said Laurie, looking amused at her maternal air.

"You may be a little older in years but I'm ever so much older in feeling, Teddy. This last year has been such a hard one I feel forty."

"Poor Jo! We left you to bear it alone while we went pleasuring."

"I had Father and Mother to help me, and the thought that you and Amy were safe and happy to make the troubles here easier to bear. How do you and Amy get on together?"

"Like angels!"

"Yes of course, at first, but which rules?"

"I don't mind telling you that she does now. At least I let her think so. It pleases her, you know. By-and-by we shall take turns, for marriage they say halves one's rights and doubles one's duties."

"You'll go on as you begin and Amy will rule you all your days."

Suddenly Amy's voice was heard calling, "Where is she? Where's my dear old Jo?"

In trooped the whole family, and everyone was hugged and kissed. Then the three wanderers were set down to be looked at. Mr. Laurence, as hale and hearty as ever, was as much improved as the others by his foreign tour. It was good to see him beam at "my children," as he called the young pair. The minute she put her eyes on Amy, Meg became conscious that her own dress hadn't a Parisian air, that young Mrs. Moffat would be entirely eclipsed by young Mrs. Laurence, and that "her ladyship" was altogether an elegant and graceful woman. And Mr. and Mrs. March smiled and nodded at each other with happy faces.

Amy's face was full of soft brightness, her voice had a new tenderness, and the cool prim carriage was changed to a gentle dignity. No little affections marred it, and the cordial sweetness of her manner was more charming than the new beauty or the old grace. Daisy found it impossible to keep her eyes off her "pitty aunty," and Demi compromised himself by rashly accepting a bribe—a family of wooden bears from Berne. His tall uncle tossed and tousled the small nephew in a way that delighted him.

How they did talk! They tried to tell the history of three years in half an hour. Tea produced a lull, and the happy procession filed into the dining room, Mr. Laurence whispering to Jo, "You must be my girl now," and a glance at the empty corner by the fire that made Jo whisper back, "I'll try to fill her place, sir."

After tea, as the party filed back upstairs, there came a knock at the porch door. Jo opened it with hospitable haste and started as if another ghost had come, for there stood a tall bearded gentleman, beaming at her.

"Oh Mr. Bhaer, I am so glad to see you!" cried Jo.

"And I to see Miss Marsch. But no, you haf a party," and the Professor paused, as voices came down to them.

"No, we haven't. Only the family. My sister and friends have just come home and we are all very happy. Come in and make one of us."

"If I shall not be Monsieur de Trop, I will go gladly see them all. You haf been ill, my friend?"

"Not ill, but tired and sorrowful. We have had trouble since I saw you."

"Ah yes, I know. My heart was sore for you when I

heard," and he shook hands again with a sympathetic grasp of the big warm hand.

"Father, Mother, this is my friend Professor Bhaer," she said, with face and tone full of pride and pleasure.

If the stranger had had any doubts about his reception, they were set at rest by the cordial welcome he received. Everyone greeted him kindly, for Jo's sake at first but very soon they liked him for his own. Laurie stood aloof at first but soon got interested in spite of himself and before he knew it was drawn into the circle. Mr. Bhaer seldom spoke to Laurie, but he looked at him often and then his eye would turn to Jo so wistfully, that she would have answered the mute query if she had seen it, but she prudently kept her eyes on the little sock she was knitting.

She stole sidelong peeps at Mr. Bhaer. "Dear old fellow!" Jo said to herself. "He couldn't have got himself up with more care if he'd been going a-wooing." A sudden thought born of the words made her blush so that she had to drop her ball and go down after it to hide her face. The Professor made a dive after the little blue ball and they bumped their heads smartly together and came up flushed and laughing.

Nobody knew where the evening went to, and at the end Amy sang Beth's songs with a tender music in her voice which the best master could not have taught her. The room was very still when the clear voice failed suddenly at the last line of Beth's favorite hymn—*Earth has no sorrow that heaven cannot heal.*

"Now we must finish with Mignon's song, for Mr. Bhaer sings that," said Jo. Mr. Bhaer cleared his throat with a gratified "Hem!" as he stepped into the corner where Jo stood, saying, "You will sing with me? We go excellently well together." A pleasing fiction, for Jo had no more idea of music than a grasshopper.

The song was considered a great success, but a few minutes afterward he forgot his manners entirely and stared at Amy putting on her bonnet. She had been introduced simply as "my sister," and he forgot himself still further when Laurie said graciously, "My wife and I are very glad to meet you, sir. Please remember that there is a warm welcome for you over the way."

The Professor thanked him so heartily that Laurie thought him delightful. "I too shall go, but I shall gladly come again if you will gif me leave, dear madame, for a little business in the city will keep me here some days." He spoke to Mrs. March but he looked at Jo, and the mother's voice gave as cordial assent as did the daughter's eyes.

"I suspect that is a wise man," remarked Mr. March after he had gone.

"I know he is a good one," added Mrs. March.

"I thought you'd like him," was all Jo said.

She wondered what the business was that brought Mr. Bhaer to the city. If she had seen his face when later he looked at the picture of a severe young lady with a good deal of hair, it might have thrown some light on the subject, especially when he turned off the gas and kissed the picture in the dark.

Chapter 39

MY LORD AND LADY

"PLEASE, Madam Mother, could you lend me my wife for an hour? The luggage has come and I've been making hay of Amy's Paris finery, trying to find some things I want," said Laurie, coming in the next day to find Mrs. Laurence sitting in her mother's lap, the baby again.

"Certainly. Go, dear. I forget that you have any home but this," and Mrs. March pressed the white hand that wore the wedding ring.

"I shouldn't have come over if I could have helped it, but

I can't get on without my little woman any more than a—"

"Weathercock can without wind," suggested Jo as Laurie paused.

"Exactly. Amy keeps me pointing due west most of the time, with only an occasional whiffle round to the south, and I haven't had an easterly spell since I was married, and know nothing about the north."

"Lovely weather so far. I don't know how long it wil last," said Amy with a matronly air which delighted her husband, "but I'm not afraid of storms for I'm learning how to sail my ship. Come home, dear, and I'll find your boot-jack. I suppose that's what you are rummaging after among my things. Men are so helpless."

"What are you going to do with yourselves after you get settled?" asked Jo, buttoning Amy's cloak.

"We don't intend to be idle," replied Laurie. "I'm going into business and prove to Grandfather I'm not spoiled."

"And Amy, what is she going to do?" asked Mrs. March.

"After doing the civil all round, we shall astonish you by the elegant hospitalities of our mansion and the brilliant society we shall draw about us, won't we, Madame Réca-mier?" asked Laurie.

"Time will show. Come away, Impertinence and don't shock my family by calling me names," answered Amy, re-solving that there should be a home with a good wife in it before she set up a salon.

As they left, Professor Bhaer opened the gate with an impatient push. Later in the evening, Laurie said suddenly to his wife, who was arranging her art treasures, "Mrs. Laurence."

"My lord!"

"That man intends to marry our Jo!"

"I hope so, don't you, dear?"

"He is a trump, but I do wish he was a little younger and richer."

"Now Laurie, don't be worldly minded. If they love one another it doesn't matter a particle how old they are nor how poor. Women should *never* marry for money—" Amy caught herself up short as the words escaped her, and looked at Laurie, who replied with malicious gravity:

"Certainly not, though you do hear charming girls say that they intend to do it sometimes. If my memory serves me, you once thought it your duty to make a rich match, which accounts perhaps for your marrying a good-for-nothing like me."

"Oh my dearest boy, don't say that! I forgot you were rich when I said yes. I'd have married you if you hadn't a penny. It would break my heart if you didn't believe that I'd gladly pull in the same boat with you, even if you had to get your living by rowing on the lake."

"How could I think so when you refused a richer man for me and won't let me give you half I want to now when I have the right?"

"May I ask you a question, dear?" his wife said slowly.

"Of course you may."

"Shall you care if Jo does marry Mr. Bhaer?"

"I assure you I can dance at Jo's wedding with a heart as light as my heels. Do you doubt it, my darling?"

Amy was satisfied. Her last little jealous fear vanished forever.

"I wish we could do something for that capital old Professor. Couldn't we invent a rich relation who shall obligingly die in Germany and leave him a tidy little fortune?" said Laurie, when they began to pace up and down the long drawing room, arm in arm, as they were fond of doing in memory of the chateau garden.

"Jo would find out and spoil it all. She is very proud of him as he is."

"Bless her heart! We won't interfere now but watch our chance and do them a good turn in spite of themselves. I owe Jo for a part of my education and she believes in people paying their honest debts."

"How delightful it is to be able to help others, isn't it?

That was always one of my dreams, and thanks to you the dream has come true."

"We'll do quantities of good, won't we? There's one sort of poverty I like to help. Out-and-out beggars get taken care of, but poor gentlefolks fare badly because they won't ask and people don't care to offer them charity, yet there are a thousand ways of helping them, if one only knows how to do it so delicately that it does not offend."

So the young pair paced happily on, feeling that their pleasant home was more homelike because they hoped to brighten other homes, believing that their own feet would walk more uprightly along the flowery path before them if they smoothed rough ways for other feet, and feeling that their hearts were more closely knit together by a love which could tenderly remember those less blest than they.

Chapter 40

UNDER THE UMBRELLA

WHILE Laurie and Amy set their house in order and planned a blissful future, Mr. Bhaer and Jo were enjoying promenades of a different sort along muddy roads and sodden fields.

"I always do take a walk toward evening, and I don't know why I should give it up just because I often happen to meet the Professor on his way out," said Jo to herself after two or three encounters.

Under the circumstances, what could Jo do but greet him civilly and invite him in? By the second week everyone knew perfectly well what was going on yet tried to look as if they were blind to the changes in Jo's face. They never asked why she sang about her work, did up her hair three times a day, and got so blooming with her evening exercise.

And no one seemed to have the slightest suspicion Professor Bhaer, while talking philosophy with the father, was giving the daughter lessons in love.

Jo couldn't even lose her heart in a decorous manner but sternly tried to quench her feeling, and failing to do so led a somewhat agitated life. She was afraid of being laughed at for surrendering after her declarations of independence. Laurie was her especial dread, but thanks to the new manager he behaved with propriety, though he exulted in private and longed for the time when he could give Jo a piece of plate with a bear and a ragged staff on it as a coat-of-arms.

For a fortnight the Professor came and went with lover-like regularity. Then he stayed away for three whole days. Jo became pensive and then very cross. "Gone home as suddenly as he came, I daresay. It's nothing to me, of course, but I should think he would have come and bid us good-by, like a gentleman," she said to herself with a despairing look at the gate as she put on her things for the customary walk one dull afternoon.

"You'd better take the little umbrella, dear. It looks like rain," said her mother, observing that she had on her new bonnet.

"Yes, Marmee. Do you want anything in town? I've got to run in and get some paper," returned Jo, pulling out the bow under her chin before the glass as an excuse for not looking at her mother.

"Yes, I want some twilled silesia, a paper of number nine needles, and two yards of narrow lavender ribbon."

The drygoods stores were not down among the counting-houses, banks, and wholesale warerooms where gentlemen congregate, but Jo found herself in that part of the city before she did a single errand, loitering as if waiting for someone. A drop of rain on her cheek made her remember the little umbrella which she had forgotten to take. "If you catch your death and ruin your bonnet, it's no more than you deserve," she told herself, and rushed across the street so impetuously that she narrowly escaped annihilation from a passing truck. She spread her handkerchief over the ribbons on her bonnet, and hurried on with increasing dampness about the ankles and much clashing of umbrellas overhead.

The fact that a somewhat dilapidated blue umbrella remained stationary above the unprotected bonnet made her look up, and she saw Mr. Bhaer looking down at her. "I feel to know the strongminded lady who goes so bravely under many horse noses and so fast through much mud. What do you down here, my friend?"

"I'm shopping."

Mr. Bhaer smiled as he glanced from the pickle factory on one side to the wholesale hide-and-leather concern on the other, but he only said politely, "You haf no umbrella. May I go also and take for you the bundles?"

"Yes, thank you." Jo's cheeks were as red as her ribbon and she wondered what he thought of her, but she didn't care for in a minute she found herself walking away arm in arm with her Professor. "We thought you had gone," said Jo hastily.

"Did you believe that I should go with no farewell to those who haf been so heavenly kind to me?" he asked reproachfully.

"No, I didn't," she answered heartily, "but I knew you were busy about your own affairs, but we rather missed you —Father and Mother especially."

"And you?"

"I'm always glad to see you, sir." In her anxiety to keep her voice quite calm Jo made it rather cool. The Professor's smile vanished and he said gravely, "I thank you, and come one time more before I go."

"You are going, then?"

"I haf no longer any business here. It is done."

"Successfully, I hope?" said Jo, for disappointment was in his reply.

"I ought to think so for I haf a way opened to me by

which I can make my bread and gif my Jünglings much help."

"Tell me, please! I like to know all about the—the boys," said Jo eagerly.

"That is kind. My friends find for me a place in a college where I teach as at home and earn enough to make the way smooth for Franz and Emil. For this I should be grateful, should I not?"

"Indeed you should. How splendid it will be to have you doing what you like and be able to see you often, and the boys!" cried Jo, clinging to the lads as an excuse for the satisfaction she could not help betraying.

"Ah, but we shall not meet often, I fear. This place is in the West."

"So far away!"

Mr. Bhaer could read several languages but he had not learned to read women. Jo's tone of despair lifted him on to a pinnacle of hope, but the next minute she tumbled him down again by observing like one entirely absorbed in the matter, "Here's the place for my errands. Will you come in? It won't take long."

When they came out of the store, Mr. Bhaer put the parcel under his arm and splashed through the puddles as if he enjoyed it. "Should we not do a little what you call shopping for the babies and haf a farewell feast tonight if I go for my last call at your so pleasant home?" he asked, stopping before a window full of fruit and flowers.

He bought several pounds of grapes, a pot of rosy daisies, and a pretty jar of honey. Then distorting his pockets with the knobby bundles and giving her the flowers to hold, he put up the old umbrella and went on.

"Miss Marsch, I haf a great favor to ask of you," he began after a moist promenade of half a block.

"Yes sir," and Jo's heart began to beat hard.

"I am bold to say it in spite of the rain because so short a time remains to me."

"Yes sir," and Jo squeezed the small flowerpot.

"I wish to get a little dress for my Tina and I am too stupid to go alone. Will you kindly gif me a word of taste and help?"

"Yes sir," and Jo felt as cool as if she had stepped into a refrigerator.

"Perhaps also a shawl for Tina's mother, she is so poor and sick."

"I'll do it with pleasure." Jo chose a pretty gown for Tina and then ordered out the shawls. The clerk took an interest in the couple.

"Your lady may prefer this," he said, shaking out a comfortable gray shawl and throwing it over Jo's shoulders. "It is a desirable color."

"Does this suit you, Mr. Bhaer?" she asked, turning her back to him, grateful for the chance of hiding her face.

"Excellently well. We will haf it," answered the Professor, smiling to himself as he paid for it. "Now shall we go home?" he asked, as if the words were very pleasant.

"Yes, it's late, and I'm so tired." Jo's voice was more pathetic than she knew, and she winked hard because she would have died rather than openly wipe her eyes. Her feet were cold, and her heart and head ached.

Mr. Bhaer saw the drops on her cheeks, though she turned her head away. The sight touched him and suddenly stooping down he asked in a tone that meant a great deal, "Heart's dearest, why do you cry?"

If Jo had not been new to this sort of thing she would have said she wasn't crying or had a cold in her head, but she sobbed, "Because you are going away."

"Ach, that is so goot!" cried Mr. Bhaer, managing to clasp his hands in spite of the umbrella and the bundles. "Jo, I haf nothing but much love to gif you. I came to see if you could care for me and I waited to be sure that I was something more than a friend. Am I? Can you make a little place in your heart for old Fritz?" he added.

"Oh yes!" said Jo. He was quite satisfied, for she folded both hands over his arm and looked up at him with an expression that plainly showed how happy she would be to walk through life beside him, even though she had no better shelter than the old umbrella, if he carried it.

Passers-by probably thought them a pair of harmless lunatics for they entirely forgot to hail a bus and strolled leisurely along, oblivious of the deepening dusk and fog.

Of course Jo was the first to speak.

"Tell me what brought you at last, just when I most wanted you?"

"This," and Mr. Bhaer took a little worn paper out of his pocket.

Jo unfolded it and looked abashed, for it was one of her own contributions to a paper that paid for poetry. "How could that bring you?" she asked, wondering.

"I found it by chance. I knew it by the names and the initials. There was one little verse that seemed to call me."

Jo looked at "In the Garret" and her eyes found the verse—

> A woman in a lonely home,
>   Hearing like a sad refrain,
> "Be worthy love and love will come,"
>   In the falling summer rain.

"It's bad poetry but I felt it when I wrote it," said Jo, tearing up the verses the Professor had treasured.

"What made you stay away so long?" she asked.

"It was not easy, but I could not find the heart to take you from that happy home until I could haf a prospect of one to give you. How could I ask you to gif up so much for a poor fellow who has no fortune but a little learning?"

"I'm glad you *are* poor. I couldn't bear a rich husband," said Jo decidedly, adding in a softer tone, "Don't fear poverty. I've known it long enough to lose my dread and be happy working for those I love."

"Haf you patience to wait a long time, Jo? I must go away and do my work alone. I must help my boys first, because even for you I may not break my word to Minna. Can you be happy while we hope and wait?"

"Yes, I know I can, for we love one another and that makes all the rest easy to bear. We'll hope for the best and leave the future to God."

"Thou gifst me hope and courage and I haf nothing to gif back but a full heart and these empty hands," cried the Professor.

Jo put both hands into his as they stood on the steps, whispered, "Not empty now," and kissed her Friedrich under the umbrella. With a glad "Welcome home!" Jo led her lover in and shut the door.

Chapter 41

HARVEST TIME

FOR A YEAR Jo and her Professor worked and waited, hoped and loved, met occasionally, and wrote voluminous letters. The second year began rather soberly for their prospects did not brighten and Aunt March died suddenly. When their first sorrow was over, they found they had cause for rejoicing for she had left Plumfield to Jo.

"It's a fine old place and will bring a handsome sum, for of course you intend to sell it," said Laurie, as they were all talking the matter over some weeks later.

"No, I don't," was Jo's decided answer.

"You don't mean to live there?"

"Yes, I do."

"But my dear girl, it's an immense house and will take a power of money to keep it in order. The garden and orchard alone need two or three men and farming isn't in Bhaer's line, I take it."

"He'll try his hand at it there if I propose it."

"And you expect to live on the produce of the place?"

"The crop we are going to raise is a profitable one," Jo laughed.

"Of what is this fine crop to consist, ma'am?"

"Boys. I want to open a school for little lads, a good, happy, homelike school, with me to take care of them and Fritz to teach them."

"There's a truly Joian plan for you! Isn't that just like her?" cried Laurie, appealing to the family.

"I like it," said Mrs. March.

"So do I," added her husband.

"This isn't a new idea of mine," continued Jo earnestly, "but a long-cherished plan. Before my Fritz came I used to think how, when I'd made my fortune and no one needed me at home, I'd hire a big house and pick up some poor little lads who hadn't any mothers, and take care of them and make life jolly for them before it was too late. Think what luxury—Plumfield my own and a wilderness of boys to enjoy it with me!" Jo waved her hands and gave a sigh of rapture.

It was a very astonishing year altogether, for things seemed to happen in an unusually rapid and delightful manner. Almost before she knew where she was, Jo found herself married and settled at Plumfield. Then a family of six or seven boys sprang up like mushrooms and flourished surprisingly, poor boys as well as rich.

It never was a fashionable school and the Professor did not lay up a fortune, but it was just what Jo intended it to be— "a happy homelike place for boys who needed teaching, care and kindness." Every room in the big house was soon full; every little plot in the garden soon had its owner; a regular menagerie appeared in barn and shed, for pet animals were allowed; and three times a day Jo smiled at Fritz from the head of a long table lined on either side with rows of happy young faces which all turned to her with affectionate eyes, confiding words, and grateful hearts full of love for "Mother Bhaer." She had boys enough now and did not tire of them. Jo was a very happy woman.

As the years went on, two little lads of her own came to increase her happiness—Rob, named for Grandpa, and Teddy, a happy-go-lucky baby who seemed to have inherited his papa's sunshiny temper as well as his mother's lively spirit.

There were a great many holidays at Plumfield and one of the most delightful was the yearly apple-picking. For then the Marches, Laurences, Brookes and Bhaers turned out in full force and made a day of it. Five years after Jo's wedding one of these festivals occurred—a mellow October day when every tree stood ready to send down its shower of red and yellow apples at the first shake. Everybody was there, and they laughed and sang, climbed up and tumbled down, and declared there never had been such a perfect day.

Mr. March strolled placidly about, while the Professor charged up and down the green aisles leading on the boys, who made a hook-and-ladder company of themselves and

performed wonders in the way of ground and lofty tumbling. Laurie devoted himself to the little ones, rode his
small daughter in a bushel basket, took Daisy up among the
birds' nests, and kept adventurous Rob from breaking his
neck. Mrs. March and Meg sat among the apple piles, sort-
ing the contributions that kept pouring in, while Amy
sketched and watched over one pale lad who sat adoring
her with his little crutch beside him.

Jo was in her element that day, and rushed about with
her gown pinned up, her hat anywhere but on her head,
and her baby tucked under her arm, ready for any lively
adventure which might turn up. Little Teddy bore a
charmed life, for nothing ever happened to him.

At four o'clock the apple-pickers rested and compared
rents and bruises. Then Jo and Meg, with a detachment of
the bigger boys, set forth the supper on the grass. When no
one could eat any more, the Professor proposed the first
regular toast, which was always drunk at such times—"Aunt
March, God bless her!"

"Now Grandma's sixtieth birthday! Long life to her with
three times three!"

That was given with a will, and the cheering once begun, it was hard to stop it. Everybody's health was proposed, from Mr. Laurence, who was considered their social
patron, to the astonished guinea pig which had strayed
in search of its young master. Demi, as the oldest grand-
child, presented the queen of the day with various gifts so
numerous that they were transported to the festive scene
in a wheelbarrow. Every stitch Daisy's patient little fingers
had put into the handkerchiefs she hemmed was better than
embroidery to Mrs. March. Demi's shoebox was a miracle of
mechanical skill though the cover wouldn't shut. Rob's footstool had a wiggle in its uneven legs that she declared was
very soothing. And no page of the costly book Amy's child
gave her was so fair as that on which appeared in tipsy capi-
tals the words *To dear Grandma from her little Beth.*

During this ceremony the boys had mysteriously disappeared, and when Mrs. March had tried to thank her children and broken down while Teddy wiped her eyes on his pinafore, the Professor suddenly began to sing. Then from above him, voice after voice took up the words, and from tree to tree echoed the music of the unseen choir, as the boys sang with all their hearts the little song Jo had written, Laurie set to music, and the Professor trained his lads to give with the best effect. This was something altogether new and it proved a grand success.

After this, the boys dispersed, leaving Mrs. March and her daughters under the festival tree.

"I don't think I ever ought to call myself 'Unlucky Jo' again when my greatest wish has been so beautifully gratified," said Mrs. Bhaer, taking Teddy's little fist out of the milk pitcher.

"And yet your life is very different from the one you pictured so long ago. Do you remember?" asked Amy.

"Yes, I remember, but the life I wanted then seems selfish, lonely and cold to me now. I haven't give up the hope that I may write a good book yet but I can wait, and I'm sure it will be all the better for such experiences and illustrations as these."

"My dream was the most nearly realized of all. I knew I should be satisfied if I had a little home and John, and some dear children like these. I've got them all, thank God, and am. the happiest woman in the world," and Meg laid her hand on her tall boy's head.

"Mine is different from what I planned," Amy said, "but I would not alter it, though like Jo I don't relinquish all my artistic hopes or confine myself to helping others fulfill their dreams of beauty. I've begun to model a figure of baby, and Laurie says it is the best thing I've ever done. I think so myself and mean to do it in marble. I say with Meg, 'Thank God, I'm a happy woman.' "

"There's no need for me to say it, for everyone can see that I'm far happier than I deserve," added Jo glancing from her husband to her chubby children tumbling on the grass beside her. "Fritz is getting gray and stout. I'm growing as thin as a shadow and am thirty. I have nothing to complain of and never was so jolly in my life."

"Yes, Jo, I think your harvest will be a good one," began Mrs. March, frightening away a big black cricket that was staring Teddy out of countenance.

"Not half so good as yours, Mother. Here it is, and we never can thank you enough for the patient sowing and reaping you have done," cried Jo, with the loving impetuosity which she never could outgrow.

"I hope there will be more wheat and fewer tares every year," said Amy softly.

"A large sheaf, but I know there's room in your heart for it, Marmee dear," added Meg's tender voice.

Touched to the heart, Mrs. March could only stretch out her arms as if to gather children and grandchildren to herself, and say with face and voice full of motherly love, gratitude and humility:

"Oh my girls, however long you may live, I never can wish you a greater happiness than this!"

THE END

What happened to the real "Jo" — Louisa May Alcott? You will find her story in the Newbery Medal book, *Invincible Louisa,* by Cornelia Meigs, a Scholastic paperback.

Orchard House, where the "Little Women" grew up, still stands in Concord, Massachusetts. The furnishings remain unchanged. As a visitor, you will see sketches drawn by Amy/May, writings by Jo/Louisa, and the low-ceilinged rooms where the March family — and the Alcotts — shared so much. For the real facts of the Alcott family closely parallel the story told in this book.